PATRON SAINTS OF NOTHING

"Lyrical. Stunning. Searing. *Patron Saints of Nothing* is the real deal, a unique and intimate look into the extrajudicial murders in Duterte's war on drugs in the Philippines. Ribay's arresting narration and knack for characterization drive a story that is unlike anything else you'll read this year."

—MARK OSHIRO, author of *Anger Is a Gift*

"A riveting, brilliantly told and deeply moving story about a young man's search for truth and personal redemption in a world that is both strange and strangely familiar."

—FRANCISCO X. STORK, author of *Disappeared*

"Complex, gripping, haunting, and deeply human, *Patron Saints of Nothing* is a powerful journey into some of life's most important questions—Who are we? What are we worth? What do we owe one another?—and a story alive with longing and pain and grace."

—KELLY LOY GILBERT, author of *Picture Us in the Light*

"How lucky we are, to live in a moment when magnificent books like this are finding their way into the world. Randy Ribay has done a brilliant job of bringing horrific events happening far away to life for readers who may know little about them, in the process showing us our own inaction, and complicity—and power."

—SAM J. MILLER, award-winning author of *The Art of Starving*

A National Book Award Finalist

A *Publishers Weekly* Best Book of 2019

A *Kirkus Reviews* Best Book of 2019

An Amazon Best Book of 2019

A Junior Library Guild Audio Selection

★ "A deeply emotional story about family ties, addiction, and the complexity of truth . . . Part coming-of-age story and part exposé of Duterte's problematic policies, this powerful and courageous story offers readers a refreshingly emotional depiction of a young man of color with an earnest desire for the truth."

—*KIRKUS REVIEWS*, starred review

★ "A deep, nuanced, and painfully real family drama . . . By deftly weaving key details into Jay's quest for the truth, Ribay provides a much-needed window for young people of the West to better understand the Filipino history of colonization, occupation, and revolution."

—*BOOKLIST*, starred review

★ "Part mystery, part elegy, part coming of age, this novel is a perfect convergence of authentic voice and an emphasis on inner dialogue around equity, purpose, and reclaiming one's cultural identity."

—*SCHOOL LIBRARY JOURNAL*, starred review

★ "Passionately and fearlessly, Ribay delves into matters of justice, grief, and identity."

—*PUBLISHERS WEEKLY*, starred review

★ "Compelling and informational."

—*VOYA*, starred review

PENGUIN BOOKS
An imprint of Penguin Random House LLC, New York

First published in the United States of America by Kokila, an imprint of Penguin Random House LLC, 2019
Published by Penguin Books, an imprint of Penguin Random House LLC, 2020

Visit us online at penguinrandomhouse.com

THE LIBRARY OF CONGRESS HAS CATALOGED THE KOKILA EDITION AS FOLLOWS:
Names: Ribay, Randy, author.
Title: Patron saints of nothing / Randy Ribay.
Description: New York, NY : Kokila, 2019. | Summary: When seventeen-year-old Jay Reguero learns
his Filipino cousin and former best friend, Jun, was murdered as part of President Duterte's war on drugs,
he flies to the Philippines to learn more. | Includes bibliographical references.
Identifiers: LCCN 2018044009 | ISBN 9780525554912 (hardback) |
ISBN 9780525554936 (ebook)
Subjects: | CYAC: Murder—Fiction. | Cousins—Fiction. | Family life—Philippines—Fiction. |
Drug traffic—Fiction. | Philippines—Fiction. | BISAC: JUVENILE FICTION / People & Places / Asia. |
JUVENILE FICTION / Law & Crime. | JUVENILE FICTION / Family / General
(see also headings under Social Issues).
Classification: LCC PZ7.1.R5 Pat 2019 | DDC [Fic]—dc23
LC record available at https://lccn.loc.gov/2018044009

Penguin Books ISBN 9780525554929

Printed in the United States of America

Design by Jasmin Rubero
Text set in Dante MT Pro

9 10 8

RANDY RIBAY

PATRON
SAINTS
OF
NOTHING

PENGUIN BOOKS

THE PHILIPPINES

LUZON

PHILIPPINE SEA

ALBAY

MANILA

CAVITE

SOUTH CHINA SEA

N E S W

MINDANAO

VISAYAS

SULU SEA

WEST
PHILIPPINE
SEA

50 MILES

For the hyphenated

This is your story
This is your son These
are our sins
   and how
did we ever get here
   without them

—Patrick Rosal

IT WAS A DAY OF SOIL, SUNLIGHT, AND SMOKE. Curtains thin as bedsheets glowed gold as roosters called out from the backyard on the other side of concrete walls and single-pane windows. On the floor of the room my father and his two brothers had shared growing up, my mom held me as I held a lifeless puppy and cried. The oscillating fan hummed, blowing warm air on us every few seconds.

I was ten, and it was my first time back in the country where I'd been born. A few days earlier, my family had driven the eleven hours along frightening roads from Manila to Lolo and Lola's house in the Bicol Region.

When we arrived, we found that their dog—an unnamed mongrel chained to the cacao tree out back—had just given birth to a litter of puppies. Only one lived. The mother refused to care for him, so I had taken the task upon myself. I held him close to keep him warm. I tried to feed him by hand, dipping my finger into a bowl of evaporated milk and then offering a drop to the puppy's impossibly small mouth.

However, the puppy would not drink the milk. Maybe because of the grief from losing his brothers and sisters, or maybe because of his mother's rejection. Whatever the reason, his breathing grew shallow. His movements slowed. Each time he blinked, his eyes remained closed longer and longer until they never reopened.

At that point in my life, I had encountered death only in fiction. I had heard about other people's relatives dying. But I had never seen death up close. I had never held it.

"Listen," Mom said in that moment, hugging me closer. So I did. Baby birds chirped just outside the window. "One thing dies, and another is born. Maybe the puppy's soul now has wings."

Gradually, I calmed down and stopped crying. But I still felt heavy with sadness as the warmth left the tiny ball of brown-and-gray fur still cradled in my arms.

When I finally stepped outside, almost all my Filipino titas and titos laughed. Not in a mean way, I think, but more like it was amusing that a dog's death affected me so much because it was nothing to them. Another day. Another dog. My cousins did not need to have someone stroke their hair and reassure them that death was part of life.

It wasn't long before the family's attention drifted away like the smoke from the garbage being burned a few houses down. My brother and my sister resumed the card game of Speed they'd been playing. My dad and Lolo returned their attention to their bottles of San Miguel. My mom gave my shoulder one last squeeze and then went over to the outdoor kitchen to help Tita Chato, Tita Ami, and Lola finish preparing lunch.

Tito Danilo rested a hand on the top of my head and spoke of finding comfort in God's love, while Tito Maning told me to stop crying and took away the puppy's limp little body. He returned a few minutes later, brushing his palms as if he had just taken out the trash. He moved to pet the puppy's mother as he walked past, but she shied away. He continued on, took out a new bottle of beer from the cooler, and sat down next to Dad and Lolo. Tito Danilo stood by in awkward silence for a few more moments before joining them, leaving me there alone.

But I was not alone for long.

My cousin Jun walked over and hugged me.

"I am sad, too, Kuya Jay," he said, using the older brother designation, which never seemed right. I had been born only three days before him, and besides that, he was one of those people who moved through the world as if he had been around for a long time. An old soul, as they say.

I almost asked Jun what his father had done with my puppy, what he had done with its brothers and sisters the previous day. But I didn't. We can only handle so much truth at any given moment, I suppose. So instead, I said nothing.

He looked at me with sympathetic eyes, eyes so brown they were almost black. "Do you want to go inside and read komiks?"

I nodded, grateful for the chance to escape from everyone without being by myself.

He threw his arm over my shoulders. We went inside. We read comics.

A few days later, the vacation ended. I flew back to pine trees, overcast skies, and a Michigan winter that could sputter till May. My tan faded. My tongue forgot the taste of tocino and Tagalog. I stepped out of tsinelas and back into my suburban life as if I had never left.

WISDOM FROM ON HIGH

Seth and I are walking across the roof of my old elementary school, which is covered in a layer of round stones that knock together like skulls with each step. A charcoal, overcast night sky hangs overhead, and the air is warmer than usual for mid-April.

We reach the end of the roof and sit down on the ledge. Seth takes up about twice as much space as me because he's basically a bear in human form. The kind of white kid who's been shaving since middle school and who's spent the last four years rebuffing the football coach's recruitment attempts. Meanwhile, I'm the kind of senior sometimes mistaken for a freshman.

We settle in and fall quiet, letting our legs dangle over the west side of the building. It's the quietest side, the one that faces the unlit field that stretches out in the darkness at our feet. The playground and parking lot are to the south, while the neighborhood pushes up against the other two sides of the building.

Even though I'm the one that lives nearby, it was Seth who, in the summer before we started high school, first realized we could get up here by climbing the fence that surrounds the HVAC units. I wouldn't do it that first time because it was the middle of the day and I was afraid of getting arrested, but he eventually persuaded me to go back later and climb it with him under the cover of darkness. It took a few more trips before he could convince me to sit on the ledge. The school's only two stories high, so if we jumped we'd probably only sprain an ankle or something. But it was high enough to make me feel scared back then, high enough to make me feel philosophical now. It's been our nighttime hangout spot ever since.

Seth swings his backpack around so it's in front of him like a kangaroo pouch and starts riffling through. It's Friday night, so I've got a pretty good guess as to what he's looking for.

Sure enough, a few moments later he pulls out a joint, grinning like he's reuniting with a long-lost friend. He lights it and takes a hit. He holds the smoke in his lungs for longer than seems possible and then exhales slowly, letting the thick smoke unfurl into the evening. He offers even though he already knows I'm going to decline. This time's no different, so he simply shrugs and takes another hit. Not that I have anything against it. My desire to smoke has not yet surpassed my fear of getting caught.

The wind picks up, rustling the leaves of the surrounding trees and tossing our hair. I reposition myself upwind so I won't go home completely reeking of pot. We sit like that for a long time, sinking back into silence as we consider our numbered days. With spring break around the corner, and then only a few more weeks after that until graduation, the future is a wall of fog obscuring the horizon.

"Oh, shit," Seth says, "I almost forgot. Hold this."

He hands me his joint as he roots through his bag again. This time he pulls out something in a white plastic shopping bag. He tosses it in my lap, and despite only having one free hand, I catch it without falling off the ledge.

"Surprise," he says.

"What is it?" I ask, passing back his weed.

"Open it."

I reach inside and pull out a hoodie, soft and smelling brand new. I hold it up in front of me. It's a deep yellow gold that's bright even in the darkness, and by the faint orange light from the parking lot lamps I can read MICHIGAN printed out in bold capital letters across the chest.

I force a smile. "Oh, cool. Thanks."

I refold it, stuff it back into the bag, and set it to the side.

He turns and stares at me for a beat. "That's it?"

"What?"

"'Cool'?"

"Yeah. It's cool. I appreciate it. Thanks."

"Not going to put it on?" he asks. I can't tell if he's actually offended or not.

"I'm good."

He takes another hit, eyes still on me. "Why aren't you more excited, dude?"

"I don't know," I say. I know I should be. Every other senior at school's been rocking their future college's apparel since the day their admissions decision rolled in.

"Still sad because of all those rejections?"

I shrug. Lean back on my hands and stare out over the quiet field.

"Seriously, dude, you're dumb as shit."

"Oh, is shit sentient?"

3

"You know what I mean. Like, out of all the schools you applied to, how many were Ivy League?"

I don't answer.

"All but Michigan and Berkeley, right?" He shakes his head. "Didn't anyone tell you about applying to safety schools?"

I try to laugh. "Come on, man. They weren't completely out of reach. Solid GPA and test scores. Plus, student government."

He considers this. "Dude. You're a treasurer."

"So?"

"Class treasurers don't get into Yale or Harvard."

"Some do."

"Maybe the treasurers who are also Olympic skiers or world champion Irish dancers or something."

"Whatever. You know how my parents are. I took the path of least resistance because if I didn't send in those apps, they would have said they were cool with it but they wouldn't have been. Can you imagine their faces if I told them I applied to some school like . . . I don't know . . . like—"

"Like, Central?" Seth finishes, smirking because that's where he's headed in the fall.

"You know what I mean."

"You do know they have, like, the ninety-third best comp sci program in the nation, right?"

"That is certainly impressive."

He flips me off. I shake my head and laugh.

When I texted my family the news this afternoon, right after I found out, I could virtually hear their collective sigh of relief at the fact that I was finally accepted somewhere. My sister, Em, replied first with, "Fuck yea, baby bro" followed by, like, fifty exclamation points. Mom messaged, "Oh, honey! We're so proud of you! (And watch your language, Em!)" while from Dad I got a "I mean, it's not Harvard . . ." joke that wasn't fully a joke. My brother, Chris, still hasn't responded.

"I never wanted to go to any of those schools anyway," I say, answering Seth's earlier question. It sounds super defensive, but it's true. I'm not sure what I want to do. For some reason, that's not okay. Everyone acts like seventeen-year-olds who don't have their career path mapped out are wasting their lives.

I consider telling Seth all of this, but he wouldn't get it. Despite his slacker stoner vibe, he already knows he wants to get his computer science degree then become a code monkey for Google or Facebook or whatever company becomes our new digital overlords.

Besides, Seth and I have been friends for a long time, but we never get too deep into things. We hang out, play video games or basketball or whatever, and that's pretty much it. If something's bothering one of us, we never really talk about it. We give each other space until things are cool again. Like sophomore year, when Seth's parents were going through their divorce. He never brought it up beyond mentioning once that it was happening, and I didn't push him to talk about it. There were a few months where the slightest thing would set him off, like kids leaving their lunch trays on their tables instead of throwing them away or someone failing to bag their dog's shit on a walk, but he eventually returned to his old self. If I had tried to get him to talk about it, it would have made things worse.

Jun really was the only person I've ever talked to about these kinds of feelings. We used to share all kinds of things back when we used to write each other letters. Actual letters—not emails or texts or DMs.

Now that I think about it, Jun should also be graduating this year—assuming he went back to school. I wish I had a way to find out what he's up to. But I don't. I messed that up a long time ago.

I stand up, walk over to the south side of the building, and sit down on the ledge overlooking the playground. The swings sway slightly, and the wind whistles through the tube slide. I look down at my feet as I kick the backs of my heels against the bricks.

Seth eventually sits down next to me. He's done smoking, but the stench still radiates from his clothes. His parents know, but they don't care, which blows my mind.

A few moments pass, then Seth chuckles to himself.

"What?" I ask.

"You know the Unabomber went to Harvard, right?"

"Yeah. And tons of the buildings are named after eugenicists."

"So it's a good thing you're not going there."

I sigh. He still thinks that's what's bothering me.

A bird or a bat flits past overhead. A dog starts barking somewhere in the distance. The wind picks up again but doesn't die down this time.

Much to my relief, Seth finally lets the college thing go and starts rambling about this top secret mod he's been working on for this first-person shooter we like to play. Without telling me what the mod does, he goes on and on about the specifics of the coding and all the iterations he had to try before it worked. None of it makes sense to me because I'm no programmer. After several minutes of this, he finally reveals that the mod replaces the rocket launcher with a cat and the rockets with babies.

"So, the cat . . . launches babies?" I ask.

He nods, cracking himself up.

"That doesn't make any sense."

"That's the point."

"I don't get it," I say.

"Exactly."

"I don't get you."

Seth considers this. "Does anyone truly get anyone, Jay?"

"Deep," I say sarcastically. "Nothing like wisdom from on high."

UNANSWERED

I sleep in on Saturday because I've got no plans beyond gaming with Seth later tonight after he finishes his shift at the sock store. I shuffle downstairs in my joggers and an old T-shirt, and after what I'll generously call brunch, sink into the living room couch, and fire up my PS4 to make some progress in this one-player game where you battle massive robot dinosaurs in a post-apocalyptic Earth.

I don't know how many hours into this session I am when my dad's suddenly standing behind me like he's learned to apparate.

"Jason, can you pause your game for a second?" he asks.

"I'm almost at a checkpoint," I say.

"Jason . . ." he starts and then falters. He tries again. "Jason, I have something important to tell you."

"Hold on." I know I'm being an ass, but I'm pretty sure this is probably going to be about college or something and I don't really want to talk about that anymore. Plus, I'm in the zone fighting this mech-T-rex that's already killed me, like, a million times.

"Jay," he says.

I slide down a hill and draw my bow and arrow, triggering the slow-motion mode. I release two arrows in quick succession. Both hit the beast's energy core, drawing heavy damage and narrowing its HP counter to a sliver.

"YES!" I say.

"Your Tito Maning called." He pauses. "Jun is dead."

My fingers slow, but I keep playing. I'm not sure I heard him right. "Wait—what?"

Dad clears his throat. "Your cousin Jun. He's dead."

I freeze, gripping the controller like a ledge. I suddenly feel like I'm going to be sick. On the screen, the mechanical creature mauls my avatar. My life drains to zero. The camera pans upward, mimicking the soul's skyward path.

The words finally land, but they don't feel real. I was just thinking about my cousin last night. . . .

"That's impossible," I say.

I sit up and shift so I'm facing Dad. He's still wearing his nurse's scrubs, and his salt-and-pepper hair is disheveled like he's been running his fingers through it. Behind his glasses, his eyes are bloodshot. I glance at the time again. Mom's at the hospital, and he should be, too.

"I thought you'd want to know," he adds.

"When?" I ask, my chest tightening.

"Yesterday."

I'm quiet for a long time. "What happened? I mean, how did he . . ."

I can't say the word.

He sighs. "It doesn't matter."

"What?" I ask. "Why not?"

"He's gone. That's it."

"He was seventeen," I say. "Seventeen-year-olds don't randomly . . ."

He takes off his glasses and rubs his eyes. "Sometimes they do."

"So it was random? Like a car accident or something?"

Dad puts his glasses back on but avoids looking at me. He says nothing for a few beats, and then quietly, "What would it change if you knew?"

I don't answer because I can't. Doesn't the truth itself matter?

I should be crying or throwing my controller down in anguish— but I don't do any of this. Instead, there's only a mild confusion, a muddy feeling of unreality that thickens when I consider the distance that had developed between Jun and me. How do you mourn someone you already let slip away? Are you even allowed to?

Since I don't know, I mirror the disturbing calm of my father, as I always do. We share the space, the silence. But on the inside, I'm a plane with failing engines.

"He's gone," Dad repeats after some time. "That's it." And then a nervous laugh escapes his lips.

I try to process the information. Jun is dead—his life has ended. And here I am, sitting in my living room on the other side of the world, a can of Coke on the coffee table, playing a video game on an enormous, wall-mounted flat-screen TV, college on the docket.

Dad wanders away.

"Wait," I call after him, "can we get there in time for the funeral?"

He stops. Over his shoulder: "There won't be one."

Confusion hits me like a wall. "Why not?"

"Your Tito Maning doesn't want to have one. The way he died . . . it wasn't . . . it's not our concern."

"What do you mean?" I ask.

But he's already gone, probably retreating upstairs.

Left alone, my confusion turns to anger, which starts to grow with nowhere to go like the roots of a plant in too small a pot. I finally drop the controller and bury my face in my hands. I take a few shaky, deep breaths. But my heart continues to race. My jaw stays clenched. My stomach remains knotted.

I think of all the letters we wrote each other over the years. What did his last one say? I don't even remember.

But this I'll never forget: I left it unanswered.

HOW HE LIVED

Not sure how long I sit there. I don't remember turning off the console, but at some point, I realize the TV screen is blue, searching for input. Like a zombie, I drag myself upstairs. The door to my parents' room is closed.

I knock. Dad doesn't answer.

I knock again. Nothing. I try the handle. It's locked. I sigh. "What happened to Jun?"

Silence.

"Dad? Please, tell me," I say, my words too thin, too pleading. Like a stupid little kid.

Still nothing. Is it possible he's on the other side of the door, covering his face with his hands and crying quietly? Probably not. I've never seen him cry once in my life.

Giving up, I retreat to my own room. I reach under my bed and pull out the Nike shoebox way in the back behind some old board games and the worn-out camo-print book bag I used in middle school. I brush dust off the lid and then open it. The smell of old paper and ink blossoms beneath my nose.

After my family's trip to the Philippines when I was ten, Jun wrote me the first of what would become many letters over the years. This shoebox contains all of them stuffed inside haphazardly, each one written on the kind of yellow paper from a legal pad. I dump them out and sort them chronologically as I search for the last one. Can it really be possible that the person who sent me all of these is no longer alive?

At this very moment, are the letters I wrote him sitting in a box somewhere, never to be opened again? I'm not sure how many I sent. Definitely not as many as Jun because I wasn't great at replying. I might go two or three months before sending one, but Jun's arrived twice a month like clockwork. Every now and then, I'd ask again if we should message each other over email instead because there was almost always a season's lag between when they were sent and when they'd arrive. Plus, I think I would have replied more often online. At first, Jun insisted we write actual letters because they were more real. But later he revealed that Tito Maning didn't allow him or his sisters to have social media or even their own email accounts.

Eventually I find the letter I'm looking for, the one dated the December when we were fourteen, shortly before Jun ran away from home.

But I'm not ready to read it yet, so I set it aside and reread a few at random.

Soon enough, my cousin feels alive again. His voice rings in my ear, and his face floats in the paper just beyond his words where he swam in the kind of feelings and thoughts most people spend their lives trying to mask from others or from themselves. I remind myself that he's dead, that I'll never have the chance to write to him again—but it's difficult to drop an anchor in that reality.

I start to feel untethered. I grab my phone and begin to text Chris, but I decide to call instead because I need to hear another human's voice. Except he doesn't pick up. Ever since he got a new boyfriend, he's been MIA. So he's probably out with him or busy doing whatever a subsea engineer does on a Saturday instead of answering calls from his little brother. I glance at the time and decide to try my sister next, figuring it's late enough in the day that she's probably recovered from whatever college party she was at last night.

Em answers midway through the fourth ring, just when I'm about to give up.

"Hi, baby brother," she says, voice groggy. I'm glad to hear it. Things were pretty rough between us for a long time. But after she moved out, I actually found myself missing her sometimes.

"Hi, Em."

She clears her throat. "What's up?"

I draw my knees to my chest. "Um . . . did you hear?" It's possible that Dad texted her the news already, but it's equally possible he didn't. Our family doesn't talk much, and usually anything important is passed along in fragments so that it feels like we're playing that telephone game, except a sadder, real-life version.

There's the sound of shifting at her end of the line. I imagine her tangled in the sheets, blurry-eyed and stretching. "Um. Yeah. I texted you back right away, remember? But if you want to hear it from me directly, fine: congrats! But that means we're rivals now."

I'm confused for a moment, then I realize she thinks I'm talking about me getting into U of M. "No," I say, "I mean . . . yeah. Thanks. But that's not why I'm calling."

"Oh?"

I run my hand through my hair. "Jun is dead."

There's a long silence at the other end, long enough that I pull the phone away from my cheek to check if I lost signal. I haven't. I'm stunned by how hard this news has hit her. I didn't know they were that close.

"Wait," she finally says, "is that one of those rappers you're into?"

"What—no," I say. "Our cousin Jun. Tito Maning's son?"

"The one who lives in the UAE?"

"No," I say. "That's Prince. He's, like, twelve. Jun is—was—my age."

There's nothing from the other end.

"The one who ran away from home?" I try.

"Oh, yeah," she says, though I'm unconvinced she actually remembers which cousin I'm speaking about. "Him. Sorry—I'm hungover."

I don't say anything.

She sighs. "Well, that sucks, man."

"Yeah. It does."

"You were pen pals or something, yeah?"

"Yeah. We were."

"So what happened?" And this is the right question but not the right tone. It feels more like she's asking out of curiosity than out of compassion. It's the same tone people use to ask about a fight at school.

"I don't know," I say. "Dad wouldn't tell me."

"Go figure. What about Mom?"

"At work still."

"Maybe he OD'd," she suggests.

I shrug, even though she can't see me.

"Murdered?"

I close my eyes. "I don't know."

"I bet it was suicide," she blurts out. "You know how some Catholics are weird about that."

I rub my eyes. This isn't even real to her. "Look, Em, I don't know. Maybe you're right, but it's not a joke, okay?"

"Chill. Didn't say it was, baby bro," she says. "Just trying to help."

"Great. Thank you. I feel so helped."

"Don't be a dick. You called me."

I don't say anything. But I'm reminded why we had trouble getting along growing up.

There's silence on the line for a few seconds. "Whatever. Anyway, you're going to love college, dude. It's, like, infinitely better than high school. Nobody forces you to go to class and you can party as much as you want. You buy any Wolverines gear yet? State's way better at football, by the way. And basketball. And pretty much everything else."

I'm quiet for a couple beats. "I've got to go, Em. Sorry I woke you up. I'll let you go back to sleep."

"O-k-a-y?" she says, drawing out the word like she has no idea why I'm upset. "Thanks for telling me about Jun, I guess."

"Yeah."

"Take care, baby brother . . . and I'm sorry this happened."

The thing is, she's not. Maybe she's sorry I'm sad, but she's not sorry he died. She didn't know him like I did.

Did anyone?

"Bye, Em." I end the call as she starts to shout something that sounds like, "Go Spartans!" and then I stare at my phone, wishing there was someone in my contact list I could call who would understand what I'm feeling. Someone like Jun.

I find Seth's number, but decide against it.

I close my blinds against the early afternoon sun and climb into bed. Still fully clothed, I pull the sheets up to my chin and stare at the ceiling. I feel like there's a heavy, oversized bolt lodged in my center that I have no idea how to remove. And each time my thoughts go to Jun, the bolt turns and burrows deeper.

I want to be held. I'm seventeen years old, but I want someone to hold me like how my mom held me when I was a little kid.

Why is this hitting me so hard? Yeah, Jun and I wrote each other. But then we didn't. I don't know a single thing about his life in the last few years. He never reached out to me, and I never bothered trying to find him. I only knew that he ran away because my dad casually dropped that fact over dinner, like, a month or so after it happened. All of us—including me—were just like, "Oh, that's so sad," and then went on with dinner, went on with our lives.

I reach over to the floor and pick up his last letter. I take a deep breath and reread it for the first time in years.

26 December 2015

Dear Kuya Jay,
I have not received a reply from you in three months. In that time, I have sent you six letters counting this one.

Maybe you have moved and forgot to give me the new address? Maybe they were lost in the mail and did not make it to you? Or maybe it is that you are too busy over in America. Now that you are in high school, you probably do not want to spend so much time writing letters to your faraway cousin anymore. Maybe you have a girlfriend. If so, I bet she is pretty and smart. Maybe you play on a sports team. If so, I am thinking it is basketball because you are a very good point guard. Much better than me.

As for me, cousin, *malungkot ako*. In English: "I am sad," or, "I am down." But translation is hard—perhaps "tired," the larger way you use it, is the better word. Tired of my *nanay* caring only about what others think of our family. Tired of my *tatay* believing he always knows what is wrong and what is right all the time just because he is a police chief. Tired of the kids at school talking about music and TV shows and celebrities like any of it matters. What is the point, you know? People are sick and starving to death in our country, in our streets, and nobody cares. They worry instead about grades and popularity and money and trying to go to America. I don't want to be another one of those people who just pretends like they don't know about the suffering, like they don't see it every single day, like they don't walk past it on their way to school or work.

I wonder, do you ever feel like this?

Anyway, sorry to annoy you with yet another letter. I am thinking that maybe you do not want to do this anymore.

If you do not reply, it is okay. I will leave you alone. But know that I would like it very much if you responded.

Sincerely,
Jun

Guilt, shame, and sadness swirl in my stomach. Yet I reread it a couple more times, forcing myself to face the sorrow, face the fact I never tried to find out where he had gone after he ran away from home, never tried to understand why.

I search his words for clues that might reveal what my dad left unsaid, that might point toward one of the grim ends Em guessed. But the letter says no more than it says. I fold it and place it back with the others, then close the lid as if to a coffin. I turn onto my side so I'm facing the wall and let the tiredness, the sadness, overtake me.

Malungkot ako.

Eventually, I feel myself drifting off to sleep. As I do, I think about how even though there's a lot I don't know, I do know it isn't right for Jun's family to deny him a funeral. No matter how he died. No matter how he lived.

AN IMPROVEMENT
TO SOCIETY

I wake to the sound of the garage grinding open. My room is pitch black, and when I check the time on my phone I find that it's almost five in the morning. There are a few texts from Seth from last night that I ignore. Downstairs, a door opens and shuts, then footsteps shuffle across the floor. I almost drift back to sleep when I remember Jun is dead. For a moment, I wonder if I dreamed that conversation with Dad, but then dread settles into my heart and I know I didn't.

I need to speak with Mom. She's always able to extract information from Dad that nobody else in our family can, so if anyone knows more about what happened to Jun, it's her.

I throw the covers back, and head downstairs through the dark house.

She's in the kitchen, back to me as she puts a kettle of water on the stove for her post-shift cup of chamomile tea. Her blond hair—which I definitely didn't inherit—is tied back in a ponytail, and she's still in her scrubs like Dad was. They work at the same hospital, where she's an oncologist and he's a NICU nurse. When Chris, Em, and I were younger, they used to work opposite shifts so that at least one of them could always be on family duty. We rarely saw them together beyond one day a week and family vacations. But after I finished elementary school, they aligned their schedules, and as we grew up, they grew closer.

"Hey, Mom," I say, looking a mess in my wrinkled clothes.

She stops what she's doing and turns around. Her weary face transforms into a picture of sympathy in a heartbeat. She crosses the space between us and wraps her arms around me. "I'm so sorry about Jun," she says. "I know you two were close. If I could have, I would have been here sooner."

Earlier I thought that I wanted someone to hold me. But now that someone is, it doesn't make anything better.

Mom kisses my forehead. "How are you holding up?"

"Fine," I say, but that's not what I want to talk about. I shed her arms and back away. "Why aren't they giving him a funeral?"

She hesitates, like she has an answer ready but is having second thoughts about going with it. Eventually, she says, "You know how your uncle is." Then she turns around and busies herself with prepping her tea.

"Yeah, but—"

"His family doesn't want to talk about it. We should respect that." She closes the cabinet door hard, like a full stop at the end of her sentence.

But I need to know more. I need to know what happened to my cousin. Maybe only for the sake of knowing—but maybe because I need to hear that it wasn't my fault. That, whatever happened, a few more letters from me wouldn't have made a difference.

"You know the reason—don't you? You can tell me. I'm not a kid anymore."

She rests her hands on the counter but doesn't answer.

I think about the words in Jun's final letter, the part about how everyone pretends like they don't see the suffering around them.

"So we're just going to act like this didn't happen? Like Jun didn't even exist?"

After a beat, she turns around to face me and crosses her arms. "If that's what's best for his family, then yes."

"Do you lie to your patients?" I ask.

She raises her eyebrows. "Not to my patients, but sometimes to their families, yes."

"You serious?"

She nods. "Sometimes my patients want me to lie for them. Nothing out of line. Mostly they want me to say something in a way that will give their loved ones relief. Or at least, something that won't leave them with too much despair."

I shake my head. Unbelievable.

"If I have a patient who is dying slowly and painfully, and he asks me to tell his family that he won't suffer in his final moments, what am I supposed to do?"

"If they ask, tell the truth."

"Even if the truth does nothing but cause the family anguish?"

"They deserve to know."

"Or do they deserve peace?"

I say nothing.

She sighs. "You aren't going to let this go, are you?"

"No."

"Just like your father . . ." she says quietly.

Except her comment confuses me because he lets everything go.

"It's not going to do anything for you," she says. "Except cause you more pain."

"I know."

The teakettle starts whistling. Neither of us moves.

Finally, Mom breaks eye contact and removes the kettle from the stovetop. She pours the water into the waiting mug, drops in the tea bag, then pushes the mug toward me. "Careful. It's hot."

"Thanks."

She glances toward the entrance to the kitchen. Then she takes a deep breath and asks, "Do you know what *shabu* is?"

"*Shabu?*" I repeat, testing the shape of the unfamiliar word in my mouth. It sounds like it could be Tagalog, but I've never heard it before. I shake my head.

"It's what they call meth in the Philippines," she says. "A cheap high. Easy to find. Devastating."

My stomach flips. "Oh."

"I don't know everything," Mom continues, "only what your dad tells me, and I can tell he doesn't know the full story either. You know how his family is. But, in this case, I don't think he wants to know any more."

"What do you mean?"

"After Jun ran away from home, he started living on the streets. At some point he started using."

I stare hard at my untouched cup of tea. A lump forms in my throat. "Overdose?"

Mom shakes her head.

I look up. "Then what?"

"He . . ." She trails off and looks around again as if to make sure Dad isn't within earshot. Then her eyes land on mine and soften. "He was shot." She pauses. "By the police."

"The police?"

She nods.

"Why would the police shoot him for using drugs?"

She takes another deep breath. "Duterte."

I wait for her to say more.

Mom blinks. "Rodrigo Duterte? President of the Philippines?"

I know she's waiting for understanding to dawn on my face, so I look down, feeling like a fool.

"You don't know about him? About the drug war?"

"I've read a little," I say, so I don't look completely stupid. But the truth is, I never made it past the headlines.

"Really, Jay, you should pay more attention to what's going on in the world outside of your video games."

"Sorry," I mumble. But it's not like our family is the model for current events analysis. There was another major school shooting a few weeks ago, and "It's so sad" and "It really is" and "I'll never understand those people" was the extent of my parents' conversation about it over dinner. They didn't even ask how I felt.

"Duterte was elected back in 2016," Mom explains. "One of those 'law and order' types. Said that if he were elected, he could eliminate the country's crime in three to six months."

"For real?" I ask.

She nods. "Blamed drugs. Said he had a plan to get rid of them, and once he did, there wouldn't be any more crime."

"And people believed that?"

"He won by a landslide." She lets that sink in, and then goes on. "Once he was president, he ordered anyone addicted or selling to turn themselves in. If they didn't, he encouraged the police—and the people—to arrest them . . . and to kill them if they resisted."

"Execution without a warrant or a trial or anything?"

Mom nods.

"Isn't that illegal?"

"The government determines what's legal."

I shake my head as I think of Jun dying because of some batshit-crazy government policy. "And they've *actually* been doing this?"

"You really haven't read any articles about this online or learned about it in school at all?"

"How many people have died?" I ask instead of answering.

She shakes her head. "Some think over ten, maybe twenty, thousand. But the government says only a few thousand."

Only.

"And Filipinos are still okay with this guy?"

She takes a deep breath. "Jay, it's easy for us to pass judgment. But we don't live there anymore, so we can't grasp the extent to which drugs have affected the country. According to what I've read, most Filipinos believe it's for the greater good. Harsh but necessary. To them, Duterte is someone finally willing to do what it takes to set things right."

"So I'm not allowed to have an opinion? To say it's wrong or inhumane?"

25

She puts her hands on her hip and flashes me a look that signals I should check my tone. Then, in a low voice, says, "That's not what I'm saying, Jay."

"What are you saying?"

"That you need to make sure that opinion is an informed one."

There's obviously no way to argue that point without sounding like an idiot, but knowing that doesn't dissolve my newfound anger. "So what's *your* informed opinion?"

"That it's not my place to say what's right or wrong in a country that's not mine."

"But you lived there. You're married to a Filipino. You have Filipino children."

"Filipino *American* children," she corrects. "And it's not the same."

"Then what about Dad—what's he think about Duterte?" I ask, not sure I pronounced the name correctly.

"He's just glad you and Em and Chris grew up here."

I don't know what to say, so I take a sip of the tea, which is bitter and lukewarm. I remember how during sophomore year, my English class read *Night* by Elie Wiesel while we learned about the Holocaust in World History. After we finished the book, we read the author's Nobel Peace Prize acceptance speech. I don't remember the exact words, but I remember how he said something about how if people don't speak out when something wrong is happening—wherever in the world—they're helping whoever is committing that wrong by allowing it to happen. Our class discussed the idea, and almost everyone agreed with it, even me. At least, we said we did. Never mind the fact we all knew most of us didn't even say shit when we saw someone slap the books out of a kid's hands in the hallway. In fact, the most outspoken supporter of the idea during the discussion was a kid who did that kind of dumb stuff all the time and thought it was hilarious.

It strikes me now that I've never truly confronted that question before, that I never had to. But I'm left to wonder, did my parents' silence—and mine—allow Jun's death in some way? Was there anything we could have done from the US?

The answer doesn't matter anymore, though. It's too late.

Jun is gone. And apparently to most people he was nothing more than a drug addict. A rat transmitting a plague that needed to be eradicated. It all still feels so absurd, so unreal.

As tears well in my eyes and a new wave of nausea roils in my stomach, I put down the mug and turn away from Mom. I rest my elbows on the counter and cover my face with my hands.

"Are you okay, honey?" comes Mom's voice from somewhere far away.

I shake my head.

She starts rubbing small circles into the center of my back, but I shrug her off and head up to my room. I sit on the floor, and then press my back against the closed door, hands shaking. My eyes gravitate toward the shoebox under my bed.

Shot.

By the police.

For doing drugs.

Not for robbing or attacking or killing.

For doing drugs.

Now he's dead.

Dead.

Maybe he was reaching out to me through those words, and I let him slip away. I stayed silent. If I had written to him more often, been more honest, would it have helped him work through some of his problems so he wouldn't have run away from home? Maybe if I tried to find him, I would have. Maybe he wouldn't have become an addict if someone were there for him.

Maybe he wouldn't have been killed in the street by the police, his death tallied as an improvement to society.

A NARROWER COUNTRY
THAN EXPECTED

I didn't think the Internet would ever fail me, but here we are.

It's Sunday night. I'm at my desk hunched over my laptop, ready to chuck the effing thing out the window.

My parents think I've holed up in my room all day to do homework, but let's get real. It's spring of my senior year, and I've already been accepted into college. Besides, Jun's death has me looking at things differently. Like, if I complete the assignments or not, what does it really matter?

No, what I've been doing is trying to find out more. I expected the info my mom gave me to get rid of that nagging feeling I had inside, but it only aggravated it. When, where, how did it happen exactly?

I need to know this level of detail.

Why? I don't know.

Truth is a hungry thing.

Maybe it's because everyone else is so willing to pretend that it didn't even happen that I'm starving for certainty. Or maybe it's my penance.

Unfortunately, after hours of devouring information about the drug war, I haven't come across anything about the recent death of a "Manuel Reguero Jr."—Jun's legal name. Since Jun was the son of a high-ranking police officer, I expected an obituary at least.

I click, scroll, skim, repeat. I keep trying different phrases and combinations with no luck. I even try using Bing, which apparently still exists.

Of course, I've found tons of articles, videos, and social media posts about the drug war in general that I check out to get up to speed on what's been happening the last few years. No matter the source, most follow the same flow: They describe the drug and corruption problems, Duterte's solution, and the mounting body count. Few include the victims' full names. Most suggest that these killings are crimes against humanity, including a note about the international community's condemnation—but inaction.

It's the photos that hit me the hardest, though. A woman cradling her husband's limp body. A crowd looking on, emotionless, as police shine a flashlight on a woman's bloodied corpse. A couple, half on the ground and half tangled in their moped, their blank faces turned toward the camera and sprays of blood on the pavement behind their heads. Sisters gathered around their baby brother's body lying in its small casket. A body with its head covered in a dirty cloth left in a pile of garbage on the side of the street. Grayish-green corpses stacked like firewood in an improvised morgue. There's even a short video of grainy security cam footage in which a masked motorcyclist pulls up next to a man in an alleyway, shoots him point-blank in the side of the head, then drives away.

In high definition, I see the victims' wounds, their oddly twisted limbs, their blood and brain matter sprayed across familiar-looking streets.

In every dead body, I see Jun. I want to look away.

But I don't. I need to know. I need to see it. These photographers didn't want to water it down. They wanted the audience to confront the reality, to feel the pain that's been numbed by a headline culture.

Most of the Filipino sites I can find in English accuse the foreign media of overestimating and sensationalizing. They praise the president for decreasing crime and drug use and improving the country in countless other ways as well. Criticisms are few and far between, which makes sense after I learn about a senator named Leila de Lima. She was apparently one of the most vocal critics of the drug war and chairing the investigation into the extrajudicial killings—and then was imprisoned on drug-related charges based on Duterte's accusation. So the majority of the opposition I find online comes from anonymous blogs or social media accounts like this one on Instagram called GISING NA PH!, which contains post after post of Filipinos holding photographs of their loved ones who the police murdered.

It's crazy and sad and shameful that all of this has been going on for the past three years, and I basically knew nothing about it.

I'm still lost in the rabbit hole when there's a light knock on my door. I minimize the browser, open a random English essay, and swivel around. "Yeah?"

Mom enters, dragging Dad in by the wrist.

"Hey, honey," she says. "We wanted to check in on you. See how you're doing."

I can tell Dad would rather be somewhere else. His eyes dart around my room, landing anywhere but on me. Mom catches his eye and gives him a look meant to urge him to speak, but he only offers a small shrug.

When I was younger, I spent a day following Dad around the hospital for a bring-your-kid-to-work kind of thing, and I remember being shocked at how friendly and comforting he was with the anxious families of the babies under his care. He was a different person from the quiet, distant man I lived with, saying all the right things in the perfect tone. It was like he used all his compassion on strangers and ran out by the time he came home.

I turn back to my laptop and type nonsense sentences into the doc like I'm actually working on this essay. "I'm fine."

"Would you like to talk about how you're feeling?" Mom asks.

How I'm feeling?

I don't know. Why does it matter? I want to go back to reading more about the drug war, to finding information about Jun. I need to *do* something, not sit around talking about feelings.

I shrug.

"It's important to process your emotions about these kinds of things," she says.

I say nothing. It doesn't escape my notice that she can't even name it.

An awkward amount of time passes, the clacking of my keyboard the only noise in the room. They're probably having a nonverbal debate behind my back about whether to push me to talk or let me be.

Eventually, Mom sighs and then walks over and kisses me on top of the head. "Don't stay up too late."

"I have to finish this essay."

"There are more important things in life," Dad says from the doorway, speaking for the first time.

I want to laugh aloud since this is the exact opposite of all they've told me my entire life—that school, my education, should be my number one priority. After all, it's why they brought our family to the US. But I hold it in and say good night.

They pull the door shut as they leave. A few moments later, I can make out the soft sound of muffled whispering from the other side. Quietly, I get up and press my ear against the door just in time to catch Dad say, "I just don't understand him."

When I walk in late to AP Calc on Monday morning, my teacher, Ms. Mendoza, blinks with surprise from where she's standing at the board reviewing the problem sets. Everyone's staring at me weird as I make my way to my seat, I guess because I'm the kid who usually gets the perfect attendance award almost every year.

"Sorry," I say, slinking into my seat. "Overslept."

Which is true, but I could have made it on time if I had rushed. After reading about what's going on in the Philippines yesterday, though, I didn't feel the usual sense of urgency this morning.

"Oh," Ms. Mendoza says. "Just put the homework on your desk, and I'll come around and check it in a moment."

"Didn't do it," I say.

I'm not sure if there's an audible gasp from my peers, or if I just imagine it. Everyone in this class does every assignment.

Ms. Mendoza gives me a curious look, as if gauging whether I'm being sarcastic or not. I don't look away.

33

"You can listen, then, I suppose." She returns to the board and picks up where she left off.

A few moments later, I feel a pencil jabbing me in the back of my shoulder. I shrug it off without turning around, already knowing that it's Seth.

"Dude," he whispers. "Why didn't you answer any of my texts all weekend?"

I don't respond.

"You okay? You look like shit."

"Screw you," I whisper.

He puts his hands up in mock surrender and leaves me be for the rest of class.

But as soon as the bell rings, Seth's giant, hairy self is looming over my shoulder. He follows me into the hallway. "Dude?" he says.

"Dude," I reply sarcastically.

"Seriously, what's going on? You didn't log in to the game Saturday night. You didn't answer any of my DMs all weekend. You were late to school today and didn't even do the homework. And now you're acting like a zombie dick."

I stop in the middle of an intersection. Kids stream all around us, clearly annoyed. Seth looks uncomfortable since he's doing most of the blocking and tries to shepherd me toward the wall. But I stay where I am. "A zombie dick?"

"Yeah," he says. "Not, like, a zombie's phallus. I mean you seem spaced out like a zombie, but you're also being kind of a dick. This isn't like you."

"Oh. I get it." I start walking again, making a left turn down the next hallway toward the school's main entrance.

"Jay—where you going?" Seth calls after me.

"Not feeling so well."

Seth jogs over. "You going to throw up or something?"

I don't answer. We walk past the front office and out the front doors. Nobody stops us. Who knew cutting was this easy?

"Need a ride home?" he asks, glancing nervously back at the school like someone's about to sprint outside, grab us by our collars, and drag us back to class.

"Nah."

It's a clear spring day. Sunny, but not so hot. Too nice to match how I'm feeling.

I keep walking. Much as I want to be alone, Seth stays with me. Soon we're beyond the parking lot and the practice fields, then in the neighborhood surrounding the school. As we pass the two- and three-story homes with their manicured lawns and two-car garages, I can't help but remember those photographs of the drug war. It seems impossible that a place like this and a place like the Philippines exist at the same time on the same planet.

"You're not actually sick, are you?" he asks eventually.

"There's so many terrible things that happen in this world," I say, measuring how much I want to reveal, how much he'd care. "But, like, nobody's even paying attention."

He shrugs. "Everyone's got their own shit to deal with, man."

"Like what? What do *we* have to deal with, Seth?"

"Finals, I guess. College."

I scoff. "But what does that stuff even matter?"

"So we can get a good job, man."

35

It's the same answer nearly anyone would give. The same answer hardly anyone ever questions. The same answer I would have given just a few days ago. But now it feels like bullshit because I think of my family. My parents, my aunts and uncles—all of them have good jobs but none of them took care of Jun.

"Look, dude," Seth says, "you're clearly in some kind of funk. Maybe you're feeling late-onset senioritis. I don't know. But look at it this way: you've only got to survive a few more days and then it's spring break. We'll play so many video games that not only will this stress fade away, but your eyeballs are going to fall out of your skull. And then after spring break, we're basically done with high school."

We reach an intersection. No cars are coming, but we wait at the light because the glowing red hand tells us to. Seth punches the walk button several times.

"You're starting to scare me, dude. I know we don't usually talk about stuff like 'feelings'"—he puts air quotes around the word—"but if you want to talk, I'm here."

I start to speak but hesitate. The light changes, but we stay on the corner as it counts down to zero and changes back to the red hand.

"My cousin died," I finally admit. A rush of fresh pain fills my heart, but I hold it in.

"Shit, dude. Sorry." He's quiet for a few moments. "No wonder you're getting existential all of a sudden. If you don't mind my asking, how?"

I tell him what my mom told me.

"Whoa." He runs a hand through his hair. "That's wild. Were you guys close?"

Yes. No. Yes and no. I don't know how to answer, so I don't, only shrug and then cross against the light.

Seth follows. "I've read about that guy Duterte. He's crazy as hell. Back before he was president, when he was mayor of some city, he had these death squads that went around killing people they thought were criminals. He even shot a few people himself and, like, jokes about it now."

I keep walking, annoyed that Seth knows more about what's been going on in the Philippines than I did before yesterday's research session.

"Man," he says, shaking his head, "I forgot you're Filipino."

"Huh?"

"You're basically white."

I stop, stung. "What do you mean by that?"

"Sorry, dude," he says, backtracking. "Never mind."

"Tell me."

He hesitates.

"Seth," I urge.

"I don't see color, man," he says. "We're all one race: the human race. That's all I meant."

"No, it's not," I say. And even if it is, that's kind of fucked up. First, to assume white is default. Second, to imply that difference equals bad instead of simply different.

"Promise you won't get offended?"

"No. But tell me anyway."

He lets out an exasperated sigh. "I just meant you act like everyone else at school."

"You mean like all the white kids?"

"Dude, our school's all white kids, so, yeah."

Except it's not. The majority are, for sure, but his generalization—spoken with such confidence, such ease—makes me feel like he's erasing the rest of us.

Seth goes on. "You talk like everyone else. You dress like everyone else. And you, like, do the same stuff as everyone else. That's all I mean. Chill."

"What would you expect me to do?" I ask. "Walk around draped in the Philippine flag?"

Seth rolls his eyes. "You promised not to get offended."

"No, I didn't." I walk away, regretting that I opened up even as little as I did.

"Where you going, Jay?"

"Home," I say without looking back.

"You want me to come with you?" he asks, like he doesn't understand why I'm upset. And that's a big part of the problem. He doesn't. He can't.

It's a sad thing when you map the borders of a friendship and find it's a narrower country than expected.

LET ME GO

I sleep the rest of the day away. And then on Tuesday Mom lets me stay home because I tell her I'm not feeling well. I'm certain she knows I'm lying since she's a doctor, but since she's a mother, I'm certain she knows that I'm telling the truth.

I've tried asking Dad about Jun a few more times, but he claims to know nothing beyond what he already told me. And I keep doing more research online and coming up empty.

But in the afternoon, I'm binge-watching old episodes of *Steven Universe* and cycling through my social media when I get a DM on Instagram from an account I don't recognize. The message only contains a link, but I'm not about to click on it because it's probably virus city.

The profile pic is a low-res shot of some Filipino guy, and the handle's a nonsense string of letters and numbers without a bio. Dude only follows me, has zero followers, and has posted exactly zero times. Definitely not clicking on this link.

A minute later, I'm thinking about setting my account back to private when I get a second message from the same number with another link.

My finger's hovering over the Block button when he sends a third message—this time it's a photo.

My breath catches. I sit up.

It's a picture of Jun.

He's sitting on a curb and leaning back on his hands in front of a wall plastered in faded advertisements. He's got a stubbly goatee and a few tattoos snaking around his left arm—telling me he's way older here than in any photo I've ever seen of him.

What. The. Fuck.

When was it taken? Who took it?

Where did you get this??? I message, heart racing.

This is your cousin, no? Manuel Reguero?

Who are you?? I ask.

No response.

WHERE DID YOU GET THIS?

Manuel did not deserve to die, he replies. **He did nothing wrong.**

How do you know??? Who are you???

Several moments pass. And then: **I was his friend.**

I wait for him to say more, to answer my other questions. But he never does.

I ask again.

As I wait for a response, I swipe back to his profile pic and zoom in on the face. He said he was Jun's friend, and he somehow found me online. I must have met him while hanging out with Jun on that trip to the Philippines, but I can't place his face at all. I take a screenshot and run a reverse image search, but no matches turn up. I Google the profile name, but that's a dead end, too.

I go back to the conversation, but he hasn't replied. I message him a few more times, but several minutes of radio silence later, I accept the fact that the guy's gone. Hopefully just for the moment.

While I wait for him to respond, I save the photo of Jun to my phone and then open the link from the first message. It takes me to an article from three years ago about Duterte's drug war, one that I've already read. It's partially a primer on what's been going on and partially a journalist sharing his observations and photos after spending a month in Manila, during which time almost sixty people were murdered by the police or by vigilantes.

Jun's friend still hasn't sent another message, so I open the second link. This one also pulls up an article, but one I haven't come across yet.

It opens with a story about a seventeen-year-old boy named Kian delos Santos that police confronted because he was on a list of suspected drug runners provided by his neighborhood. They tried to arrest the boy, but he fought back and pulled a gun. In self-defense, they shot and killed him.

Only that's not what happened.

A CCTV camera happened to record everything. The video showed a group of police officers dragging him into the middle of a vacant lot, hands tied behind his back and a sack over his head. Then, they removed the sack, untied him, and slapped a gun into his hands. They stepped back and raised their own, pointing the barrels directly at his face. The boy immediately dropped the gun and raised his hands to shield his face. His last words according to an anonymous witness: "Please no—Please no—I have a test tomorrow."

There are other stories. Two brothers on their way to buy snacks.

A boy going to meet up with a teammate for their basketball game. Five friends playing pool. A mother out late buying medicine for one of her kids. A teacher eating at a canteen. And more.

All the stories follow a similar pattern: Someone is accused without evidence, they are killed without mercy, then the police cover it up without regret. Of course, the official report reads that the suspect resisted arrest. But this is contradicted by videos, anonymous eyewitness accounts, or forensic evidence.

The government never apologizes. They deny mistakes, asserting that they had reliable information or evidence, and that nobody, not even family members, should assume they know a person completely. "People hide their sin," one police chief explained.

Of course, the victims are almost always poor and don't have the means to bring legal action against the government.

The article goes on to talk about the mass incarceration; the imprisonment of Duterte's political opponents on drug-related charges that lack credibility, such as with Senator de Lima; the system in which police officers earn certain amounts of money for killing specific types of suspects, creating an economy of murder—especially since there are no bonuses for arrests.

So the drug war continues. The body count rises.

"They are exterminating us like we are rats in the street," ends the article, a quote from a mother who lost all five of her sons to the antidrug campaign, known as Operation Tokhang locally.

I clench my jaw and fight back tears.

I return to the conversation with Jun's friend. There's still no response, but my eyes land on his second-to-last message: **He did nothing wrong.**

The possibility that Jun died like one of the people from this article transforms my sorrow into white-hot anger.

If that's true, why isn't anyone talking about it?

The article included the fact that four low-level officers were eventually charged for killing that seventeen-year-old, but their punishments were minimal and only happened after massive protests. But what about the other victims who never got a hashtag? What about Jun?

Would there be justice?

Definitely not if nobody even knows what truly happened.

So maybe that's it—maybe I can find out. If his friend is right, maybe there are witnesses; maybe there's video; maybe there's a flawed report.

I stand up from the couch and start pacing the living room. For the first time in a few days, I feel like I have the opportunity to do something that matters. Something real. Something for Jun.

Except I know I can't do it from here, from behind my laptop.

I need to go to the Philippines.

I laugh. That's impossible. I can't just up and fly halfway across the world.

Or can I?

Spring break starts in a couple days, and I don't have plans besides playing video games with Seth. I wouldn't have to miss that much school, and at this point in senior year most of the classes are filler anyway. I have a passport, so that's not an issue. And even though a last-minute ticket to Manila will be pretty damn expensive, we've got the money.

No, the real problem won't be getting my parents to pay for it.

It will be convincing them to let me go.

GROUNDED

Later that night, Mom and Dad are standing at the island in the kitchen, reviewing the details of the flights I've pulled up on my laptop. I could leave the day after tomorrow, on Thursday, and then return a couple days after spring break. All they have to do is enter the payment information.

"No," Mom says. "No way."

Dad says nothing.

"Why not?" I ask.

"It's too expensive," she says.

"We just bought a Land Rover," I counter.

"Yes, *we* have the money." She gestures between Dad and herself. "But *you* don't."

Dad laughs.

"It can be my graduation present," I say.

Mom says, "What about the new computer?"

"I don't need one. And this even costs less."

Mom raises an eyebrow. "Weren't you just complaining about how this one keeps crashing unexpectedly?"

We all look at the computer, as if waiting for it to crash at that exact moment. Thankfully, it doesn't.

"It's fine," I say. "That's a quirk. It's quirky and lovable."

"That's not what you're going to say in the fall when you lose a term paper you've been working on for days."

"Everything saves to the cloud now, Mom."

She looks to Dad. He gazes at the screen.

"You guys always talk about how you learned so much from traveling. The best classroom is the world and all of that. How it opened up your eyes and changed your life. How you wouldn't be the people you are today if you hadn't taken some of those trips. You wouldn't even have met if Mom never went to the Philippines. Don't you want me to experience some of that?"

They hold their silence.

"Would you rather I sit around the house all week and play video games?"

Mom sighs, crosses her arms over her chest.

"And remember how much Em matured after she studied abroad in France?" I add, omitting the stories Em told me about hitting the clubs every weekend.

"You want to travel instead of getting a new computer?" Mom says. "Fine."

Dad looks at her. I smile.

She nods, then adds, "But not to the Philippines."

My face falls. "Why not?"

"I mean . . . with what happened . . ."

A tense silence settles over the kitchen.

It drives me crazy that nobody will say Jun's name. But I keep myself in check because getting angry isn't going to get me what I want right now.

Thankfully, Mom senses the discomfort and redirects before anyone has a chance to answer her question. "You should go somewhere you haven't been before. You really enjoyed our trip to England last summer, didn't you? Why not somewhere else in Europe, like Spain? I have some friends in Valencia who live right on the Mediterranean coast. I bet they'd love to host us, and it would be a great chance to practice your Spanish."

"Wait—'us'?" I ask.

"Is there a problem with that?"

A problem? No. *Many* problems? Yes. But I need to tackle one at a time. "Um, can you guys take off work like that?"

"I'm sure we could make it happen."

Dad clears his throat. "Actually, I don't have any vacation days left."

"We can afford for you to take unpaid time off."

"I'd rather not, Dana."

Mom turns to me. "Fine. A mother-son trip."

Suppressing my urge to cringe hurts. But I manage. "As wonderful as that sounds . . . I was thinking I could travel alone."

"Oh?" she says. "Too cool to hang out with your mom?"

Yes. Definitely yes.

"No," I say. "I just think it would be a good way to celebrate graduating high school, you know? Like becoming a man, and all that." It's corny, but whatever it takes. I would never be able to find out the truth about Jun with Mom hovering over my shoulder.

I gauge their reactions and can tell they're still not convinced. I take a moment to go over the Hail Mary speech I've prepared in my head. Of course, I can't just tell them straight up that I want to investigate Jun's death since they've already made it clear Tito Maning's family would rather forget about him completely. But I know a bit of the truth might help me make my case.

"What happened with Jun," I start, "made me realize how little I know about Dad's side of the family, about that side of myself. I mean, we see your relatives in Ohio almost every summer, Mom, but I haven't seen Dad's family or been to the Philippines in almost a decade. I don't speak Tagalog. I can't even name more than a handful of cities in the country. But all of that's part of me, isn't it? Or, I mean, it should be. It's like I only know half of myself."

My parents exchange a look. I can't tell if it's good or bad. I'm afraid what I've said came out more like an accusation than an explanation.

"I understand all of that, and I do think it would be good for you to go back." She uncrosses her arms and takes Dad's hand, lacing their fingers together. "But maybe the timing's not right."

Except I'm ready for this.

"The truth is, Grace asked me to go," I lie.

Dad cocks his head. "Really?"

I nod.

"You've spoken to your cousin since . . . ?"

I look him straight in the eye. "She's been having a really hard time and wants me to hang out with her for a bit. You know, to help her through it. But please don't tell Tito Maning—she doesn't want him to know it was her idea."

"I didn't know you two were close."

"We text sometimes," I say.

"But Maning doesn't allow her to have a phone."

"Oh. I meant message. Online."

He looks at Mom for a moment then back at me.

"She's having a *really* hard time," I repeat, hoping he cares enough about his niece's emotional well-being that it will sway him.

Dad lets go of Mom's hand and angles the laptop toward himself. He gazes at the screen and drags a finger across the trackpad to scroll the page. Mom leans back against the counter and watches.

"Jay's almost eighteen," he says.

"Almost," Mom says.

Dad scrolls up and down the page, making it clear he's killing time while he thinks instead of seeking information about the flight. Eventually he stops, runs a hand over his mouth, and then makes eye contact with Mom for several seconds.

Something passes between them, and a moment later, Dad pulls his phone from his pocket then turns his attention back to me. "I need to make sure it's okay with Maning."

"You serious?" I say.

He nods, then disappears to make the call.

I look at Mom expecting her to protest. But she sighs, mutters something about her baby boy growing up, and then wraps me in a hug.

Though Dad speaks to Tita Chato and Tito Danilo every few weeks, it's not unusual for him to go months without speaking to Tito Maning. And when he does, his conversations with his older brother typically last only a few minutes, more an exchange of news than a conversation. I'm counting on their lack of communication to work in my favor now, on him believing my lie that Grace doesn't want him to know it was "her" idea and honoring that, and on Tito Maning's desire to keep up appearances, to pretend that Jun's death really doesn't matter. If he were to refuse to host me, then that would be admitting that it does.

While Dad's gone, Mom eventually releases me from the hug and then asks about half a dozen more times if I'm sure I wouldn't rather go with her to Spain or Iceland or the Czech Republic. Dad rejoins us like ten or fifteen minutes later.

"Is it cool?" I ask.

He nods.

I want to wrap my arms around him, but that's not something we do. So instead, I tilt my head in a gesture of appreciation and say, "Salamat po. Thanks."

"You will stay with family the entire time," Dad says. "You won't go anywhere by yourself."

"Of course," I say.

Dad turns the laptop to face him and starts typing in the payment information. "Go get your passport," he says.

I do and then hover over his shoulder as he enters the last of the information. When he clicks to confirm the purchase, I can't believe this is really happening. A strange, fluttery feeling stirs in my chest. My heart wants to soar, but it's like a bird with clipped wings, the real reason I'm going keeping it grounded.

THINGS INSIDE

4 March 2012

Dear Kuya Jay,

I decided I want to be an astronaut when I grow up. We learned about the planets today in science class, and I wish I could see them for myself. Even though most everyone wants to visit Saturn because of its rings, I would fly to Jupiter. Did you know it has a storm that is thousands of kilometers in diameter that has been going on for hundreds of years? If I could go into the middle without being killed, I think that would be so beautiful to see. And if I got bored, I could go to one of its many moons. Teacher said one of them has water, and where there is water, there will be Filipinos.

I told Tatay at dinner, and he said it was stupid, that everyone knows the Philippines has no space program. Maybe it will one day, I said. Then I pointed out how we were some of the first people to cross the oceans, so why couldn't we be among the first to cross space? He shook his head and said I have been watching too many American movies. The

Philippines will never have a space program, he said. When I told him that I will move to a country that has one, he said no, that I was born here and I would die here.

After dinner, Grace told me she did not think my idea was stupid. She said she would like to visit Neptune. But when I told her how cold Neptune is, she switched her answer to Venus.

It is fun to dream about, but I think Tatay is right. So maybe you could become the astronaut instead. And if you're a very good astronaut, maybe they will let you take someone along and you could choose me. We could go to Jupiter, or we could go wherever you want. Anywhere but this planet.

Sincerely,
Jun

I am on the floor next to my bed rereading one of Jun's letters after dinner—still in disbelief that my parents have agreed to let me go on the trip—when there's a knock on my door.

"Can I come in?" Dad says from the other side.

I put the letter away and slide the box back under my bed, wondering if he's here because they've changed their mind. "Sure."

Dad enters, pushes aside some clothes draped over my desk chair, and takes a seat. He leans back and looks around. I wait for him to say something. Finally, he points with his lips at the poster of Allen Iverson on the wall above my bed—one of the very few recognizable Filipino habits he's retained. "That's new, yes?"

I shake my head. Iverson's still wearing a Sixers jersey in the picture. He used to be Jun's and my favorite player.

"Oh," he says. He looks around. Taps the statuette of the Forsaken Queen from *World of Warcraft* that's on my desk. "But this is, right?"

"Sure," I say, even though it was a Christmas gift from him and Mom three years ago. Another thing shaded with Jun's ghost because when we were in middle school, he snuck out to an Internet café so we could play online together a few times. He was terrible, of course, but I didn't care.

"I knew it." Dad goes back to letting his gaze wander, and I go back to waiting for him to say why he's here.

Eventually, I can't take it anymore. "So what's up, Dad?"

"'What's up?'" he repeats. "That's a very American phrase, isn't it?"

"Yeah, I guess so."

"You're very American. Like your mother. No accent like me."

I shrug.

"That's why I moved us here. I wanted you, your brother, and your sister to be American."

"Mission: accomplished." I draw my knees to my chest, seeing this for what it is.

"You may not speak Tagalog or know as much as you would like about the Philippines, but if we'd stayed, you wouldn't have had all the opportunities that you've had here."

I don't say anything, but I wonder if Jun would still be alive if our family had remained or if his family had joined us in the US.

"It's easy to romanticize a place when it's far away," he goes on, making this officially the most I've heard him speak at once in a long time. "Filipino Americans have a tendency to do that. Even me. Sometimes I miss it so much. The beaches. The water. The rice paddies. The carabao. The food. Most of all, my family." He closes his eyes, and I wonder if he's imagining himself there right now. After a few moments, he opens them again, but he stares at his hands. "But as many good things as there are, there are many bad things, things not so easy to see from far away. When you are close, though, they are sometimes all you see."

I want to tell him that I understand, but I don't because I don't. Instead, I ask, "Like what?"

"Just be careful and keep that in mind," is all he says, rising to leave. "I forwarded the flight info to your email. You'll be there for ten days. You'll spend three with Tito Maning, three with Tita Chato, three with your lolo and lola, and then one more with Tito Maning since he'll take you back to the airport."

"What about Tito Danilo?" I ask.

"He was assigned to a parish in Bicol a few years ago, so you'll see him when you are with your lolo and lola."

"Thank you, Dad," I say. "I really do appreciate it."

He stops in the doorway. "But, Jason, you must promise one thing."

"I know," I say, "stay with family at all times."

"Well, yes, but that's not what I was going to say. You must promise not to bring up your cousin while you're there. It will be too painful for them. Too shameful. They want to forget. To move on. Honor that."

"Of course, Dad," I say. "No problem."

He searches my face for the truth. Satisfied, he nods and leaves.

I may not have learned to speak my native language from him, but I learned to keep the most important things inside.

LIKE A FOG

I stay home from school again on Wednesday to prepare for a trip that does not feel real. I message my teachers to let them know I'll be out and to ask for work, and then I make a checklist of all that I need to bring. I select books; charge my electronics; and download music, TV shows, and movies onto my phone for the long-ass plane ride. I text Seth to let him know what's up. I DM Jun's friend again, but he's still MIA.

When Dad comes home from work, his car is loaded with stuff he picked up from Costco. I help him unload everything.

"*Pasalubong* for the *balikbayan* boxes," he explains.

"Huh?"

"*Pasalubong:* Gifts for the family. *Balikbayan:* One returning home."

I nod, vaguely remembering this happening before our last trip to the Philippines.

He sets up two cardboard boxes in the living room and then lays out everything he bought: clothing, medicine, toiletries, SPAM, ginormous tins of coffee, toys, school supplies, a couple pairs of shoes, and more. There's no way it's all going to fit in two of those boxes.

He starts methodically filling the first one, and I wander over and start with the second. He keeps glancing over and frowning. After a couple minutes, he stops what he's doing and tells me, "Like this." He gestures toward his box. "You need to put the heavier stuff on the bottom."

"Oh." I begin unpacking everything to start over, ashamed.

"Don't worry. I'll take care of it. Will you get the scale, please?"

I back away and let Dad finish.

After both boxes are full, Dad weighs them. One is a bit over and the other a little under the fifty-pound limit, so he swaps a few items until both are good to go. He then tapes them shut, writes Tito Maning's address on the sides in large letters with permanent marker, and binds them with nylon rope for good measure. He pats one and says, "For Maning and Chato." And then the other. "For Danilo and your lolo and lola."

When I think I'm finished packing my suitcase, Mom comes in and makes me run through my checklist with her to ensure I have everything. It's all there, but I can't shake the feeling that I'm forgetting something important. After she says good night, I pull Jun's letters from the box, bind them with a thick rubber band, and shove them inside my backpack.

It takes me a long time to fall asleep. When I do, I dream what I think is a memory. I am ten and back in the Philippines. I have spent the day at school with Jun, and now we are walking back to his house. Everyone's wearing the slacks and short-sleeved Barong of their school uniform, even me since I borrowed Jun's clothes. We're laughing because one of his classmates looks like a giraffe when he sticks out his neck, then everyone goes their separate ways at an intersection. I try to follow Jun, but he tells me I can't and picks up his pace. I try to follow him through the afternoon streets, which are crowded with people and cars and jeepneys and motorcycles. It's not long before I lose him.

We arrive at the airport in a predawn hush. My parents wait with me in a long line of Filipinos, each bearing their own balikbayan boxes. When it's my turn to check in and my boxes get weighed and tossed onto the conveyor belt, it strikes me that even though Dad took care of them up until now, I'll have to claim the boxes by myself in Manila. They'll be my responsibility.

I hug my parents. Dad holds on to me longer than I expect, and when we separate it looks like he's about to say something but stops himself. I say good-bye and head through security without looking back, relieved to be on my own at last but also feeling kind of adrift thinking about the long journey ahead. Detroit to South Korea, then South Korea to Manila. Almost twenty hours in all.

My flight is one of the first of the day, so the airport is still waking up. The terminal's halls are filled with bright, fluorescent light, but more workers than passengers. Most of the shops and newsstands are closed. The only place with a line is Dunkin' Donuts.

I find a seat right next to my gate. Through the windows, I watch the crew get comfortable in the cockpit and the flight attendants start to prep the plane. The handlers load the luggage into the cargo hold, my boxes somewhere in there. The sky lightens, but with the clouds I can't distinguish east from west.

The gate gradually fills with people until it's standing room only. As we begin to board, the knot in my stomach tightens. And as I make my way down the ramp, onto the plane, and into my seat, Jun's ghost follows like a fog.

THE STRENGTH OF MY
CONVICTION

I wake up certain I am about to die because an alarm is blaring in my ears. But when my eyes fly open, nobody else is panicking. All of the other passengers are sleeping or reading or talking softly. Yet, the alarm is still blasting, a shrill, urgent pulse drilling into my brain.

Finally, I realize the sound is coming from my headphones. It's some sound effect in the movie I fell asleep watching. I tap pause on the seat-back screen, and the alarm is immediately silenced. I laugh to myself and slip off my headphones. Relieved I am not about to die, I stretch in my seat a bit and rub my eyes, then I navigate to the flight map. The little plane symbol is partway across the Pacific Ocean. Four more hours to Seoul, where I have a layover, and then, for the first time in almost eight years, I'll be in Manila. No parents or brother or sister. Just me.

I try to look out the window, but I can't see much from my middle seat except for the blue of the sky. An old Filipino man sits in the window seat to my left. He's staring straight ahead with his eyes open, but his screen is blank. This is the same position he was in when I fell asleep, making me wonder at his ability to do nothing for hours on end. No book. No in-flight movies. No small talk. Just a rosary clutched in his hands. Maybe he's sleeping with his eyes open. Dude does look pretty old, so I guess he could be thinking back on his life.

A middle-aged white woman was to my right—the kind who seems like she probably posts a lot of photos of herself doing yoga on social media alongside inspirational quotes—but her seat's empty at the moment.

I consider resuming my movie or playing some game, but I don't really feel like doing either. I cycle through some of the available TV shows and movies, but the only thing that catches my attention is *Hitch,* starring Will Smith. I hit play, even though I've already seen it. I've seen all of Will Smith's films since Chris was obsessed with the guy when we were growing up. According to my brother, the first *Bad Boys* is the man's finest work, followed closely by *Independence Day.* It was mostly downhill from there. If you tell Chris *After Earth* is a great film, he will slap you, even though he saw it on opening day.

It's not too long before *Hitch* loses my attention. I dig through my bag and pull out Jun's letters. I've gone back and started rereading them chronologically, so I take out the next one. I lower the tray table, smooth the paper flat, and take a deep breath. I read.

29 September 2013

Dear Kuya Jay,
Did you know that if you eat mango and chocolate you will

have to go to the bathroom so much? It is true. Just ask Grace!

Sorry if that was a gross way to begin my letter, but I thought you might find it interesting. It could also be useful to know if you are ever having trouble with your bowel movements.

Anyway, I need to tell you about this thing that happened yesterday after Mass that is bothering me. Our family went to the mall—the big one we took you to when you were here? The driver dropped us off in front of the entrance like normal. It was very crowded and as we walked toward the door, this woman approached us. She was very dirty and smelled bad, like all of the other street people who beg. Except instead of holding out her palms for some coins, she held out something to my nanay. At first, I thought it was just a bag or a bundle of rags, and I wondered why she would be trying to give that to Nanay.

But then I looked closer and saw it was a baby, Kuya Jay. A baby.

Except it did not look like any baby I had seen before. It was so thin, and its skin was a weird color. Not really pale, but almost. Closer to gray, maybe. Anyway, it could not have been more than a few weeks old. It was not even crying.

"Please, ma'am," the woman said, and then coughed a few times.

My nanay kept walking. Everyone in my family kept walking. Everyone around us kept walking as if this woman were a ghost, as if she did not exist.

Except for me, Kuya. I stopped and looked at the woman's face. Her eyes were yellow. Her cheeks were hollow. Her teeth were crooked and incomplete. She held out her baby to me. "Please," she said again.

I reached to take the child—but then a hand clamped my arm and dragged me away. Away from the woman, past the security guard, through the open glass doors, and into the mall. In a flash, the woman was gone, replaced with the bright lights and bright smells of a thousand stores.

"Stay with us," Tatay said to me, still dragging me to catch up with my sisters and Nanay, hurting my arm.

"But that woman . . ." I said.

"What about her?" he said.

"She was trying to give me her baby."

"And what were you going to do, eh? Raise it?" He laughed.

I thought of the sermon we had just heard at Mass that morning. It was about the Good Samaritan. You know the one? I think everyone does. Or, at least, everyone has heard it. Every time I do, I think, surely, if I were in that situation I would be like the Samaritan and help the man in need. But how many times have I instead walked past?

And so I did not say anything, Kuya. I stayed silent. I let Tatay drag me through the crowd of shoppers until we rejoined Nanay and Grace and Angel. And when he finally let me go, I did not try to return to her.

I cannot stop thinking about that woman and her baby.

I feel like I should have taken her baby and given it to an orphanage or something. I told Grace this later, but she said there was nothing I could do, that I am too young to take care of a child. She also said that there are probably millions of children that need to be taken care of and even if I was old enough I could not take care of them all. Even though she is young, I know she is right. And that makes me feel like my chest is hollow.

But, it seems to me that there are so many older than us who are able to take care of those in need. If everyone did a little bit, then everybody would be okay, I think. Instead, most people do nothing. And that is the problem. Does that make sense, Kuya?

Anyway, I hope to hear from you soon. It has been a few months since your last letter. I want to know how you are doing and if you ever beat that video game that was giving you so much trouble.

Sincerely,
Jun

I feel a hand lightly touch my right arm. It's the woman in the aisle seat, back from the bathroom or wherever she was. "Are you okay?" she asks, her face colored with concern.

I blink and find my eyes are brimming with tears. I sit up, wipe them away with my hoodie sleeve, and clear my throat. "Oh . . .

um. Yeah. I'm okay. It's just the movie." I point at the screen. "It's really sad."

The woman's eyes follow my finger. We both watch as Will Smith tries to teach that stocky white guy how to dance.

It does not go well.

In Seoul, my connecting flight's been delayed. I'm sitting on the floor because there are too many people and not enough seats at the gate. But it's okay because South Korea is apparently decades ahead of the rest of the world. This place is as bright and as clean as a spaceship in an optimistic sci-fi film. There are outlets and USB ports everywhere you look. There are computers and touch screens set up throughout the terminal with free Internet access. But most impressively, the toilets have these sci-fi doors that slide out of the wall with the push of a button.

When you grow up in a country like the United States, you're constantly told it's the greatest place in the world. But then you go somewhere else one day and find out that bathroom doors like this exist, and you start to question everything.

But adults lie, I guess. That's what they do.

Sure, there are a bunch of reasons they do it, and people would probably say most of them are pretty good. When you're a kid, they lie and say you did a great job in a game even if you sucked. Then you grow up a bit and your mom and dad lie to you about how strong their relationship is and how much they love each other after they have a big fight. Then you grow up a bit more and they tell you the lie that life is as simple as studying hard, getting into a good college, and finding a decent job.

Sometimes I feel like growing up is slowly peeling back these layers of lies.

The truth of what happened to Jun is under there somewhere. And its burial seems increasingly intentional the more I think about it. Since Tito Maning's a big deal in the police force, it wouldn't have reflected well on him if his son was murdered as part of the drug war. I'm sure he has all kinds of connections, so maybe he leveraged one of them to keep Jun's name out of the press. Who knows what else he's hidden.

I pull my bag closer and shift to a more comfortable position, then put up my hood and close my eyes. I turn up the volume of my music to drown out the airport crowd, then I imagine the moment when Tito Maning will pick me up from the airport. Standing straight, I'll greet him, look him in the eye, and then ask him point-blank how his son died. I will not look away or be intimidated or be silent. I'm not a little boy anymore. I will hold his gaze until he gives me an answer, and if he lies, I will demand the truth. Like a tree in the wind, he will bend before the strength of my conviction.

A NEW SILENCE ARRIVES

As soon as I step out of the plane, the scent of Manila hits me. It's a smell I've forgotten I know, but its familiarity rushes back in an instant. It takes me back eight years to when I was here last with my family, and maybe even back to almost eighteen years ago when this air was the first that filled my lungs.

I follow the other passengers to immigration. The line moves quickly, and when I get to the front, the tired-looking immigrations officer asks, "Balikbayan *ka ba?*" as he examines my passport, which states the Philippines as my place of birth, and then compares the picture to my face.

I give the man a blank look since I don't know how to respond. I mean, I know he's asking if I'm a Filipino living abroad who's returning home—Dad had told me to say yes to this question as it makes things easier and grants me a longer visa just in case I should need it. But saying yes feels like a lie, even if the Philippines is listed as my place of birth in my passport.

He sighs, then says something in Tagalog that I don't understand. When I don't respond, he looks up. "You speak Tagalog?"

"No," I say. "Sorry."

He shakes his head like he's disappointed, stamps the page, and hands my passport back. I thank him and walk past, checking out the status he granted me. Surprisingly, it's the year long balikbayan visa.

Feeling somewhat more legit than I did a few seconds ago, I slip my passport back into my backpack and make my way to the baggage claim. I grab a luggage cart, throw my carry-on atop, and wait for the carousel to start moving.

I pull out my phone and check my Instagram messages thanks to the international SIM card Mom set me up with before I left. Nothing from Jun's friend's account, though, and his profile still has no posts. Maybe he only created it to reach out to me. But then why stop responding after dropping that bombshell?

In case he logs back in, I let him know I'm in the Philippines for the next week and a half and that I'd love to meet up and talk. After all, he's probably my best bet for finding out anything concrete. Next, I shoot a quick text to my parents to let them know I landed safely, then I put my phone away.

Except for a handful of white folks, Chinese, and Koreans, everyone else here looks Filipino. Black hair. Brown skin. Broad noses. Short statures. I've forgotten what it's like to be around so many people who look like me. I feel like I belong in a way I never do back in the States. But then again, my skin is noticeably lighter, and I can't decode any of the non-English words that fill the air. The in-flight magazine said that even though the national Filipino language is based on Tagalog, there are around 170 languages spoken throughout the country. I can't even begin to tell the differences between what people are speaking around me right now.

Eventually, there's a loud buzz and then the carousel kicks into motion. Bags and balikbayan boxes start sliding down the ramp, but I hang back as everyone else jockeys for better position.

Eventually, my boxes tumble down to the conveyer, and I drag them onto my cart. Then I push through a surprisingly lax customs line and past the crowd of families waiting outside of arrivals. I step out of the Ninoy Aquino International Airport into noise and sauna-like air. The parking garage across the way blocks the sun, but it doesn't block the humidity that's already making me sweat.

My dad told me Tito Maning would meet me in the passenger pick-up area, so I push my heavy-ass luggage cart outside. Except there are only hotel shuttles and taxis. I look around for signs while trying not to appear lost. A few people wander over offering, "Taksi? Taksi?" and then drift away when I shake my head. Eventually, I ask a security officer, and he directs me to a ramp across the way that leads to a lower level. But my relief at having found the correct spot is short-lived because there's no sign of Tito Maning in any of the looping cars or in the crowd of waiting faces on the other side of a low gate.

Ten minutes pass. Twenty. Thirty.

I'm sweating even more now, and not only because of the temperature. We still arrived on time even though we were delayed out of Seoul, so there's no reason for my uncle not to be here yet.

A low-level panic begins to bloom within my chest as I realize how completely helpless I am. Nobody thought to give me Tito Maning's number, so I message my dad to ask for it. But it's the middle of the night back home, so I don't expect a quick response. Of course, my uncle's address is written on the side of the boxes, but I don't have any pesos, and I'm not sure taxis here will take American money.

Maybe coming was a mistake. I don't even know how to get picked up from the airport. How am I ever going to discover the truth behind Jun's death?

I'm a few shallow breaths away from a full-on panic attack when an SUV with windows tinted so dark they're almost black pulls up to the curb. The passenger-side window slides down, revealing Tita Ami sitting shotgun and sporting expensive-looking shades. Her black hair is gathered into a bun, and she's wearing so much makeup her face is an unnatural shade of white. She offers a restrained smile and a stiff wave.

"Hello, Jason," she says. "Get in. Tomas will take your things."

I hear the driver's-side door open and close, and then a man who is not Tito Maning appears. He's bald and overweight, wearing flip-flops, jeans, and an untucked polo shirt. My adrenaline dissolves as I realize I'm not going to get the confrontation I have been waiting for. At least, not right now.

As the man approaches, he nods and points to himself. "Hello, sir! I am Tomas."

"Jay," I say as he takes my hand and shakes it vigorously.

He opens the hatch and starts hurriedly loading my boxes and suitcase. "Sir Jay, you speak Tagalog, sir?"

"No. Sorry," I say, wondering how many more times I'll have to apologize for that on this trip. Each time I do is like admitting to some deep moral failing.

He opens the rear door for me and motions for me to enter.

Angel waves to me brightly from the middle spot in the backseat. "Hi, Kuya!"

On the other side of Angel, Grace looks up from a book she's reading and nods, but she says nothing.

Seeing the two of them without Jun stings. But I put on a smile, say hi, and climb in.

The last time I was here, they were seven and four, and now they're fifteen and twelve. Grace is no longer the little kid I remember from before. There's a seriousness about her, a maturity, even in the way she sits calmly with her jet-black hair pulled back into a tight ponytail. Angel's changed so much, too, it's almost hard to believe. She's deep in that awkward preteen phase complete with pimples, braces, and gangly limbs. However, the top of her right ear is still squished down, and her medium brown skin—darker than mine or Grace's—is still a perfect match for Jun's. But both sisters have the same eyes that their brother did, deep brown and bright with intelligence.

The interior of the vehicle smells overwhelmingly like leather and air freshener, and it's chilly thanks to the AC and the tinted windows that block the sunlight. There's a statuette of Santo Niño affixed to the dash and a rosary dangling from the rearview mirror.

"How are things?" I ask nobody in particular. And, of course, I regret the question immediately. How do I think they are when Jun died about a week ago?

There's an awkward span of silence, and then instead of answering, Tita Ami asks, "How was the flight?"

"Long," I say, suddenly sad, thinking of all of Jun's letters I reread, thinking of how this family feels incomplete without him here.

Tomas returns to his place behind the wheel and pulls his door closed, instantly shutting out the noise and light and chaos of the airport pickup area. With rushed and practiced movements, he makes the sign of the cross, taps the rosary, and then pulls away from the curb.

"Kuya, when we flew to Singapore last year, I ate sushi on the plane," Angel says randomly. "It made me throw up."

"Cool," I say.

Conversation stalls and the car falls quiet sooner than I expected. Even the radio is turned off.

Grace keeps reading. Tita Ami checks her makeup in the mirror set into the sun visor. Angel stares at the people in the neighboring vehicles, occasionally nudging me to point out someone particularly funny-looking.

We creep forward, stymied by the bumper-to-bumper Friday morning traffic surrounding the airport. The only vehicles moving quickly are the swarms of motorcycles threading dangerously between cars.

After a few minutes, I ask casually, "Where's Tito Maning?"

"Working," Tita Ami says. "Your uncle is very busy these days."

I understand without her having to say it that it's the drug war keeping him busy, and I want so badly to use the moment to ask about Jun. But I hold my tongue. It's not that I'm intending to keep my promise to Dad. It's that I'm convinced nobody in this car knows the truth. After all, he hadn't lived with them for nearly four years. If anyone knows anything about what happened last week, it's Tito Maning.

"Will I see him tonight?" I ask.

"Don't count on it," Angel says, then points to the driver in the car to our left. "Kuya, that man looks like a sad frog, no?"

Tita Ami tells her not to be rude, but Angel insists it's okay since he can't see us. Grace's eyes stay glued to her page.

"What are you reading?" I ask.

"A book."

"Any good?"

She shrugs.

Eventually, we reach the highway entrance, where there's even more traffic. Most of the vehicles are headed into the city, but it still takes us about half an hour to move a few blocks. And there's so much honking. It's like people are using their horns for echolocation, so there's an unending cacophony of beeping over the rumble of engines.

At some point, we finally start moving. I gaze out the window and watch the city roll past. The high-rises of downtown Manila are behind us, but the billboards persist, advertising shampoo, fast-food restaurants, new housing developments, local politicians, cell phone plans, and anything else it's possible to sell. Almost all the models have skin as light or lighter than mine.

On the other side of the thin wall that lines the highway, I catch glimpses of small homes with unpainted cinder-block walls and corrugated metal roofs. Palm trees and dense tropical vegetation I can't even begin to name dot the landscape, sprouting from wherever there's a patch of earth.

It doesn't seem like there is a war going on—a war the country is waging against itself in the name of public safety, a war that has taken Jun's life plus thousands of others. Things don't appear much different from what I remember them being like eight years ago.

So with each silent mile, questions build inside of me.

Why did Jun run away from home in the first place? Where did he go? Did he ever contact his family? Why, exactly, was he killed? If not for drugs, then what? Why deny him a funeral?

Do they miss him?

I glance at Grace's book. The text is in English, but I don't recognize it. I try again. "What are you reading?"

She doesn't look up. "*El Filibusterismo*, Kuya. By Rizal."

"Oh," I say. I know she means José Rizal—the national hero of the Philippines who inspired the movement for independence when the country was still a Spanish colony—but I haven't read it. Come to think of it, I've never even read a book with a Filipino character. "Do you like Harry Potter?" I ask, reaching to build some connection.

Grace ignores me.

"Every student in the Philippines is required to read *El Fili* in grade nine," Angel explains. "In grade eight they read *Noli Me Tángere*."

Another book I haven't read. Another way I'm not Filipino enough.

She goes on. "I only just finished grade seven, but I have read them both already."

"Cool," I say, and make mental note to buy copies of each while I'm here.

Grace continues reading and Tita Ami continues being silent in the front seat while Angel and I chat about school in the Philippines. Like how high school used to end after tenth grade but was extended to twelfth a few years ago. How instructors speak in English instead of Tagalog except for in Filipino class. How in the public schools, there are so many kids that they only attend for half a day, either in the morning or in the afternoon. And even still, there are fifty or sixty in a classroom without AC. She and Grace go to private school, though, where they have full days, half the number of classmates, and perpetually cool air—except during brownouts.

After that, Angel bombards me with questions about Em. Where she's going to college, what she's studying, how she wears her hair now, her favorite band/movie/TV show, and so on. The girl seems to have an unhealthy obsession with my sister.

But eventually she runs out of questions, and the car falls quiet again. Tomas exits the highway and turns onto one of the smaller main roads that connects the region's neighborhoods. It's narrow with small awning-covered storefronts and kiosks occupying the shoulders on each side, selling everything from tropical fruits to tires to roast pigs to handmade furniture to headstones to empty aquariums to construction materials. It's like a shopping center deconstructed and laid out horizontally over the length of several miles.

I thought the highway driving was frightening, but it's even more terrifying on this road where people cross the street like it's some ultra-advanced level of that old game *Frogger*. Tomas pulls startlingly close to the rear ends of garishly painted jeepneys stuffed over capacity with passengers, swerves into oncoming traffic, and then cuts back into the right lane just in time, making motorcycles and tricycles dodge to avoid us. And every other driver employs the same technique, creating a chaotic world of abrupt braking and acceleration, of narrow misses and near-deaths, leaving imagined collisions lingering before my eyes. All the while, the rosary swings and nobody bats an eye but me.

Eventually, we slow to a stop at a clogged intersection. There's no traffic light, just a cop with a whistle in the middle of it all, trying to control the chaos.

I'm watching the cop's impressive effort when I'm startled by a knock on my window. It's a young girl, maybe a bit younger than Angel. Her hair is a tangled mess, her face is sweaty and smeared with dirt, and her raggedy dress hangs loosely on her thin frame. She looks at me with big, pleading eyes and holds out her hands.

Only Grace and I look up.

"Palimos?" I hear her say through the glass. *"Palimos?"*

"Do not worry, Jay," Tita Ami says, "she cannot see you. The windows are too dark."

I think of Jun, of all his letters I left unanswered. All his words that mourned how people ignored those in need.

I take a few American dollars out my wallet and Grace discreetly presses a few Philippine pesos into my hand. I roll down the window, hand the money to the girl, who thanks me with a straight face and a mumbled, "Salamatpothankyousir," and then moves away quickly.

I roll up the window with a small glow in my chest. Things are much cheaper here than in the US, so even though it was just a few dollars, it should last her a long time. Maybe she'll even be able to pay for a term of school.

"I know you mean well," Tita Ami says, "but you should not have done that."

76

"Why?" I ask.

A moment later, two boys—just as young and dirty and hungry-looking as the girl—approach and start knocking on the glass with their knuckles. Their knocking is more insistent, their pleas more demanding.

"They are like ants," Tita Ami explains. "You will never get rid of them all."

As I reach for my wallet again, traffic finally starts moving. The boys jog alongside the vehicle, but we leave them behind before I can take out any money.

I give Grace a pleading look, but she shrugs and goes back to her book.

Tita Ami says, "You cannot give money to everyone who asks for it while you are here. There are so many poor in this country. If you gave even just a peso to each one, you would be poor yourself before long."

I want to tell my aunt that she's wrong. But I remember what my mom said about how I can't truly understand what it's like to live here.

"Besides," Angel says, "Tatay says they will only spend it on shabu."

I sense a collective mental flinch in the car at the mention of the drug Jun had been supposedly using. It's like we've been dancing around broken glass and just stepped on a piece. But nobody reacts, nobody says anything.

"We give to the church, and they do what they can," Tita Ami says a few moments later in an artificially pleasant voice, as if to move us past the thought. "At least that way we are certain our donations will be put to good use."

If Jun were here, I bet he'd argue the hell out of that statement.

But he's not, so it goes unchallenged. The thought crosses my mind to step up and say what he might have, but I only half remember the criticisms he leveled at the church in his letters. Nothing I could say in this moment would do him justice. No, the best way I can honor my cousin's memory is to find out what really happened to him.

"Can we turn down the air?" I ask, the AC suddenly feeling too cold for me to bear.

Tita Ami makes a face. "It is very hot outside, I think."

"Yeah, but it's arctic in here."

Nobody moves to turn it down. The cool air keeps blowing. A new silence arrives.

SOME SMALL REBELLION

After driving for a while longer, we come to a freestanding cement archway that has what I'm guessing is the name of the neighborhood hand-painted across the top in large letters.

"Our *barangay*," Tita Ami explains as we pass underneath.

After a few blocks, we turn off the main road and Tomas rolls down the window, beeps his horn, and waves at a security guard as we pass his booth.

Like many of the neighborhoods on the outskirts of Manila, it's a collection of densely packed houses on narrow streets. Windows are covered with bars, garages have locked gates, and the property walls are lined with barbed wire or broken bottles set in the cement. Some of the houses have fresh paint and look immaculately maintained, while others look run-down or half-completed. Yet, even these have signs of life, like clothes hanging on a line or people peeking out from the openings where windows would go.

People are walking or biking down every side street we pass. Kids play alongside chickens and stray dogs. A carabao grazes on tall grass in an empty lot next to a basketball court shielded from the sun by a hangar-like canopy. An old woman sweeps the street with a straw broom, while nearby a group of men are gathered around a car's open hood, gazing at its engine.

"Do you remember all of this?" Tita Ami asks.

"Barely," I say.

"You were last here how long ago, Sir Jay?" Tomas asks, speaking for the first time in a while, as if nearly arriving at our destination has awakened him.

"About eight years." But it feels like a million.

He whistles, long and low. "That is a long time to be away from home, sir."

"This isn't his home," Tita Ami says.

Tomas laughs. His eyes meet mine in the rearview mirror. "It is in your blood, *di ba?*"

"Half of my blood, I guess." Not that I know what that counts for.

"Sir Jay, maybe while you are here you find yourself a nice Pilipina?" He winks.

I don't say anything.

"Or maybe you already have a girlfriend in America?" he asks.

Everyone's attention shifts to me. I shake my head. "No time to date," I say. "Too much homework."

Tomas nods knowingly. "Focus on your studies. That is good. Time for girls later!"

"Exactly," I say as if my singleness were a conscious decision. "And you don't have to keep calling me 'sir.'"

"Okay, sir!"

We make a few more turns, and then Tomas brings the SUV to a stop in front of the gated driveway and beeps the horn three times.

The house on the other side looks like it was teleported here from one of the billboard advertisements along the highway. Yeah, it has the same security features as the other homes and then some, but it's all tall windows and modern angles, accent stones and terra-cotta roof tiles, strategically placed mini–palm trees and walkway lights. Plus, this place seems to take up at least twice the space of the other lots and rises an extra level above the surrounding houses.

I realize it's Tito Maning's only when I spot the tiny shop—that I remember is called a sari-sari store—built into the next-door neighbor's faded pink cement wall. A memory of Jun buying every type of Filipino snack there one night so that I could taste each one blinks in my mind like a firefly. His favorite: a chocolate stick called Choko Choko. Mine: shrimp chips.

A weary-faced woman emerges from Tito Maning's house, a towel slung over one shoulder. She unlocks the gate and pulls it open, and Tomas drives through. We climb out of the car, squinting into the bright midday sunlight. The air feels like a wall of heat, and I start sweating immediately.

Book tucked under her arm, Grace immediately slips inside the house. Angel follows after her.

"We did some remodeling since you were last here," Tita Ami says.

"Looks nice," I say because I'm supposed to. But it's only Jun's room I'm interested in. I remember the posters of basketball players, the action figures, the boxy TV connected to a Wii, an acoustic guitar leaning against the corner, a journal hidden under the mattress. The focus of the room, though, was three tall bookshelves on the wall opposite the windows that were packed with books arranged by color. Like me, Jun was in the fifth grade. Unlike me, he was already reading novels while I was still all about *Diary of a Wimpy Kid*. When I asked how long it took him to read one, and he said a day or two, so I called him a liar.

I also remember that the room was clean and well-organized. At first, I assumed it was because of their housekeeper, but after just a few days of staying with his family, I noticed she cleaned every room in the house except his. When I asked him about this, he shrugged and said, "Why should someone else have to clean up after me?"

He hasn't lived here in a few years, but he must have left something behind that will tell me more about who he eventually became, about what happened to him. And once I'm left alone, I'll find it.

I start for the back of the SUV to unload my things, but Tomas waves me away and tells me that he'll take care of it. I start to protest, but Tita Ami says that that's what they pay him to do.

As soon as we enter the house, the AC hits me like I've walked into a refrigerator. The air smells like new construction and Filipino food. I follow Tita Ami's lead and step out of my shoes, leaving them by the door—something my parents stopped making us do back home years ago.

Surprisingly, the inside seems unchanged from what I remember. The foyer still leads into the living room, with the dining room, the kitchen, and the outdoor kitchen beyond. The crucifix above the entrance, the four seasons panels made of shells, the leather sofas arranged around an oriental rug, the tapestry of the Madonna and Child in a Renaissance style, the beige floor tiles—they're all the same as they were when I was here as a kid. The only updates I spot are the huge, flat-screen TV next to the tapestry and the new family photos that hang on the walls, none of which feature Jun.

Tomas brings in the last of my stuff and then says good-bye. When he pulls the door shut, the house is quiet except for the hum of air-conditioning and the muffled sounds of someone moving around outside.

"María," Tita Ami explains. "Our *kasambahay*."

I'm guessing that means "maid." I don't remember if it was the same woman as the last time I was here. Nobody ever bothered introducing us, not even Jun. He expressed regret about this in a letter at some point, but while we were visiting, she would go about her work as if invisible. A silent spirit who left behind a trail of fresh laundry, hot food, and clean dishes.

"Come. I will show you the house," Tita Ami says, handing me a pair of brand-new house slippers that I dutifully put on.

"Tita Chato and Tita Ines going to come by?" I ask. Last time, my aunt and her partner were already waiting here to greet my family when we arrived.

Tita Ami turns and starts to walk up the marble staircase. "You will see them on Monday."

"Not until then?" I ask, following.

"We do not speak to them anymore," she says over her shoulder.

That's news to me. Another thing Dad probably knew and chose not to reveal.

"Why not?"

Tita Ami offers no further explanation. Instead, she starts the tour. The core of the house—the living and dining rooms and the kitchen, along with the three bedrooms I remember from last time—are still in place, but there is a new wing, a new third floor, and even a new rooftop patio. In most parts of the house, the bathrooms have been remodeled and updated, the walls repainted, the furniture replaced. Minus the Santo Niños, the paintings of St. Mary, and the other Catholic paraphernalia scattered throughout the place, a lot of it looks like something out of a Williams-Sonoma catalog, which feels out of place in the tropics. All the while, Tita Ami's movements are controlled and composed. She tells me the exact cost of each renovation, translating the peso amount into American dollars. I make sure to nod and act appropriately impressed.

"That seems like a lot of work," I say. "Wouldn't it have been easier to move into a new house?"

She stops short and glares at me. "This is where we have always lived. This is our home. We try to improve it, not abandon it."

The last time my family visited, she and Tito Maning kept making passive-aggressive comments like this about Dad in front of everyone. Though Tita Chato would defend him, he never called them out on it. He'd just look down like a dog that's been reminded of its place in the pack as the third-born. As a little kid, I didn't know what was going on between them and nobody bothered to tell me. It was only later, from Jun's letters, that I came to understand how they resented Dad for leaving.

Too much my father's son, I let this fresh dig stand and follow her for the rest of the tour.

Eventually, we reach Jun's old room. We stop outside the closed door.

"You will stay here, in the guest room," she says. "You will take a rest now."

"'Guest room'?"

She ignores my question and all that it implies. If she feels strange about having me stay in her dead son's room, she doesn't show it. But neither does she open the door.

"We will eat after you wake," she says, and then walks away.

I'm exhausted from all the travel, but there's no way I'm napping before I have the chance to go through my cousin's old stuff.

I've seen a lot of movies where when a kid dies, the parents leave their room untouched. Like, model airplanes are left hanging from the ceiling, their wings collecting dust. The paint on the walls fade. The *Star Wars* bedspread is never replaced. A book lies on the desk, forever open to the same page. The room becomes a sort of museum as the years pass, or maybe a shrine. Time is frozen within those four walls. The kid still lives. He just stepped out for a moment and could return any second.

This is what I expect, but this is not what I find. Not at all.

Now, there is nothing in this room.

Well, nothing of Jun's. The basics are all here. A bed with a nightstand next to it. A dresser with a mirror. A wooden chair in the corner. There are no decorations. No pictures or artwork of any kind on the walls. Not even any of the Catholic trappings. A quick search confirms that the drawers are empty, the closet holds a few musty sheets and pillows, and the bed hides nothing except for a dusty floor.

All his things are gone.

The only signs of life are my suitcase and backpack sitting against the wall, which María must have brought up while Tita Ami was giving me the grand tour.

I sit down in the middle of the floor, in the middle of this monument to denial. A lump forms in my throat, and I feel the urge to cry approaching like a tidal wave. But I close my eyes, take a deep breath, and hold it back. The wave settles. The water calms. I'm not a little kid anymore.

I didn't expect to find all the answers here, but I expected to find something of what used to be. I didn't think that they would have erased him from their lives so thoroughly. I wonder how long it took them to transform his room—did they do it four years ago or just last week? And his stuff—Did they throw it away? Burn it? Donate it? Did they keep *anything* at all? Whatever the answer, did Tito Maning and Tita Ami take care of it themselves, or did they have Tomas or María or someone else do it?

Hopefully they boxed all of Jun's things up and shoved them into the back of a closet somewhere else in this house. If so, I'll find it the first opportunity I have.

But maybe I should know better than to think they'd grant him such a mercy. These people who were content to let him live in the streets, who didn't give him a funeral, who instructed Dad to tell me not to mention his name while under their roof. His "parents."

Needing to pull Jun back into this world, I reach into my bag.

2 December 2013

Dear Kuya Jay,

I received your letter dated in September. Europe must have been so beautiful—even if you were bored much of the time listening to tour guides, and even if you fought with Kuya Chris a lot. I am glad that you and your family had a chance to travel and that you returned home safe. Please tell me more about your trip in your next letter, and if you can, include some pictures. I would like to go there someday, and to visit you in the United States. It is very difficult for Filipinos to get visas, though. I guess many countries think that if they let us in, we will never leave.

Maybe they are right.

As for me, I recently visited the squatters in Legazpi with Tito Danilo (or Father Danilo? I am never sure what to call him ever since he was ordained). We were all spending time together when he said that he needed to go. I asked why, and he said he had to help feed the poor. I asked if I could go with him. Nanay said no, that it would be too dangerous, but Tatay said yes.

"We drive past the slums every day," he said to everyone, "and this boy has never actually stepped foot in them. It will be good for him to see how many of his countrymen live. To see how spoiled he is."

So I accompanied Tito Danilo to an old church in the city, we helped make sandwiches, and then we handed them out.

It is very difficult to describe what the slums are like. Many of the right words I do not know how to translate into English, and since you can probably find pictures and videos online, I will not try. Anyway, it is the kind of thing you need to experience for yourself to begin to understand. Like a full moon or a typhoon or love (so I am told).

Instead, I will say three things about my experience: first, it felt good to be doing something for other people. I spend so much time thinking about my troubles that I often feel very bad about life. But when I was handing out sandwiches, it made my problems go away for a time. It made me feel useful to the world in a simple way. Second, the Church may not be all bad. I met one old woman who had been doing this every week for the last forty-eight years. Even if God does not exist, this woman has been doing good in His name so maybe it does not really matter. I only wish the Church were more like her and less like the priests who abuse their powers. Third, the slums were not as bad as everyone makes them seem. There was not as much garbage as I expected, it did not smell as bad as I thought it would, and the people did not seem to be as miserable as I have been led to believe they are. Yes, it is VERY crowded and unsanitary and hot. But people still go to work, they still watch TV and look at the Internet through their phones, they still bathe and wash their laundry, they still have children that laugh and play and cry, they still love their families. Life persists.

I think Tatay wanted me to observe serious poverty and

then return and fall at his feet, thanking him for letting me
live in a house in which I have my own air-conditioned room.
Instead, I am thinking that in some ways it might be easier to
live there than here with him. But maybe I can only think that
because it is not my life.

Sincerely,
Jun

An overwhelming exhaustion overtakes me as I finish reading, and a queasiness settles in my gut. Did I grasp the depth of his unhappiness when I first received the letter? I can't remember.

I get up from the floor and move to the bed. I feel gross from traveling, but the prospect of showering strikes me as tiring as it does pointless. Instead, I lie down and pull thoughts of Jun over me like a blanket, like to do so within this house is some small rebellion.

EVERY SINGLE
SURVIVING WORD

It's dark when I wake to someone shaking my shoulder lightly. I shrug it off at first, feeling like I'm at the bottom of a well. But the shaking persists, and I slowly open my eyes. The hallway light spills through the doorway, silhouetting a figure next to the bed.

"Tita?" I guess, my mouth stale.

"Kuya," comes the sound of Grace's voice. "*Kain na*. Time to eat."

I glance at the time on my phone and feel a low-level panic because it's just after seven. I napped for almost eight hours. "Be right down."

"Okay, Kuya, but hurry or Angel will eat your flan," Grace says before leaving.

I lie in bed for a minute, rub my eyes, and then throw back the covers and head downstairs. The smell of sautéed garlic and spiced meat gets stronger the closer I get to the kitchen, making my stomach rumble. When I round the corner to the dining room, I stop short. The food is already on platters on the table, and everyone is already in their seats—including Tito Maning.

He's at the head of the table, looming like a volcano, his violent potential simmering under the surface. He's still wearing his police uniform—a short-sleeved, navy blue button-down shirt with darker blue pinstripes that's stretched tight across his barrel chest and biceps. A single silver star sits in the center of each epaulette on his shoulders. His badge gleams over his left breast, while over his right sits rows of ribbons atop a tag that bears our shared last name: REGUERO.

"Ah, Nephew," he says in his gravelly voice as he leans forward and runs a hand over his bald head. "It is nice of you to finally join us." He doesn't move to hug me or shake my hand. "We have been waiting for quite some time. Hopefully the food is not cold."

I stand there for a few seconds, holding his gaze, still disoriented from having woken up moments ago. My heart pounds like a drum. A feeling of dread settles in the pit of my stomach. My mind reaches for the first words of the mini-speech I had prepared for this moment, the speech in which I would demand the truth about Jun.

But under the weight of his gaze, I come up with nothing. I look away, like I usually do—like Dad would—and the opportunity dissolves.

"Sorry, Tito," I say. I feel his eyes following me as I make my way to the empty seat set at Tito Maning's right, next to Grace. Where Jun used to sit, maybe. I pull back the chair, and it scrapes across the tile.

"You should have set an alarm," he says.

"I did," I lie. "Jet-lagged, I guess."

"You need to keep yourself awake until nighttime if you want to overcome it," he says.

Everyone else around the table stays quiet. Motionless. Steam rises from the waiting garlic fried rice, chicken adobo, and what looks like oxtail soup.

I pick up the rice bowl and start to serve myself, but Tito Maning clears his throat pointedly. I freeze, rice paddle in midair, and look up. Everyone has joined hands except for me.

Right. Prayer.

"Sorry." I set the paddle down and take Tito Maning's and Grace's hands.

We close our eyes and bow our heads. Tito Maning recites the prayer that my family stopped saying long ago, then we all say "amen." Not wanting to do anything else wrong, I let everyone else start serving themselves before I dig in.

For a long time, nobody speaks. Not even Angel. There's only the clinking and scraping of forks and spoons against plates, the quiet sounds of chewing, the occasional lifting of a glass and gulping of water. It's awkwardly formal compared to back home, where we usually all eat at different times, typically while in front of the TV or a book or our phones. Loneliness and noise. The American way.

There's a strong sense it will stay like this until Tito Maning decides otherwise.

"Jason," he eventually says. "How was the flight?"

"Long," I say.

He glances at me like that was the stupidest answer ever.

"It was fine," I correct. "On time and everything."

He nods. "How is your tatay doing?"

I clear my throat. "He's good—I mean, well—he's doing well."

"Not well enough to visit home, eh? I told him to study medicine instead of nursing."

I don't know what to say to that, so I don't say anything. I long for the awkward silence of earlier.

"And your nanay?" he asks.

"She's also doing well. Busy, though, ever since her promotion."

He shakes his head. "It is not good for a woman to be away from her family so much. Who is to raise the children?"

"Um," I say.

"I hear your kuya is doing very well in Texas. Very successful, no?"

"Yeah, I guess. I don't hear from him much, though. He's pretty busy. Plus, he started dating this new guy a few months ago and then fell off the face of the earth."

He makes a face. Then gestures toward Grace with his lips. "This one will be even more successful, I think. She is at the top of her class in both appearance and intelligence. Every test they have, she scores the highest."

Grace shifts under his attention, clearly uncomfortable with the praise.

He gestures toward Angel. "That one is lazy. She needs to work harder and eat less."

Angel stiffens.

"And your ate Emma?" Tito Maning asks.

"Emily," I correct.

"She is still wasting your tatay's money studying 'art'?"

Not sure what to correct here. "Graphic design," I say.

"And your father tells me you were accepted into Michigan University?"

"Yup."

93

"'Yup'?"

"I mean, yes."

"Did you not apply to Harvard like your kuya?"

"I didn't get in."

He nods as if expecting that.

"Grace will attend Harvard when she finishes her studies here. But you are at least on scholarship?"

"No . . ."

"No?" He lets out a small scoff then shakes his head.

Jesus. Jun dealt with this constant judgment for fourteen years.

"What will you study?" he asks, moving on. "Engineering, medicine, or law?"

I take a drink from the bottle of distilled water that I know they buy specially for me since my American stomach can't handle their water.

"Engineering," I lie, hating that to people like him those are the only three career paths. In reality, I'm planning to go in undeclared and then change my major eventually to something to do with making video games. But I'm pretty sure if I told him that, he'd slap my plate off the table.

Tito Maning nods, like I've answered correctly.

Since we're doing a round of updates, this is a perfect opportunity to bring up Jun—but I can't bring myself to broach the topic. It's less a space for someone else to enter the conversation and more a vacuum sucking us into Tito Maning's judgment.

I'll ask him about Jun another time, when it's just the two of us alone. Without an audience, maybe I'll be less scared and less self-conscious, and maybe he won't feel the need to make me feel small if there's nobody there to witness it.

When Tito Maning speaks again, it's in Tagalog and to Tita Ami. From where I'm sitting, though, their exchanges sound less like natural conversation and more like interrogations. He asks. She answers. He comments. He asks another question. She answers. He comments. This cycle repeats for some time with her and then with each of my cousins in turn while I stay quiet and keep eating. They slip in some English every now and then, but it's not enough for me to follow the conversation.

As dinner winds down, Tito Maning turns back to me. "Tomorrow, I work, and your tita Ami must take Angel to dance class. So Grace will show you around the city. Tomas will drive you."

"Okay," I say, as if I have a choice.

"You wasted today sleeping," Tito Maning says, "so I am thinking Grace can take you to some of our historical sites tomorrow." He says something in Tagalog to Grace, probably suggestions of where to go. And then to me, "I am thinking your tatay has taught you nothing about our history."

I don't say anything.

"Do you know when Rizal was executed?"

I shake my head.

"How much America paid to 'buy' this country? How many the Japanese killed and raped during the occupation?"

I don't say anything.

He sighs. "It is a shame. When your kuya was first starting to speak, I said to your tatay, 'You must teach him Tagalog and Bikol,' and do you know what your tatay said to me?"

"No," I respond, not wanting to know.

"'The boy does not need to be confused,'" he says in a feminine, mock-American accent meant to imitate my dad. "'Christian will be going to America, so he needs only good English.'" He lets out a sarcastic laugh. "And what is the result? None of his children knows their mother tongue. And if you do not know your mother tongue, you cannot know your mother. And if you do not know your mother, you do not understand who you are."

If I were braver, I would defend my dad right now. I would ask Tito Maning where his own son is. But I keep my head down, push around the fatty pieces of meat still on my plate, and hold my tongue.

I feel Tito Maning's eyes on me. "It is not your fault. While you are here, you will learn. Grace and Angel will teach you some Tagalog. We will take you to important places. You might even find yourself a nice Filipina. By time you leave, you will be more Filipino than your tatay, eh?"

I know it's his attempt at a joke, but my blood is boiling since this dinner has transformed into an accounting of my failings. I put down my fork and spoon and wipe my mouth with my napkin.

"But make sure to stay out of the sun while you are here," Tita Ami adds. "Your skin will get dark and ugly. You have very good skin already."

"Um, okay," I say because even though this seems wildly prejudiced, I don't want to get into it with Tita Ami. I just want to retreat upstairs.

I push my chair back and start to rise—but Tito Maning hisses.

Everyone looks at me.

"You have not been excused, Nephew. I know my brother did not teach you about our history, but did he fail to teach you manners, as well?"

"Sorry, Uncle. I'm not feeling well. May I be excused?"

"No," he says. "Everyone is still eating, and there is good food on your plate. This is not America. We do not waste in the Philippines."

I hover above my chair, half standing, half sitting, trying to decide what to do. If I walk away, would he hit me? I doubt it. At the same time, something about the tone of his voice—a voice accustomed to giving orders and having them immediately carried out—compels me to wait for his permission to leave.

"Is something wrong with the food?" he asks as my indecision lingers in the air between us like some nasty odor. "I know it is not hamburgers or pizza, but I think María is a very good cook. It is why we hired her even though she is not very smart and barely speaks Tagalog."

Now I feel like I should defend María even though I don't even know her, but I don't know what to say. Tito Maning seems to have this effect on me where I know what is right, but I feel too weak to do it. I place a hand over my abdomen. "It's my stomach. All the travel is messing with it. Or maybe it's something I ate on the plane."

"Maning," Tita Ami says nervously, "if Jay is not feeling well, why should we force him to stay at the table?"

"It is the least he can do to show us respect. Besides, we still have not done pasalubong."

I give up, but this tension's making me uncomfortable as hell and I need some kind of break. "May I take my plate to the sink?"

He nods.

In the kitchen, María is standing by the sink as if waiting to be called. Seeing her up close, I'm guessing she's in her late twenties or early thirties. Her black hair is gathered in a messy bun, and her skin is much darker than anyone else's in Tito Maning's family. When she notices me, she rushes over to take the plate from my hands, head bowed.

"I can wash it myself," I say. "It's okay."

"No, sir," she says, smiling. "No, no." Then she says more in Tagalog, or maybe in her native language, voice quiet and low. But it's clear she's not going to let me near the sink, so I finally hand it over.

"Thank you," I say, trying to make it seem like I really mean it. "It was very good. Very sarap."

She smiles at the small bit of the language I probably just butchered, but I still feel guilty.

I take my time returning to the dining table and then sit quietly while everyone finishes. After they do, we move to the living room and sit around Tito Maning, who opens the balikbayan box Dad marked for him and Tita Chato. I'm a bit nervous since Dad didn't tell me who's supposed to get what, but Tito Maning doesn't bother consulting me. He sifts through the items, examining each one before passing it to someone in the family, setting it aside for himself, or putting it back into the box. When he's emptied about three-quarters of the contents, he declares the rest for Tita Chato and Tita Ines and then dismisses us.

I immediately retreat to Jun's old room, close the door, and lie down on the bed. I try to fall asleep but can't. The sense that I betrayed my cousin by letting my silence bury him buzzes around my brain like a mosquito I can't brush away. How am I going to confront my uncle when I couldn't even distribute Dad's gifts by myself?

The fact that it's so cold in this house isn't helping me fall asleep.

I get up, shut off the AC window unit, and then lie back down.

The room quickly warms. Like, real quickly. I actually switch the AC back on a few minutes later.

Eventually, I hear people walking around, pushing in chairs, clearing dishes. Then the TV turns on and there's the muffled drone of evening news anchors. Outside, I hear construction noises, people calling to one another and laughing, cars honking, dogs barking.

An hour passes. Two hours. Feet stomp up the steps, the hallway light turns off, and doors slam shut. The neighborhood's sounds gradually quiet, but there's always a low hum of activity, never the complete suburban silence I'm used to. Despite my emotional exhaustion, sleep doesn't come.

Finally, I give up. I reach over to my backpack, unzip it, and fish for a letter to read.

But my fingers can't find the stack of folded papers.

I pull my bag closer, open it all the way, and dig through, using my phone's flashlight to illuminate the contents.

But I still can't find them.

I know they were right here—I read one before my predinner nap.

I get up and turn on the room's light. I remove every single item from my backpack. I check every pocket. I turn it upside down and shake it until crumbs and dust fall out. And then I search my suitcase, every corner of the room, my empty backpack again, my suitcase again, my backpack again.

Nothing.

Every single letter is gone—and with them, Jun's every single surviving word.

NOT AN ANSWER TO
THE QUESTION

The roosters start crowing way before sunrise. I know this because I'm still awake when it happens.

I've been thinking about how to bring up the issue of my missing letters. María was the only one who wasn't in sight during dinner, so it must have been her. But why? What would she possibly want with them?

Since we don't speak the same language, I'll have to ask someone else about it, but how can I do that without sounding like some spoiled brat accusing the help of theft?

I keep waiting for the sound of a door opening or a toilet flushing or footsteps walking down the hall—any signal that someone else in the house is awake.

I didn't fall asleep the first night we were in the Philippines the last time I was here, either. In fact, I stayed up all night in this same exact room. Jun was so excited that I was there, so relieved to have another boy in the house who was his age. Unlike whenever I spent the night at my friends' houses, Jun didn't want to play video games for hours on end or watch movies. Instead, he wanted to talk, to know about me. He asked question after question about my life, the hunger of his curiosity surprising me. Up until that point, I thought only girls could talk for as long as we did. I don't know why I thought that, but I immediately realized what I'd been missing out on.

We are bound to family by blood, but there's no guarantee any connection exists beyond that. Look at Dad and his brothers and sisters. Look at Chris and Em and me. I get along well enough with my siblings, but I don't feel like they understand me, and I'd guess they feel the same. It was different with Jun, though. That first night I knew that if we would have been classmates, that we would have been best friends. There was something we recognized in each other, I think, even if we couldn't name it, even if I still can't all these years later.

And the questions he asked, I still remember. They were surprisingly deep for a ten-year-old, not the usual superficial stuff like favorite color, food, TV show, basketball player, etc. No. Jun asked me if I liked my family. He asked me what I found beautiful. He asked me if I believed what the Bible said and what the priests said during Mass, if I thought heaven and hell really existed, if I believed that those who committed suicide really were damned forever. He asked me if I ever felt lonely.

I answered all of them as honestly as I could, even if my answers were dumb. I mean, I'd never had to give much thought to most of that stuff before. And even if I had, the answers lived inside of me, and when I pulled them out into the light they were pale, weak things.

There was something about Jun, about the way he asked the questions, that didn't even make me hesitate before speaking, that didn't make me feel self-conscious or like I had to give the right answer or try to sound smart. It was like he actually wanted to know what I had to say no matter what it was, like he wanted to know me. He wasn't just waiting for his turn to speak; he wasn't waiting to judge.

So I told him I liked my family okay, but that sometimes I thought they were disappointed in me or thought I was weird, even if they never said it. I told him I found Rihanna and Katy Perry beautiful. That I believed the Bible because God wrote it. That, yes, I felt alone all the time, even when I was surrounded by people.

He never gave me his own thoughts on these topics unless I asked, and his letters would later reveal that he remembered most everything I ever told him.

The letters.

Damn.

I finally hear someone stirring downstairs, so I jump out of bed. I find María—who I was hoping I'd find—in the kitchen, preparing breakfast. As I approach, she looks up and offers a small, forced smile before returning to her work.

"Magandang umaga," I say.

She returns the greeting.

My knowledge of Tagalog exhausted, I proceed in English. "Thanks for bringing my bags upstairs last night."

She nods and smiles. Of course, I can't tell if it's because she's acknowledging what I said or just the fact I said something.

"Umm . . . but I can't find some letters that were in my backpack." Even though her attention's focused on the food she's prepping, I trace the shape of a rectangle in the air with my free hand, followed by a gesture like I'm writing. "They were definitely in there before.

But they're not anymore." She says nothing. "Maybe they, like, fell out while you were carrying my stuff upstairs, or something?" I suggest so I don't sound too accusatory, even though I know they couldn't have since I read one before I had taken my extended predinner nap.

I search her face for some form of recognition, but María simply nods and smiles again without looking up and starts slicing a pepper. She's either a masterful liar or has no idea what the hell I'm saying.

Why would she take letters written in a language she can't speak?

I sigh. I've lost the only piece of my cousin that seems to remain in this world. I wish we would have just messaged online like normal kids. It wouldn't have been the same thing as being able to hold the pages and smell the ink, but at least I would still be able to read his words.

And then it hits me: María works for Tito Maning. Maybe he asked her to search my stuff for whatever reason. Jun said his father periodically did that to make sure he and his sisters weren't bringing home drugs or anything else illegal. Jun hated it, of course, hated the mistrust. In the letter where he first mentioned it, he said that it almost made him *want* to bring home something illegal just to spite Tito Maning.

I peel away from the kitchen and drift across the dining room, across the living room, and into the new wing. One of the rooms they added to the house was an office for Tito Maning. If María took the letters at his command, I'm guessing that's where they'll be now. And since it's not even five a.m. yet, I've probably got at least an hour before any sane person would wake up. I wish I would have thought to do this even earlier, but oh, well.

The door is closed. I knock lightly in case he's in there, but when there's no sound or movement from within, I push it open, step inside, and close it quietly behind me.

The air is cool from the air conditioner that's humming despite the fact the room's empty, and since the sun hasn't risen yet, I can only make out the vague shapes of furniture in the dark. I almost flick on the light but decide not to in case someone should wake up and notice it shining under the door. So instead, I take out my phone and turn on the flashlight.

I remember the simple layout from the grand tour. At the end of the room, there's an expansive desk, its back to a large window. Shelves run along the side walls, one filled with books about history and politics while the other displays a collection of knives. So many knives.

I step out of my house slippers to mute my steps and then make my way behind the desk. I shine the light over the desktop and notice there are no family photos like on the desk my parents share back home. There's only a blank calendar showing the wrong month, a small clock with unmoving hands, a statuette of a bull rearing its horns, an award of some kind from the government.

I sit down in the desk chair and check the drawers. The first couple contain pens, pencils, paper clips, and the like. I sift through the office supplies to make sure there's nothing hidden at the bottom or the back of each, but the most incriminating thing I find is half a pack of cigarettes and a lighter. A guilty pleasure, perhaps?

The next drawer, much to my surprise, is crammed full of Toblerone bars and packages of those Ferrero Rocher chocolates that are wrapped in gold foil—maybe the reason the AC runs 24/7 in this room? I consider pocketing a couple since they're so effing good, but he seems like the type of person who takes daily inventory.

The last two drawers, one on each side of the desk, are the kind that contain hanging file folders. I pull out the one on the left, and it's so light that I already know it's empty. Sure enough, there's only dust and stray folder tabs. I try the one on the right—but it won't budge.

There's a small keyhole, so I search through the other drawers for a key. I don't find one, but there are plenty of paper clips. I straighten one out and then poke the thin metal into the keyhole. I have no idea what I'm doing, of course, but it always looks so easy in the movies. Maybe if I keep poking it will hit a release?

"Kuya Jay?" comes Angel's voice from across the darkness, startling me so I drop the paper clip and my phone, sending them clattering to the floor.

"Um," I say, gathering them quickly and trying to think of a believable excuse. I lift the light to see my cousin approaching in her pajamas, hair loose and falling down her shoulders and back. "Oh, hi, Angel. I'm just . . . I'm . . . um—"

She crosses the room. As she starts to move around the desk, her eyes land on the lock. "Are you trying to break into Tatay's desk?"

I freeze. "No, I—"

"Because you will need the key."

"Huh? Oh, like I said, I'm not—"

Angel laughs. By the blue-white spotlight of my phone, I watch as she makes her way to one of the bookshelves. Going up on her tiptoes, she tilts one of the books upward and slides something I can't see from underneath it. Turning to me, she points at the spot. "When you are finished, you return it here." Then she walks back over and sets a small key on the desk in front of me. "You will not find anything interesting. It is all boring police files."

"Thanks," I say, picking up the key, amazed. Seems Jun wasn't the only rebel in this family.

"What are you looking for, anyway, Kuya?" she asks.

As I think of whether to tell her the truth or not, I unlock the drawer and pull it open. Sure enough, it's a bunch of files. I'm afraid of making her too sad by bringing up Jun, but I do go with some measure of the truth considering she helped me out. "Some important papers I had in my bag are gone."

"What kind of papers?"

I start flipping through the files with my fingertips, scanning for lined paper and Jun's handwriting, for my letters. "Research," I say. "For a project. On Duterte." Not entirely a lie.

"And you think Tatay took them?"

So far, all I see are official-looking documents. Nothing that remotely resembles anyone's personal letters. "Maybe."

I expect her to ask why I think her father would go through my stuff and confiscate my possessions, but she seems to accept it as a possibility because all she says in response is, "Be quick—Tatay will wake up soon."

"Okay. Thanks again. See you at breakfast, cousin."

"Not if he catches you."

I laugh.

She doesn't. "Seriously, Kuya, do not forget to put the key back."

Angel disappears as quietly as she appeared. The silence resettles. I keep flipping through the files, still finding nothing but what looks like police reports or documents—why Tito Maning would keep them at home and not at the station, I have no clue.

By the time I've made it to the last folder at the back of the drawer, I still haven't found any of Jun's letters. I flip through the files one more time to make sure I didn't skip over any by mistake. I'm ready to give up when I make it to the last file again, but then I think of one more place to search—I push the folders all the way to the back.

My stack of letters isn't at the bottom of the drawer, but there is a piece of white paper folded in half. I slip it out and unfold it to discover a long list of names and addresses. The top corner is torn a bit, as if it was ripped from a stapled packet.

I'm about to put it back when my eyes land on Jun's name about three-quarters of the way down, circled in pencil. But it only says UNKNOWN in the address box.

What is this?

I flip it over to see if there's any more information and find a few messy, handwritten sentences that end with a question mark.

Unfortunately, I have no idea what it says since it's entirely in Tagalog. The only words I recognize are "Chief Reguero" and "anak," which I know means "child."

I pull up a translation app on my phone and start typing in the words, not sure if I'm spelling them correctly thanks to the bad handwriting.

Halfway through the first sentence, I hear a toilet flush, then the rush of water moving through the pipes.

Damn.

My heart starts racing. I try to hurry, but that only causes me to mess up more. Then it finally hits my dumb ass—I snap a pic, slip the note back, slide the drawer closed, and lock it.

I hear someone start down the steps, and my brain screams at me to get out of there. I scramble around the desk and over to the bookshelf to rehide the key—but which book was it under? Panicking, I tuck it away at random, rush out of the study, and duck into the bathroom across the hall.

As I pull the door closed, whoever's coming downstairs reaches the main floor. There's a pause, like the person's deciding which way to go, and then I hear the shuffle of house slippers approaching.

Shit.

A moment later, they're right outside the bathroom. Right outside the study.

Shit—did I remember to close the door when I hurried out?

I jump as the bathroom doorknob jiggles. But I locked it, so it holds.

"Occupied," I say. But it feels more like a squeak.

"Oh, Jason," comes Tito Maning's voice, thick with sleep. "Why is the light closed?"

Shit. I'm standing here in the bathroom in the dark. "Um . . . it's more peaceful?"

There's a moment of hesitation on his end, and then, "*Kain na*. Breakfast."

"Be right there." And then I listen.

Except I don't hear him leave.

I imagine Tito Maning's spidey sense tingling, as if my presence in his study moments ago left some temporal residue lingering in the air. A moment later, though, he walks away.

I exhale with relief and drop to the floor. Then I pull up the picture on my phone to finish typing the note into the translator.

But the photo—taken in a rush—is out of focus and blurry as hell.

Over breakfast, I mention the papers missing from my bag. The ones for my "research project." I describe the thick bundle bound by a rubber band.

"They might have fallen out," I say. "Did anyone happen to see them somewhere?"

Nobody says anything at first. They keep on eating their tapsilog and drinking their instant coffee or Four Seasons juice.

"Sorry, Kuya," Angel says, shrugging. "I lose things all the time, too. It helps to retrace your steps."

Grace shakes her head.

Tita Ami: "No, but I will tell María to look for them today while you are out."

Tito Maning's face betrays nothing. A moment later he scoffs, keeping his eyes on the last bit of meat he's scraping into his spoon. "If the papers were that important, you should have stored them somewhere safe."

The DM from Jun's friend. The stolen letters. The list of names.

There's more to Jun's story than anyone here is letting on.

"I thought I had," I say, observing that my uncle's response was not an answer to the question.

LEAD THE WAY

After breakfast, a car picks up Tito Maning to take him to the station. Tita Ami and Angel head to Angel's dance class a few minutes later. Then Grace and I hop in the SUV with Tomas to spend the Saturday checking out Rizal Park and Intramuros, two of the major tourist attractions in downtown Manila. It'll be cool to learn a bit of history while I'm here, although I'm more interested in the opportunity to talk to Grace alone.

But as in the car yesterday, she hides behind her book like it's a shield. I scroll through that GISING NA PH! Instagram feed, trying to decide if I should casually tilt the screen her way and ask if she's seen it yet. Doesn't seem like the most sensitive way to broach the topic of her brother, though.

Small talk. I'll start with small talk.

"What's it like being one of the only teenagers in the world without a cell phone?" I ask.

Grace presses a finger to the page to mark her place and then lifts her head. She eyes me for a moment as if sizing me up. "There are many teenagers in the world without a cell phone, Kuya."

"Yeah, I know. I meant, like, of your friends. A lot of them have phones, right?"

She nods.

"Back in America, pretty much every kid has one starting in middle school. Most would die without them."

Shit.

Why'd I say *die*?

She continues reading. Tomas catches my eye in the rearview mirror and shoots me this look like I'm a total dumbass.

I try again. "I mean, it must be weird that you're not allowed to have one even though your family can afford it."

"It seems to me it is better."

"Why's that?"

"Many of my friends spend so much time worrying about likes or favorites or followers. But none of that is real."

Okay. Not what I expected from a sixteen-year-old girl.

"Also, I do not think I would read as much if I had a phone," she adds.

"Yeah. But still. That's a strict rule, you have to admit. Your dad . . . he's intense. Don't you ever wish things could be a little different?"

Grace considers this. *"Bahala na."*

"Huh?"

"Whatever will be, will be."

"Oh."

"Tatay loves us very much and wants us to be safe and successful. I trust his decisions."

"But Jun—"

"I don't want to talk about Kuya Jun," she says, her tone suddenly icy.

I notice Tomas glance at me again in the rearview mirror—then I jerk forward as he slams on the breaks. A stray dog with mangy fur trots across the street, inches from our bumper. Tomas lays on the horn, rolls down the window, and curses out the animal for some reason.

Then he turns to us, wide smile and bright voice again. "Sorry, sir. Sorry, ma'am."

We lapse back into tense silence. Several more minutes pass before Tomas mercifully says, "Sir, ma'am—we are here."

He pulls up to the curb, Grace says something to him in Tagalog as she tucks her book into her purse, and then we hop out into the heat and noise. We wave good-bye to Tomas, and then the car disappears into the maw of traffic.

Rizal Park is an expansive greenspace several blocks long sur-rounded by high-rise condos and a bustling business district. People stroll up and down wide stone walkways lined with Philippine flags, palm trees, topiaries, and grass lawns that are almost well-maintained. At one end there's a pond and a stone obelisk. At the other stands a large statue and some ancient-Rome-type buildings that I'd guess are museums or government offices.

"Which way?" I ask Grace, taking it all in.

She doesn't answer, and when I look over, I see why—she's staring at a phone in her hand.

"Wait—I thought . . . ?"

She raises her eyes to me, waiting for my reaction.

"I won't tell anyone."

She almost smiles. "Good."

Her attention lingers on me for another beat like she's about to say something else, but then she goes back to whatever she was doing on her secret phone.

Good for her.

"So . . . shall we check out that monument-looking thing or that big dude with the sword?" I ask.

"No."

"Um."

"Follow me," she says, stuffing her phone into her purse and then taking off swiftly down the street away from the park.

The scenery shifts as soon as we turn the corner. Stalls and street food vendors and crowds pack the sidewalk so densely I can't even see the park anymore. People sleep on flattened-out cardboard wherever there are slices of shade. Flyers are pushed toward our hands. A small kid swings a loose tree branch to which a kitten's desperately clinging. A man is sitting in a chair with a paper cone in his ear, the end of which another man is lighting on fire. A crowd gathers around two people at a game board. Every few feet, scents alternate between sunbaked garbage and fried food.

"Stay close, Kuya," Grace says, stepping off the sidewalk and through a row of parked tricycles.

I follow, and we make our way along the side of the street where the crowd is thinner but the chances I'm going to get hit by a car are much, much higher. Then Grace turns and flags down a jeepney with the Chicago Bulls logo hand-painted on its side. We climb into the back. People scoot over to make space for us on one of the benches, but it's a tight squeeze.

"Guessing we're not going to Intramuros?" I ask.

"We are not." Grace fishes a couple of coins from her purse and calls out, *"Bayad po."* She hands them to another passenger who passes them up to the driver whose dashboard is a plywood panel without any meters.

"So where we going?"

"The mall," Grace says.

"The mall?"

"Yes, Kuya."

"Why?"

"To meet someone."

"Who?"

"Do you always ask so many questions?"

"It's kind of a new thing," I say.

"Maybe for now you stop. Enjoy the ride."

One jeepney transfer and about twenty minutes later, we're in front of a huge building with a metal globe out front. SM MALL OF ASIA reads the sign.

"What does SM stand for?" I ask as we walk toward the main entrance.

"Shoe Mart," she says.

"Shoe Mart? Does the entire mall only sell shoes?"

"They are a big company that began as a shoe store. In the US, you name things after big companies, *di ba*?"

"Oh, yeah, I guess," I say. "The Detroit Pistons play in a stadium called Little Caesars Arena."

"The pizza restaurant?"

"That's the one."

She shrugs. "See, Kuya. You name a basketball court after a pizza restaurant. We name a mall after a corporation that grew from a shoe store."

"Ah, the poetry of capitalism," I joke.

Grace smiles for the first time since I've arrived.

We pass through security, cross the atrium, and step onto the escalator. The place is packed, and like most malls I've been to, it's all linoleum and skylights, pop music and perfume.

When we reach the second floor, there are two girls standing there waving at us. Sisters, I'd guess. Around our age. The taller one has straight black hair with stylish bangs and is wearing the kind of dress/thick-framed glasses combo that makes me think she has a lot of Snapchat followers. While the shorter girl is in all black and has one of those hairstyles where one side of her head is shaved close to the scalp, which makes me think she doesn't even use Snapchat.

Grace hugs them and introduces me as her cousin. Then she points to the shorter girl: "Mia." Then touches the taller girl's arm: "Jessa."

"Um, hi." I don't know if I'm supposed to shake their hands or what, so I stand there and wave awkwardly.

"They are sisters," Grace says, confirming my initial impression. Then she starts speaking to them in Tagalog. There's enough English mixed into their conversation to make me feel like I might be able to figure out what they're saying, but not enough for me to actually do so. There's also some laughter and glances cast my way, so I pull out my phone to have something to do other than feel self-conscious.

But they only carry on for a few minutes before Grace turns back to me. "Okay. We will meet you two back here at four."

"'You two'?" I ask.

She draws a line in the air connecting Mia and me.

My stomach tightens. "But I was hoping we could catch up today. There's a lot I'd like to talk to you about." Then to Mia, "No offense."

"I'm not as boring as I look," Mia says to me. Then, to Jessa and Grace, she says something in Tagalog that makes them laugh.

"What?" I say.

"Nothing," says Mia, grinning.

"She said that you probably are," Jessa translates for me.

Mia slaps her arm. I resolve for the hundredth time to learn the language.

"We will talk later, Kuya," Grace says. "I promise."

"Fine. Have fun," I say, trying but failing to sound sarcastic.

And with that she leaves me alone with this random girl for the next several hours.

"Do you like laser tag?" Mia asks.

"Is there seriously a laser tag arena here?" I ask, still watching Grace and Jessa walking away.

She nods.

Right before they turn the corner out of sight, Grace takes Jessa's hand.

"Lead the way."

YOU CAN HOLD ON TO ME
IF YOU NEED TO

In a massive disappointment to both of us, the laser tag place is closed because their gear isn't working. Mia lists all the other attractions in the mall, as if desperate to fill the time with activities. Ultimately, we decide to visit the newly opened aquarium instead.

On the way there, I make a few brilliant observations about the stores we pass like "Oh, we have that one in America," or "That chicken mascot looks super buff," and she replies politely enough but seems less than impressed by my insight. I ask why most of the celebrities and models that grace the advertisements in the store windows are so fair-skinned, and she answers only with, "Colonialism." Then there's a lot of awkward silence.

The walls outside the aquarium are painted with ocean scenes, and there are a few tanks set facing outward, in which neon fish swim among bright coral that may or may not be artificial.

I follow Mia inside, and she starts talking to the teenage kid at the entrance in Tagalog. I zone out, gazing around at the place. The only light sources are the glowing tanks. A few people in the semidarkness are walking around quietly and slowly, as if they were in a museum instead of a mall. The entire effect is as if we are underwater ourselves.

We each pay the entrance fee and head inside.

Turns out the aquarium's running a special exhibit on jellyfish. They look cool, floating around like aliens. Or ghosts. Yeah, ghosts is more accurate. Some are almost invisible, while others are red or purple or some other neon color brought out by the UV lights. Some have long, threadlike tentacles several times longer than their bell-shaped bodies, while others just have little nubbins that constantly undulate. We watch them move through the water, mesmerized by their slow-motion drifting.

"Did you know there's a type of jellyfish that's essentially immortal?" I ask Mia after a while, breaking the spell of silence.

"Really?" she says standing next to me, her face lit by the blue glow of the illuminated water.

I nod. "When it starts to get old, it can somehow revert its cells to its younger state. It can keep doing that forever, theoretically."

"That's cool," Mia says. "Life is weird."

"Yeah. Except I remember reading that most of them don't end up living very long. They usually get eaten by predators. And they're like this big." I indicate the space of about an inch between my thumb and forefinger.

"Oh," she says. "Poor little guys."

Suddenly, I feel sad. Even though they're just jellyfish, I feel bad for them. It's stupid, I know, but still. I lead us over to a different tank. The jellyfish here kind of look like semitransparent, blue mushrooms. They're upside down, gathered in a corner.

Mia comes up next to me. I feel her eyes on me, but I keep mine locked on the jellies.

"What if humans could do that?" she asks after a few moments.

"Float upside down in a corner?"

"No," she says. "Live forever. Imagine an old man hobbling down the street with his cane and oxygen tank. Then he suddenly stops, drops everything, and shakes his body like a dog stepping out of water. Then—poof—he's a baby again."

We laugh, things starting to loosen up.

The jellyfish keep bumping into the corner.

"So," I say, "your sister and Grace—they're together, aren't they?"

Mia nods. "Four or five months now. A record for Jessa."

"Cool."

"You didn't know?"

I shake my head. "Turns out there's a whole lot I don't know about my family."

We wander over to the next tank which contains bulbous, sack-like jellies in water glowing purple.

"How'd they meet?" I ask.

"Online."

"Like a dating site?" I ask.

She shakes her head. "A fan forum for some anime they're both obsessed with about gay figure skaters. And then it turns out that we live in the same village as her tita."

"Weird."

"I know—figure skating, right?" She smirks.

We move to the next tank.

Mia seems so confident and self-assured, I wonder how old she is. I'm not sure if it's considered rude here, but I go ahead and ask, "How old are you?"

"Thirty-one," Mia says.

This blows my mind. I turn to look at her. "For real?"

She breaks into a grin. "Nineteen. You?"

"Seventeen."

"Aw, you're just a baby!"

She tries to pinch my cheeks, but I slip away, smiling.

"I graduate in a few weeks," I point out.

"Ooh, all grown-up," she teases. "What's next?"

It's refreshing that there's no assumption in the way she asks. Not sure if that's a cultural difference or if that's just Mia. But I like it.

"I don't know," I say. "College, I guess."

"You don't sound excited."

"I'm not," I confess in a straightforward way I haven't been able to admit to anyone, not even Seth.

"College isn't for everyone," she says like she means it, not in the judgmental way people back in the States say it.

Mia leads us over to a different tank where the jellyfish have red, velvety bells and long tentacles that trail like shimmering threads.

"What about you? Are you studying somewhere?" I ask.

"Sophomore at UP-Diliman."

I don't want to ask her what she's studying. It's such a boring line of conversation, and I don't want to come off as boring. But I want to keep talking to her and it's the only thing I can think of so I go ahead and ask.

"Journalism," she answers.

I raise an eyebrow. "Really?"

"Yes, really."

"Is that . . . safe?" I ask, thinking of all the articles I've been reading about the drug war, about the consequences to those who criticize it, or even shed light on it.

"Have you heard of the Maguindanao Massacre?"

I shake my head.

"It happened in Mindanao. A few hours away from where my mother is from. Where I was born and lived until I was almost twelve."

She pauses. I wait for her to go on.

"A large group of people were on their way to file candidacy papers for a man who was going to run for office. Many were family members or supporters of the filing candidate, but most—thirty-two of the fifty-eight—were simply reporters. Thugs hired by his opponent intercepted and then killed them . . . all of them."

"Jesus," I say. "That's horrible."

She nods. "Some say it was the deadliest attack on journalists in the world."

"That happen in, like, the sixties or seventies or something?"

"2009."

I fall quiet trying to reconcile the violent vision of that relatively recent event with the mundane middle-class fantasy of this mall, with the international stereotype of Filipinos as friendly and subservient.

"So that's a no on safety," I say.

"Not if you want to do political or crime reporting. Not if you want to find the truth."

"Let me guess: That's the kind of reporting you want to do?"

"Of course," she says with conviction.

I want to ask her thoughts on Duterte and on the drug war, as I'm sure she has many. But what if she supports all of that? What if she's one of the supposedly 80 percent of Filipinos who approve, who are willing to accept Jun's death as sacrifice for the greater good?

We reach the end of the exhibit and exit the aquarium. The brightness of the mall makes it feel impossible to continue the conversation.

"What do you want to do next?" Mia asks.

"I don't know," I say.

She thinks for a few moments. "Ice-skating?"

"Sure," I answer, unsurprised by everything this mall contains, as if it's a microcosm for all the contradictions in this country.

Mia walks slowly by my side and keeps glancing over like she wants to ask if I'm okay. But she doesn't, and I'm thankful for it. There are moments when sharing silence can be more meaningful than filling a space with empty chatter.

Eventually, we make our way to the third floor and find the ice-skating rink. We join the long line in front of the register at the entrance. The air is chilly, so Mia wraps her arms around herself. Then she huddles up next to me so our arms are touching. "Okay if I steal some of your body heat?" she asks.

"Steal away."

I check out the price on the sign boards, then watch the people already out on the ice. A few wear helmets and cling to the side boards. Most drift awkwardly in a slow circle. A few in the middle look legit, practicing figure-skating jumps and spins.

"Do you know how to do this?" Mia asks.

I nod. "I played hockey when I was growing up."

She pretends to be impressed.

The line moves forward. We pay, pick up our skates, stow our things in a locker, and then sit down on one of the sections of low bleachers where it smells like every skating rink ever—that gamey combination of concession stand food and feet.

As we lace up, Mia continues our conversation from earlier. "If you're not excited about college, then why go?"

I shrug. "Because it's what I'm supposed to do."

"What if you don't?"

"That's not even a possibility."

"Why not?"

I double-knot my laces. A group of kids shuffle past us, walking awkwardly across the floor on their skates. Someone falls on the ice.

"I'll never find a job," I say. "And my parents will disown me. So there's that."

"I doubt that's true," she says. "If they love you, they won't disown you."

I think of Jun.

"All right, they won't disown me. But they'll be horribly disappointed."

"Isn't that better than spending four years studying something you don't care about to get a job you don't really want to do for the rest of your life?"

"Easy for you to say."

"My parents wanted me to study nursing and then go abroad."

"And how do they feel about your rebellion?"

She finishes tying her skates and sits up. "They worry about my safety. About job prospects after I graduate. But it's what I want to do, and they respect that."

"What if I don't have a clue what I want to do?" I ask.

"It takes time, I think. Follow your interests. Develop your strengths. Stay open to trying new things." She hesitates, then adds, "Maybe you haven't developed a passion yet because you've spent your entire life doing what others wanted you to do."

The realness of our conversation's starting to remind me of my exchanges with Jun.

"What made you want to be a journalist?" I ask.

Mia stretches her legs out and touches her toes. "An investigative piece I read while I was in high school about child trafficking in Metro Manila. Everyone here was talking about it for days, and then the article eventually led to dozens of arrests. Business owners. Policemen. Even politicians."

"Damn."

"I was always nosy, and I was a good writer. That article showed me I could use those skills to expose the truth and make the world a better place."

"So how does one find the truth?" I ask.

"Depends on the story."

I consider offering more, but thankfully, Mia goes on.

"Most of the time you start with research. But here in the Philippines, the records are often incomplete or inaccessible."

"So then what do you do if you hit a wall?" I ask, holding my breath.

"Talk to people. Find a lead."

"Like witnesses?"

"Yes, or anyone else who might know something else you can research or someone else you can speak with."

The only person I can think of who fits that description is Jun's friend who sent me those DMs. But I've given up hope of him ever replying to my messages. That leaves Tito Maning.

"What if the person won't talk, but you know they have important information?"

Mia studies me.

"Hypothetically speaking . . ." I add.

"Then you figure out how to get them to talk—or you steal that information."

My mind goes to the blurry photo of the note I found in the desk. Maybe I'd make a good journalist.

"Of course, stealing's not entirely ethical. Or legal. And might make it impossible to publish."

Maybe not.

She goes on. "So usually you would find someone else who might know something."

Is there anyone else? Jun ran away years ago. He didn't contact me—but maybe he had been in touch with someone in the family. Possibly. But nobody seems willing to so much as utter his name.

I'm about to ask another question when the music, the lights, the TVs on display—all suddenly shut off. Thanks to dim emergency lighting and the whiteness of the ice, we haven't been plunged into complete darkness. Still, all of the ice skaters come to a gradual stop.

"Brownout," Mia says. She pulls out her phone, as everyone else does the same. "Even the cell towers are down."

It's quiet for a few moments as we wait for the power to kick back on. When it doesn't, the hum of conversation returns, people continue walking to wherever they were on their way to, and the ice-skaters resume circling the rink.

"Why isn't anyone leaving?" I ask.

"People will stay inside as long as it's cooler than outside, and they'll keep the mall open as long as people have cash."

I think for a moment. "What about the jellyfish?"

"They'll be okay. This happens often enough that the aquarium probably has a backup generator."

"So you still want to do this?" I ask.

She gestures to the skates on our feet. "We've already committed."

I nod, relieved that we don't have to part ways yet.

Mia looks at me for a moment. "Is everything okay, Jay?"

"Huh?"

"Your face looks like this." She makes an exaggerated grumpy face.

I consider lying and just saying that nothing is wrong, that I'm fine. Tired from jet lag or something. But fuck it. There's something about Mia that unfolds me. And I'm never going to find out what happened to my cousin if I don't learn to talk, to ask difficult questions.

I run my hand through my hair and shift on the bench so I'm facing her. "Has Grace told you and Jessa about what happened to her brother?"

Confusion sweeps across Mia's face. "Grace doesn't have a brother."

Now it's my turn to look confused.

"She just has the one younger sister, right? Angel?"

I shake my head in disbelief. I understand why Tito Maning might want to erase his son from his life, but I can't even begin to grasp how Grace could let her brother fade so completely that she wouldn't even tell her girlfriend about him.

"She does—I mean, did—have a brother," I say. "Jun."

"*Talaga*?" Mia says, looking at me with new interest. "Really?"

"He was two years older than her—just like me. But he ran away from home four years ago."

"Why?"

I think of his last letter to me, feeling a fresh sting of guilt at knowing I'll probably never hold it in my hands again. "Why does anyone run away from home?"

She doesn't answer.

"But he was killed last week," I continue. "Shot by the police for using drugs—supposedly."

Mia puts her hands over her mouth, then her heart. "I'm sorry, Jay, I had no idea. I . . ." She's quiet for a few moments, gazing at me sympathetically. Then she touches my knee. "But you said 'supposedly.' Your questions earlier—you're trying to find out what happened to your cousin, aren't you?"

I lift my eyes to the rink. Fog is starting to rise as the ice evaporates. I nod.

Then everything tumbles out of me. The messages Jun and I used to exchange, the DMs with the links to those articles and the recent picture of Jun, my missing letters, and the list with Jun's name on it.

I expect her to say I'm reading too much into things, but instead, she asks, "Can I see the picture of the note?"

I pull it up on my phone and hand it to her. She squints at the screen. Zooms in.

I say, "It's blurry, I know. I'm going to try to take a better one when I have a chance."

She shakes her head, face lit by the phone's glow. "You don't need to."

I freeze. "You can read it?"

"Not all of it—but most."

"What does it say?"

Still squinting at the screen, Mia says, "It's to your uncle. The person who wrote it sounds like he was one of your uncle's subordinates. Maybe a detective? He says that per your uncle's request, they located his son—"

"Where?" I interrupt.

"It doesn't say. They only ask how your uncle wants to proceed."

I don't say anything.

"Do you have any idea when this might have been written? There's no date on the note."

"I don't." Then, "It's a list of drug dealers, isn't it?"

"Most likely," she says. "Every barangay captain is asked to keep a list of suspects for the authorities."

"How do they know the people on the list are guilty?"

"They take the barangay captain's word for it."

"And then they just kill them?"

"They are *supposed* to try to arrest them first."

I pull my phone back and stare at the blurry picture again. What was Tito Maning's response? Did he pay someone to remove the name? Did he ask the detective to confirm? Did he tell them to kill his son? Is he capable of such a thing, is any father? There's that story from the Bible where Abraham was ready to kill Isaac because God told him to and only didn't because God was like, "JK lol."

"Do you think you could help me?" I ask.

"Of course," she answers without hesitation.

"Thank you."

"I'm guessing you've already searched the Internet, but I have some connections at the newspapers and in the police. I'll see if they know about his specific case. Do you have a picture of the list where you saw your cousin's name?"

I shake my head.

"If you can take one that would help. I might be able to figure which barangay he was living in and then we could go from there."

"I'll try."

"In the meantime," Mia says, "talk to your uncle."

"He's not going to tell me anything."

"Find a way to get him to." She takes out her phone. "What's your number?"

I tell her. A moment later, a text comes through: **This is Mia!**

"That's me," she says. "Let me know if you find out anything else."

"Okay," I say, excited to have some help. Excited to have Mia's number in my phone.

She sighs, slaps my skate, then stands. "Ready?"

"Sure."

We wobble over to the entrance to the rink, where an employee hands us each a helmet.

"Oh, I don't need one," I say.

"Sir, it is policy, sir," the employee tells me.

"Just put it on," Mia says.

As I do, I tell Mia, "You can hold on to me if you need to."

"My hero," she says, taking my arm.

Then we finally step onto the ice.

The air is cool and damp. The fog now rises above most people's heads. The other skaters are vague shapes that gradually appear and disappear like ghosts.

Together, we make a slow circle once around the rink. Then I lead her to the boards and say, "Watch my feet."

I skate ahead by myself a short distance, trying to exaggerate my movements to show her how it's done. I'm about to turn around when a little kid darts in front of me. I try to stop but catch an edge and hit the ice hard.

While I'm trying to stand, Mia emerges from the fog, cracking up. She glides over effortlessly and tries to help me but is laughing so hard she's not very useful. "*Magaling magaling!* Salamat for that beautiful demonstration!"

I manage to get back to my feet. "A kid got in my way."

"*Talaga?*"

"For real!"

"If that's what you need to tell yourself, okay."

I rub my left hip as I start to skate away from her. "You could have told me you already knew how."

"Why did you assume I didn't?"

I don't answer. The pain is fading, but the embarrassment is a lingering sting.

Mia catches up a few seconds later, still laughing, and offers her arm. "You can hold on to me if you need to."

ALL THAT IT MEANS

Grace and Jessa have this blissful look in their eyes when they meet up with us, like they're waking from a dream.

"Did you two have fun?" Jessa asks.

"No," Mia says. Dread is just about to settle in the pit of my stomach when she breaks out laughing. "Yes," she admits, looking at me. Then she turns to her sister and rattles off a few sentences in Tagalog. All three of them laugh.

"Did you just make fun of me again?" I ask.

"Yes," Mia says without missing a beat.

"Okay, Kuya," Grace says, "enough flirting. We do need to get to Intramuros before Tomas."

So we say good-bye to Jessa and Grace, then go our separate ways.

Outside, the wind is making the palm trees sway and garbage skitter across the cement. Dark clouds hang overhead, and it smells like it's about to rain.

Grace walks a few steps ahead of me with her arms folded across her chest and head down. Any of the lightness and joking from only moments before has disappeared. The walls are back up.

"So," I say, making my way to her side. "You and Jessa?"

She doesn't answer at first. Then, "Yes."

"Cool."

"Please do not tell anyone," Grace says.

"Sure. But everyone seems fine with Tita Chato and Tita Ines."

"You should hear what Tatay says about them now that they're not around." She laughs for some reason. "Anyway, did you really have fun with Ate Mia?"

"Yeah. I did."

"Too bad she has a boyfriend, *di ba?*"

Oof. "Oh. Yeah."

"Seriously," she says. "You cannot tell anyone. Not even your family."

"Of course I won't," I say.

"Thank you, Kuya Jun."

I flinch.

She stops short. "I mean—Kuya Jay."

"Yeah," I say. "No problem."

We lapse back into silence and continue walking, pretending like it didn't happen, like saying his name didn't summon within both of us all that it means.

A VISIT

At dinner, Tito Maning interrogates everyone about their day, like he did last night. When it's Grace's turn, she makes up an elaborate fiction about our day walking around Rizal Park and then Intramuros, the walled section of Manila that hails back to the Spanish colonial days. She recounts everything in impressive detail, even throwing in a story about paying a worker to allow us into some of the areas of Fort Santiago—where José Rizal was executed—that are usually off-limits to the public. Tito Maning nods approvingly and turns to me.

"What did you think, Jason?"

I read up on some of the history of the place on the way back to bolster our story. But I don't want to overplay my hand, so I simply answer, "It was cool."

"Cool?"

I nod, meaningfully. "Powerful."

He stares me down for a few seconds. I was pretty sure he was buying Grace's lies without question, but the gaze he's giving me now makes me wonder if he sees through all of it.

Thankfully, he looks away, shifting to address the entire table. "Tomorrow, I do not work. After Mass we will go to Malacañang

Palace and the National Museums. We will continue Jason's education."

I nod.

The conversation lulls. I try to work up the courage to ask my uncle about Jun, as I assured Mia I would do. As I know I need to do.

Where did your people find Jun? I want to ask.

How did you tell them to proceed?

Did you have your son killed, Uncle?

But every time I almost speak, the words catch in my throat. If the answer to that last question is yes—if he did give the order to kill Jun—then who knows what else he's capable of. I doubt he'd straight have me shot by his underlings, but maybe he'd arrange something to happen to me that wouldn't cast suspicion. People die in car accidents all the time.

I'm starting to feel like I'm a couple more conspiracy theories away from claiming the US government faked the moon landing. But the possibility spooks me enough that I drop my gaze back to the rice and beef lengua on my plate and resolve to confront him tomorrow instead.

After dinner I head back to my room. First thing I do is check my bag again—even though I already did so immediately after we got back from the mall. I guess I'm still holding out hope that a guilty conscience prevailed and the letters were returned. Unfortunately, they're still not there.

My phone starts buzzing in my pocket. I'm suddenly nervous thinking it might be Mia, but turns out it's Mom. I answer, and we chat for a while. I catch her up on the flight and my fake trip to Rizal Park and Intramuros. I leave out everything having to do with Jun or Mia for obvious reasons. She tells me things are the same as usual back home and that they miss me and whatever. Then she asks if I want to speak to Dad for a few minutes. It's not really a question, though, because I can already hear her passing him the phone before I say anything.

Whenever I talk to Dad on the phone, it reminds me of this show my family used to watch together where these people race around the world in teams of two and complete crazy tasks. In this one episode, they traveled to a village in Botswana and had to milk a goat until they filled a bucket to a certain line. Most of the teams struggled but eventually accomplished the goal. But one team's goat was only giving up a few drops of milk, no matter how much the team yanked. The camera kept cutting between shots of the goat's smug face and the desperate squeezing of its unyielding teats. I said, "That's like trying to talk to Dad on the phone," and then we all cracked up for, like, six minutes straight. Needless to say, from that day forward, every time I talk to Dad on the phone, I think of that goat.

This conversation's no exception. Unlike Mom, he asks few questions. He mostly offers bits of advice, like to ignore anyone who tries to talk to me on the street or to keep my backpack in front of me whenever I'm in crowds. There's also a lot of silence, but not the good kind. I try to ask him some questions to keep the conversation going, like how work is going and stuff, but he only gives monosyllabic responses. I want to tell him about the note from Tito Maning's desk, but I can't figure out how to without admitting I snuck into my uncle's office. Instead, I ask him if he knew that Tito Maning and Tito Chato aren't on speaking terms.

"Yes," he says.

"Do you know why?"

"No."

"You never asked?"

"It is none of my business."

"Oh," I say. "Really?"

"Yes."

More silence.

"And it's none of yours," he adds.

Then he makes some excuse for needing to leave and we say good-bye.

I wake in the middle of the night and immediately sense that there is someone in the room with me. It's dark and the house is quiet. A sliver of moonlight slips through a crack in the curtains.

I prop myself up on one elbow and try to rub the sleep from my eyes.

There's someone at the desk. A man. A burlap sack covers his head, but his left hand lit by moonlight is writing furiously. The pen scratches across the paper. Relentless. Hushed. It's like rolling waves under a dark sky.

"Tito?" I ask.

He continues writing.

I throw the sheet back, surprised to find the air so cold that goose bumps rise on my skin. They really do love their air-conditioning in this country. Nonetheless, I swing my legs around to the side of the bed and set the soles of my feet upon the tile floor. It's like stepping on ice. Ignoring the cool burning, I drift across the room to the desk. I lean over the man's shoulder to peer at what he's writing.

Only, it's gibberish. A tangled mess of lines like a toddler's scribbles.

Then the pen stops.

Slowly, he shifts in the seat, and I know he's looking at me even though his face is covered by the sack. Then, with stiff, deliberate movements, he pushes away from the desk and rises. I back away until I'm against the window and have nowhere else to go.

As he approaches, I see his feet are bare, and he's wearing a pair of old jeans and a dark polo shirt, both dirty and torn. There are a few dark stains around his chest and stomach, each one with a trail of dried blood. Holes, I realize. Bullet holes.

He starts to walk forward, bare feet whispering as they slide across the tile.

He's only a few feet away now.

Then a couple of steps.

I want to run, but I can't. My muscles are disconnected from my brain, like a marionette with cut strings.

He stops. Reaches up and pulls the sack off his head.

It's Jun. His hair's a mess, tangled with sticks and dirt, and the lower half of his jaw is missing, a gory mess in its place. His eyes meet mine. Two stars in a clear winter sky.

"What happened to you?" I ask.

The exposed muscle and sinew where his lower jaw used to be twitches as he continues moving toward me.

"I'm sorry for what they did to you. I'm sorry I lost your letters.

I'm sorry I was too afraid to speak to Tito Maning again tonight. But please tell me, what happened to you?"

He doesn't answer. He can't. Instead, he stops a step away. Then he reaches out and places his palm against my chest.

I wake.

I'm in the same room. It is just as dark and cold and quiet. The same sliver of moonlight slips through the curtain. My eyes flick to the empty chair at the desk. But I'm alone.

A dream, then.

Or perhaps a visit.

THE WORD OF GOD

It's drizzling on Sunday morning as we pull up to the church. The building is all fancy stonework, tall windows, and biblical statues.

Tomas lets us out right in front where an usher is waiting with an umbrella. As we step out of the car, he holds it over Tita Ami and leads us through the huge crowd that overflows from the doorway despite the rain.

Inside, the church is a more imposing version of others I've been to. Rows upon rows of mahogany pews lead to an altar with an empty dais, above which hangs an enormous crucified Christ. There are columns and arches and sconces. Golds and browns and whites and deep reds. The scent of frankincense hangs in the vast emptiness between our heads and the high ceiling, and even though there must be at least a thousand people here, nobody is talking. A boys' choir sings a hymn from the rear balcony, their voices powerful and angelic, amplified as they echo against the granite walls and soar over the sounds of the oscillating fans that are mounted on every column. Enormous, stained-glass windows depicting the Stations of the Cross line those walls, muted without the sun.

The usher leads us through the unbelievable crush of the Sunday crowd to a reserved section near the front. Tito Maning sits closest to the center aisle, then Tita Ami, Grace, Angel, and me at the end. Next to me is an old Filipina, head bowed in prayer.

As we wait for the priest and his acolytes to enter, I scratch under the stiff collar of the ill-fitting Barong Tito Maning insisted I borrow since I didn't have my own. I'm actually taller than he is, but since his chest is much broader, the Barong is somehow too short and too baggy at the same time.

It's been a while since I've been to Mass. When I was growing up, my family went every Sunday, and Chris, Em, and I all made our First Communion and Confirmation. But I wouldn't say we were religious. I mean, we never prayed before eating, read the Bible, talked about God at home, or anything like that. Even right after we got home from Mass, we'd all immediately change out of our church clothes and go about our day, nobody ever commenting on that morning's sermon. Then, when Chris graduated high school and moved out, we stopped going. Nobody said anything about it. It kind of felt like taking us kids to church was a thing our parents did to make sure we were raised right, and then we got old enough and they figured the job was done.

Jun often referred to church in his letters. He complained about the boredom that made his eyelids heavy as soon as Mass began, about the hypocrisy of everyone praising Jesus's holy works but then completely ignoring the poor, about the corrupt and abusive clergy that hid their sins behind their frocks and crosses.

When Tito Danilo was ordained, I remember Jun's words: "Another sheep to the slaughter."

At the same time, though, Jun spoke of his belief in God a lot. I remember in one particularly long letter he wrote that if God existed at all, it probably wasn't in the way everyone assumed.

I didn't know what I thought about all of that—I still don't—but I actually liked the act of going to church. I found comfort, I found peace, in those hushed Sunday mornings. The scents. The sunlight. Christmas, Lent, Easter. The prayers that told you exactly what to say. The stories and songs about some dude just trying to do good and convince others to not be horrible to one another.

When my family stopped going, I didn't tell anyone that it made me sad. Em had always openly despised going, and at school, the kids who admitted to enjoying church were labeled weirdos. This was also around the time Seth became an outspoken atheist.

I'm brought back to the present when the organ begins and a thousand people stand in unison. I rise to my feet with everyone else, and we all watch the procession walk slowly down the long center aisle, draped in their vestments and carrying a tall, ornate cross, tapered candles, and the other sacred objects. They pause in front of the altar, and the music stops. In the silence, the priest—a younger guy than I expected, with a fresh haircut—bows and mumbles a prayer as he makes the sign of the cross. The acolytes set down their objects in the appropriate places and then move to their seats on the side, staying on their feet. The priest finishes the blessing, turns to the congregation, and leads us through the call-and-response opening, his voice booming throughout the church thanks to a lapel-mic.

Then the organ starts playing again and the choir leads the congregation in "Gloria." After it finishes, silence returns. The priest does his call-and-response thing again, then walks over to the throne-like chair up front and sits. We all sit.

A woman takes the podium, cracks open the enormous Bible to a marked page, and starts reading.

I have no idea what she's saying since it's all in Tagalog, so it's not long before my mind drifts to that weird-ass dream I had about Jun's corpse hanging out in the room last night.

I texted Mia about it this morning. **Maybe it wasn't a dream,** she replied. Then she went on to explain that superstitious Filipinos believe a visit from the dead means that the deceased has unresolved business that needs to be taken care of before their soul can move from this world onto purgatory.

Maybe you will keep seeing him until you find out the truth.

I don't buy the ghost theory, but it does make sense to me that the dream was a manifestation of my own guilt from losing the letters and being too nervous to confront Tito Maning again last night.

I told her so, then she replied, **TALK TO YOUR TITO!**

I will, I texted.

When?

. . . later.

Good, she texted, followed by a winky-face emoji.

I thanked her and considered asking how her boyfriend was doing. But I didn't. I had, however, already tried to sneak back into Tito Maning's office, only to find the door locked.

At the podium, the woman finishes the reading from Acts and the Mass proceeds. We cycle through the sitting and standing and kneeling, the calls-and-responses, the prayers and the hymns. At some point during the sermon, the rain picks up, drumming loudly on the roof. My eyelids grow heavy. My head bobs forward. . . .

Angel nudges me awake with her elbow. I rub my face and sit up straight. I glance at Tito Maning at the other end to see if he noticed. As if he senses me looking at him, he turns and meets my eyes, his own beaming a silent ray of disapproval. I turn my face back toward the altar and try to pretend like I'm paying real close attention to the Word of God.

THAT LAST PART ALOUD

"That is where the president lives," Tito Maning says from the front seat of the car as he taps the window with his knuckle.

Tomas pulls over at the side of a road that loops through a park across the murky Pasig River so we can all peer out through the rain at Malacañang Palace. It's a white, two-story building in the Spanish colonial style that's not nearly as large as I expected. It's surrounded by newer-looking buildings with similar architecture, and tall trees bowing in the wind and rain.

"Cool," I say.

"President Duterte might be in there right this moment figuring out more solutions to our country's problems," he adds. "He is a great man, you know."

"Have you met him?" I ask, imagining such "solutions" would be just as condemned by the human rights groups and the UN as his current ones.

"Twice," he says.

"He awarded your tito a medal just last month for the excellent work he is doing to protect the people in our region from drugs," Tita Ami says.

The rain beats down on the car. The windshield wipers swoop back and forth. Grace shifts in her seat next to me.

There's no way we're not all thinking about Jun, but nobody says anything. Not even me, despite the fact it's another perfect opening. The moment passes, and Tito Maning starts conversing with Tomas in a mixture of Tagalog and English.

Then Tito Maning turns to me and explains the history of the palace as if he were a tour guide. Everyone seems to tune him out, and I'm itching to check for messages from Mia. But since Tito Maning's lecture is for my benefit, I stare out the window and try to listen intently as he traces the building's history from a private residence built by a Spanish colonist in 1750, to a state house officially used by the Spanish governors and then the US governors when Spain ceded the Philippines to the US in 1898 (despite the fact the Filipinos had declared independence), to finally being used by the Philippine presidents after the country earned its full independence in 1946.

"Marcos lived there the longest," he says. "From 1965 to 1986. He was our greatest president—it was a shame what happened to him. A stain on our country's history."

I'm not an expert on Philippine history or anything—it's not like it's even mentioned in US history textbooks beyond maybe a sentence or two—but from what I've been reading, Marcos is widely regarded by the world as a brutal dictator, continuing to stay in power after the end of his presidential term by declaring martial law. His political enemies and most vocal critics would be "disappeared"—dragged from their homes in the middle of the night and never heard from again. He closed the newspapers. He granted lucrative contracts to his friends. His family embezzled billions during his rule—money that should have been spent on infrastructure or the schools or helping the poor. I came across one site that listed everything they took with them to Hawaii after being ousted during the People Power Revolution, and it included jewels, crowns, tiaras, golden statues, and other valuables whose total worth was several million dollars. However, the "stain on our country's history" Tito Maning is referring to is not all of that, but rather the nonviolent revolution.

"*Isang tunay na bayani*," Tito Maning says wistfully. "A true hero." He knocks the window a couple of times with his knuckle. "But I think President Duterte's legacy will be greater."

After we finish driving around the palace, we head to the National Museums of the Philippines. They're enormous white stone buildings with columns and other Roman features. Angel points to each one: "Natural history. Anthropology. Art." Then she adds in a whisper, "Natural history is the best, Kuya. There's a submarine you can walk through and a *butanding*. The others are sooo boring."

"I'll keep that in mind," I whisper back even though I don't know what a *butanding* is.

Tomas pulls over along the opposite side of the street where he dropped off Grace and me yesterday. Right as we're about to get out of the car, though, Tita Ami clears her throat and says, "Maning, I have many errands to run today, and since the girls have been to the museum many times already . . ."

In the front seat, Tito Maning pauses with his hand on the door handle. He doesn't say anything for a few moments as he considers this. "Have they no more to learn about their country? Do they know it all already?"

Grace and Angel stay quiet.

"The museum is not going anywhere," Tita Ami says.

"I bet the ancient Egyptians said that about the Library of Alexandria," he says.

"You go in with Jason, and I will take the girls with me. I could use their help. They can come back another day."

There's a tense silence as everyone waits for Tito Maning's answer. I know I should be hoping for him to agree so I can have the chance to talk to him about Jun, but it's not like I'm thrilled at the possibility of spending a few hours alone with this man.

"Very well," he finally says. He tells Tomas something in Tagalog, then says to me, "Come, Nephew."

When nobody else is looking, Angel sticks out her tongue at me. I roll my eyes.

"Should I take off the Barong?" I ask, fingers already working the collar button.

"And go in your undershirt?"

I stop. "I don't want to damage it."

"You can always buy a new Barong," he says. "You cannot buy self-respect."

"Um, okay."

I follow Tito Maning out into the warm, heavy rain, where this time there's no usher waiting for us with an umbrella. We shut the doors, the SUV pulls away, and we follow the pathway. I shield my head with one hand like that's going to do anything, while Tito

Maning keeps this hard-ass look on his face as if he doesn't notice the torrential downpour. We go around the statue of Lapu-Lapu—"He killed Magellan with a spear through the face," Tito Maning notes proudly—and up the wide stone steps to the main entrance of the Museum of Anthropology.

We're drenched by the time we reach the tall doors. After we pass through security, a couple of employees immediately greet Tito Maning by name. They hand us towels—something they don't do for others that entered at the same time—and we pat ourselves dry.

As Tito Maning signs us in, I reach for my wallet. "How much is the entrance fee?"

"Nothing. All the National Museums are free."

"Really? That's cool. In the US it's, like, thirty dollars to get into one of these, and then, like, another thirty dollars for a hot dog or something at the museum café."

Tito Maning nods. "You can thank President Duterte. He understands how important it is for all of the people—from the richest to the poorest—to know and honor their history." He looks down one of the quiet, nearly empty hallways, and then down another. "The only shame is that more do not take advantage of this great opportunity."

Tito Maning begins walking, hands clasped behind his back, as if expecting me to follow.

I do.

He leads us down a long, dimly lit hallway. I ready myself to speak, to ask about Jun. My heart starts hammering in my chest.

I can wait, I decide. We've got all afternoon.

We wander through the museum, and despite Angel's warning, I find it interesting. There are the recently discovered butchered remains of a rhinoceros that suggest human relatives lived on Luzon around 700,000 years ago. Stone artifacts from fragments of tools, statuettes, jars, and weapons from early inhabitants. A dark room full of jars shaped like people filled with human remains that were found in a cave. A bunch of porcelain from China's early trade presence. A collection all about the Muslim cultures of the southern islands. A room dedicated to rice cultivation. An exhibit about Baybayin and the other syllabic scripts used in various regions long before the Spanish arrived. A collection of illustrations and photographs depicting the elaborate tattoos traditional in some tribes.

Tito Maning and I don't hold any actual conversations as we check all of this out. Mostly, he points to things and says, "Jason, I am thinking you know nothing about this," or, "This is what they wanted us to forget." Occasionally, he quizzes me on background knowledge I obviously don't have. It doesn't take me long to realize that this trip is less about educating me and more about exposing my ignorance.

It's a lot of information, and as much as I'd love to remember it all, the only thing staying in my head is how badly I'm failing. I think of what Mia said when I told her about my dream, and I keep expecting to see Jun's ghost around every corner, asking me why I'm keeping my silence.

After a couple of hours, Tito Maning decides we're done and that we should go to the National Museum of Fine Arts next. As we walk over to the adjacent building, I form the question I'm going to ask about Jun in my mind. Except this time, not only does my heart start racing as I prepare to voice it, but I get this light-headed feeling like

I'm going to pass out. So I say nothing, hanging back a couple steps.

I was thinking an art museum would be a reprieve from Tito Maning's disappointment, but I am gravely mistaken. It has a decidedly historical bent, but there are few placards besides those with the basic identifying information for each piece. This allows my uncle to assume the role of lecturer to an even greater extent than before, wielding his knowledge like a club.

He begins by explaining how the National Museums exist thanks to Imelda Marcos, the wife of Ferdinand Marcos. Without a trace of irony, he informs me that this very building used to be where the House of Representatives and Senate met until they were dissolved when Marcos declared martial law.

The first several exhibits are populated with sculptures and paintings of Jesus, Mary, the angels, and the saints. Tito Maning points out a sculpture of a bored-looking St. Michael stepping on the devil's neck about to stab him in the face with a trident and comments, "Beautiful," then continues expounding on the over three hundred years of Spanish colonial rule—which he seems to despise, except for the fact they brought Christianity.

Gradually, Filipinos themselves and scenes from rural life start appearing as subjects. Tito Maning explains the Filipinos finally started to see themselves as men, leading to the fight for independence in 1898, which he tells me more about when we reach an exhibit focused on Rizal. From here, the museum jumps nearly fifty years to a room depicting the horrors of the Japanese occupation during World War II, where the works are titled with words like "massacre," "doom," "torture," "burning," and "atrocity."

"Do you notice what is not emphasized here?" Tito Maning asks, stopping me in the hallway on our way to the next exhibit.

And here's a question I can finally answer. "American colonialism?"

He nods, for once. "Yes. We had declared ourselves free, and then your country ignored that, stepping in where Spain left off. Do you know the names of the heroes of the *Katipunan*?"

I can't tell if it's a rhetorical question.

"Do you know the Americans stole entire villages and then displayed them in your country as if they were animals in a zoo?"

There's a long, painful silence. I don't say anything because of course I don't know any of this—what does he expect? They never taught us the specifics in school. I think there was, like, a paragraph on the Philippine American War in my US History textbook.

Thankfully, the moment is disrupted by a docent who walks up and says, "Hello, sirs. We are closing already. Please make your way to the exit, sirs."

Tito Maning nods. The employee scurries away.

"We didn't get to the upper floors," I say, curious about the creations from the era of Marcos and the People Power Revolution.

"Modern art," Tito Maning says dismissively. "Garbage."

As we wander toward the exit, I feel a building pressure. I need to do it now. I need to ask about Jun while we're still alone.

"Tito—"

He holds up a finger for me to wait and takes out his phone. He types out a text, probably telling Tomas to bring the car around, and then keeps walking as if I hadn't started to say something. I follow as he leads us back downstairs toward the exit.

Great. An entire afternoon alone with Tito Maning, and I've failed to work up enough courage to ask him a single question about Jun. Why did I ever think I could do this? I am a seventeen-year-old child.

As we cut through the middle of the building on our way to the exit, an enormous oil painting the size of the side of a barn catches my eye over my shoulder. I break free from Tito Maning's orbit and make my way over even though he continues walking.

Spoliarium by Juan Luna, 1884. It depicts a life-size Roman scene in which a few men drag dead gladiators across a stone floor by their arms. There's a crowd watching on the left half—though I can't tell if they're curious or horrified or mourning. The colors are dark and grim, interrupted by a few bright red cloaks, streaks of red-brown blood trailing the bodies, and the illuminated pale skin of the central corpse. In the shadows are the shapes of even more dead bodies, so faint I almost didn't notice them.

A rush of emotion courses through me—something I've never felt looking at a painting before. And then I realize why: it reminds me of the photographs from the drug war.

Tito Maning walks up next to me.

"What happened to Jun?" I ask quietly, trying to sound brave.

I turn to face my uncle. I spoke before I even realized it, before I had time to be intimidated. But he doesn't say anything. He holds the silence like a knife, eyes glued to the painting and hands clasped behind his back.

With every passing second, the awkwardness expands. After what feels like forever but is probably only a minute, I start to wonder if he even heard my initial question. My heart thumps in my chest, and I feel my palms starting to sweat. "Tito Maning," I say, throat suddenly dry, "what happened to—"

"I heard you the first time," he interrupts, his own words hard and simmering with anger. "Did your father not tell you?"

I nod, even though it was technically Mom who told me. "Killed by the police for using drugs."

"Why do you ask a question, then, to which you already know the answer?"

I take a deep breath. "Is that the truth?"

He looks at me now. His eyes are the thick black of clouds that precede a volcanic eruption.

"Maybe—" I start.

"Were you with him when he died?" he asks.

"No."

"Were you in communication with him before he died?"

"No," I admit.

"Then why is it you think you know what happened to my son?"

"I . . . I don't know. I read some articles—"

He laughs, low and derisive. "You read some articles?" This is not really a question. "I am guessing they were written by your Western media?"

I stay quiet.

He laughs again. Unclasps his hands, uses one to rub his chin, and then folds his arms across his wide chest. "Do you think they know what is happening in this country?"

"For one article, the journalist and photographer spent something like forty days in Manila."

"Forty days? Let me know when they've been here for forty years."
He mutters something to himself in Tagalog, and then holds his arms
out as if to encompass the room. "I know you knew nothing when
you arrived, but have you learned nothing today? Our country's history is full of invading foreigners who thought they knew us better
than we knew ourselves. And many of us believed them over and over
again. Many of us welcomed them with open arms, learned their
language, joined their churches, asked for positions in their crooked
governments." He folds his arms over his chest again, turns his face
back toward the painting, and shakes his head. "No more."

"They're not trying to take over," I say. "They're only journalists.
They're trying to show the truth."

"Are you stupid?" he asks.

The bluntness of the question catches me off guard. I don't know
how to respond.

"Tell me," he says. "Have you seen reports in these newspapers
about the problems we face with drugs?"

"I don't know. Maybe they did some reporting on that."

"I am sure they did not. I am thinking they have said nothing about
how your government has propped up corrupt officials in the Philippines for years simply because they agreed to support US interests?
Nothing about those officials taking money from foreign drug cartels
to look the other way as they peddle their poison to our sisters and
brothers, our daughters and sons?"

I wonder how much of this is true. Since I don't know, I don't say
anything.

He gestures around us. "Have they said anything about President

Duterte making the museums free? Building bridges and repairing roads that have lay crumbling for decades? Making contraceptives free for all women, regardless of income? Banning cigarettes so we can breathe cleaner air? Reducing crime to its lowest rates ever so that people finally feel safe walking around their own barangay at night?"

I stay silent.

"No?" He continues. "These people—the ones writing these articles you have been reading—they do not care about the Filipino people. They sensationalize the worst of what is happening here and ignore the best in order to sell copies or win awards. It is that simple."

"But Jun wasn't a drug addict. He wasn't a drug pusher."

"What do you know about Jun?" he asks, practically growling.

"I—"

"Did you raise him?"

"No, but—"

"Do you know why he ran away from home four years ago?"

I turn away, run a hand through my hair. But Tito Maning's eyes stay on me.

He shakes his head again. "He was using drugs, Nephew. I found them in his room myself. I saw them with these eyes." He points to his eyes. "I held them in these hands." He shows me his palms, which then curl to fists. "Then I gave him a choice: stop using or get out. What do you think he chose?"

I don't answer.

"He chose to leave, Nephew. He *chose* to leave. To leave his tatay and nanay. To leave Grace. To leave Angel. He *chose* the drugs."

Dad never told us why Jun ran away, only that he did. Did Dad know this? Is it even true?

No. Jun wouldn't have done that. He had a good heart. Of course Tito Maning would lie to conceal his own guilt over whatever he did.

But if I'm being honest with myself, a sliver of doubt creeps into my mind. Jun's letters always conveyed a sense of isolation, an undercurrent of sadness. Maybe even depression. Don't those feelings sometimes cause people to self-medicate?

Maybe he did start using. Maybe he continued to and that's why the police killed him. Maybe that's the truth, plain and simple.

No. Not the Jun I knew.

Jaw clenched and arms crossed, I shake my head.

Tito Maning smirks and turns back to the painting. "Jun was nothing but an addict, and I was not going to let him bring that into my home. I know this might sound harsh to you, a spoiled American, but I have seen over and over how drugs destroy the lives of not only the user, but everyone around them. We all make choices, and we all must deal with the consequences of those choices. If we do not hold people accountable for their decisions, then we leave them free to destroy our society. That is how the world works. It is simple."

A curtain of silence falls between us.

My head reels trying to decide if I believe him or not, trying to grasp—even if this is true—how a father could be so brutally cold toward his son. My dad isn't the most communicative, but at least I know he would never throw me out like that, no matter what I did.

The lights at the end of the hallways start to click off. Another docent approaches and tells us the museum's now closed. Tito Maning peels away from the painting and starts toward the exit. He lets out a short, high-pitched whistle and gestures with a small nod for me to follow. I do, arms still crossed, hanging back a few steps.

Outside, the downpour has stopped, but the air is muggy and smells of damp concrete. Some of the streetlamps and city lights have turned on, and the world is bright in that muted gray way it can be beneath an overcast sky. We walk slowly down the stone steps still slick with rainwater toward the curb where Tomas waits.

"Why did you take the letters Jun wrote me?" I ask after a few moments. I mean this accusation to sound strong, like a powerful beam of light banishing the darkness to reveal the Truth. Instead, my words come out quiet and weak and shaky, poisoned by my doubt.

"Letters?" he asks.

"They were in my bag when I arrived. Then they were gone."

"Ah, you think I took them."

I nod. Barely.

He shakes his head. "I don't know anything about your letters."

I search his face. Either he's the world's best liar or he really didn't take them. I have no idea which it is.

"So that is why you were in my office."

I stop short.

He raises an eyebrow. "You thought I wouldn't notice that my key was in a different place?"

Since he already knows, I may as well ask about the contents of the note on the back of the list I found in his desk, about how he told his subordinate who located Jun to proceed. But I feel drained, lost. A compass missing its needle. What would be the point when

I can't sense whether anything he says is truthful or not?

Tito Maning reaches the car and turns to me. "I am disappointed my brother did not teach you to respect your elders."

He expects an apology. I stay quiet.

"You do not live here. You do not speak any of our languages. You do not know our history. Your mother is a white American. Yet, you presume to speak to me as if you knew anything about me, as if you knew anything about my son, as if you knew anything about this country." His words are measured and even. The slow suck of the sea gathering for a tsunami.

"When we return to the house," he continues, "you will pack your things and Tomas will drive you to Chato's."

I uncross my arms, let them dangle at my sides. "I thought I was supposed to stay with Tita Chato starting tomorrow?"

"That was the plan," he says. "But you have outworn your welcome in my home."

"Oh," I say. "Okay. Well, fuck you, too."

Except I don't really say that last part aloud.

A COMPLETE WASTE

I slouch low in the backseat and watch the city pass under the night sky as Tomas drives me to Tita Chato's. It started raining again, so the water runs down the windshield, blurring my view of the orange streetlamps, the billboards, the crowded homes and shuttered store-fronts and empty stalls along the roadside. The wipers swish back and forth, and the headlights from oncoming traffic light up the inte-rior of our vehicle intermittently. The Beatles are playing over the radio, and Tomas is singing along softly to himself.

I'm kicking myself for how weak and submissive I was with my uncle. There's no way he was telling the truth about Jun, and no way he didn't steal my letters. It kills me to know that they remain behind somewhere in my uncle's house. But he's right about one thing: This isn't my country. It hasn't been since Dad persuaded Mom to return to the US when I was one. Maybe I don't deserve to know about Jun's life. Maybe I gave up that right when I stopped writing him back, when I let him slip from my thoughts so easily. Who was I to step off the plane and demand anything of this place?

Maybe I shouldn't have come here. I should have stayed in Michigan, playing video games and completing my spring break homework. I should have accepted the fact that Jun was dead and that there was nothing I could do—nothing I should do—about it. Fall would have come, and I would have been in Ann Arbor, secure in my ignorance.

Thinking about all of this makes my stomach turn. I start feeling ill and am about to ask Tomas to pull over so I can vomit when my phone starts buzzing.

It's Dad. Great.

I hit ignore.

A few moments later, there's a voice mail. I delete it without listening. Then comes a text.

What happened with your uncle? Chato said you're going there early?

I don't respond. Instead, I pull up Mia's number and send her a long text about my argument with my uncle.

Only a few moments pass before she replies.

No wonder Grace hasn't told him about her and Jessa.

Yeah, I don't think he'd be too happy about that.

At least we'll be closer now! ;)

What do you mean? I ask.

Remember I told you that your tita lives in my village? When Grace visits her, she usually finds some time to sneak away and meet up with Jessa;)

I smile. **Oh.**

BTW, sorry, but I couldn't find out anything about your cousin today:(

That's okay, I say. **Appreciate the effort.**

I'll keep trying, she replies. **Txt tomorrow if you want to meet up. I'll be around.**

Ok. I will.

Magandang gabi! (That means g'night!) ;)

Magandang gabi, Mia.

I slip my phone back into my pocket. Three winky face emoji in that exchange. Grace said Mia has a boyfriend, so maybe they mean something different here? Maybe Filipinos don't use them to flirt. Maybe they use emoji like punctuation.

I don't know, but I do know my nausea has passed. At least for now.

Maybe this trip won't be a complete waste.

FAIL HIM IN DEATH

"So you made *Manoy Baboy* angry, eh?" Tita Chato says, wrapping me in her arms as soon as I step out of the SUV. She is a stocky woman who smells of cooking oil and soap. Her partner, Tita Ines, stands behind her, hands on her hips. Both are wearing traditionally patterned dresses in different colors and bamboo house slippers. Tita Ines is slightly taller, and her skin is much lighter since she's half-Chinese.

"Huh?" I ask.

"Maning," Tita Ines explains. "Your tita is mixing languages to make a rhyme. 'Manoy' means 'older brother' in Bikol, and 'baboy' means 'pig' in Tagalog. *Manoy Baboy.*" Then she smirks at Tomas, clearly not caring if he tells my uncle.

"Oh," I say. I hug Tita Ines, then step back. "Yeah, I made him pretty angry. But I didn't mean to."

"That's too bad," Tita Chato says.

Tita Ines shakes her head and laughs. She and Tita Chato help Tomas pull my bags and the two balikbayan boxes out of the SUV. We say good-bye to Tomas and then he drives away.

"Sit," Tita Chato says, gesturing toward the plastic lawn chairs that are gathered around a plastic patio table.

I do as she says, even though I'd rather just go to bed. Tita Chato and Tita Ines join me. Light from the house spills from the open doorway and windows. A thin tendril of smoke rises from a lit cigarette in an ashtray at the center of the table, and the rain continues to fall in the darkness on the other side of the gate. A small lizard races up the wall and behind the porch light.

"*Butiki*," says Tita Chato, following my gaze. Then she leans forward, picks up the cigarette, and takes Tita Ines's hand with her free hand. She takes a long drag and exhales the smoke slowly through pursed lips.

"I thought smoking was illegal now?" I say, remembering Tito Maning's diatribe.

"Only in public," she says.

"*Ay naku*, I try to get her to quit a thousand times," Tita Ines says, fanning the smoke away from her face. "But she listens only to herself."

"There are many ways to die in this country," Tita Chato says. "This is the one I am least concerned about." She takes another drag. Exhales. Smiles.

"Do you eat dinner?" Tita Ines asks.

I shake my head.

"I fix you a plate," she says, getting up. She disappears into the house, leaving me alone with Tita Chato.

We sit in silence for a few minutes, watching the rain fall. "Is this a typhoon?" I ask after some time.

"This is just rain," she says. "When it is a typhoon, you will not have to ask that question." She leans forward, resting her elbows on the table. "So, Nephew, what did you do to anger my brother? Not that that is a very difficult thing to accomplish. . . ."

Probably from her years as a lawyer, she has the kind of voice that demands the truth. I tell her what happened. Tita Chato listens attentively, nodding and shaking her head in all the right places.

When I finish, she snuffs out her cigarette in the ashtray and leans back. "And then he kicked you out just like he did his own son?"

"Tito Maning said he gave Jun a choice. That Jun chose to leave?"

Tita Chato shakes her head. "My brother is a liar. Just like the government that he serves. Never forget that."

My heart lifts. I scoot forward. "What are you saying, Tita?"

"The first part is true—Maning found drugs in Jun's room."

My face falls.

"But the second part is a lie—he gave Jun no choice. Maning made him leave immediately."

"How do you know?"

"Because like you, Jun came here."

I lean back and let that sink in. I thought I was getting nowhere with all of this, but as if I'm living in some parallel shadow universe, I seem to be following the course of my cousin's life without knowing it. I imagine him sitting on this same covered patio, maybe even in this same plastic chair, telling Tita Chato what happened between him and his father.

"That's why Tito Maning doesn't talk to you anymore, isn't it?" I ask. Tita Chato nods.

"Did my dad know about that? About Jun?"

"No," she says, confirming what he told me last night.

166

"But you talk to him so often?"

"We talk about many things. You and your kuya and your ate. Your mother. Ines. Our jobs. But your father . . . he doesn't like to think about our troubles here so much. I think it makes him feel guilty, so I don't bring them up if it can be avoided."

"Why would it make him feel guilty?"

"Because he left."

This hits me hard. For some reason, I've never thought about the guilt he carried across the ocean.

Tita Ines returns in that moment with a steaming bowl of soup.

"Sinigang," she says, and places it on the table in front of me along with a spoon, a glass of water, and a slice of white bread. Then she takes her place beside Tita Chato again. As I dig in, Tita Chato rattles off some Tagalog to Tita Ines. I hear my name several times, so I assume she's catching her up on what happened between my uncle and me. Tita Ines keeps shaking her head, making a face, and muttering under her breath.

I'm scooping the last of the sour but savory soup into my mouth when she wraps up the story.

"Ay," Tita Ines says. "Why God allows that man to have children, I do not understand."

Tita Chato lets out a bitter laugh. "I think that Maning considers it a great mercy that he did not kill his son on the spot. Maybe he would have if Duterte would have been in power then."

Damn.

That is what Jun had to deal with when he was fourteen years old. Meanwhile, I was worrying about math homework, being shorter than most of the girls in my grade, and making the basketball team.

"Was it shabu?" I ask.

"No—marijuana."

I shake my head in disbelief. All of that not over meth, but over weed—a drug probably half of humanity has tried at least once. Seth smokes up all the time but never has to worry about being killed for it thanks to where he happened to be born and the color of skin he happened to be born with.

"I know," she says.

"How long did he stay with you?" I ask.

"Almost one year," Tita Chato says.

And now my mind is blown. My dad told me Jun had run away from home, but he never told me that he had lived with Tita Chato afterward for any amount of time. I always imagined that he simply disappeared into the city.

Jun was not lost to the streets—at least not at first. He was within reach. And I did nothing. Like a rising tide, my own guilt returns.

Tita Chato looks down. "For that year, we lived together, the three of us. We went to work. He went to school. We even went on a few short vacations together. Boracay. Batangas. Palawan."

Tita Ines takes her hand. "We are like a little family during this time."

"But," Tita Chato says, "when Jun had been with us almost one entire year, Maning called. Not to ask Jun to return, but to tell us that since Jun was our son now, we should know that the school had contacted him to say that our son had not attended classes for three weeks straight and would fail the term."

"Wait—Tito Maning was still paying for him to attend school?"

She nods.

So, he had someone searching for Jun, and he continued paying his private school fees. Why would Tito Maning do that?

"Anyway, we were very confused about the call because every day during that time he had put on his school uniform and left the house the same time we left for work. When we returned, he would be sitting at the table, books spread out all around him. At dinner, he would tell us about his day in detail, recounting what he had learned or what he and his classmates had done."

"So what did he say when you confronted him?"

Tita Ines laughs. "He is honest. He admits it and says that school is useless, that it is not teaching him anything new anymore."

"He was probably right," Tita Chato says. "He was a very sharp boy. Had real brains. All of that memorization of facts that our schools spend so much time emphasizing was child's play to him. He needed something more than the system knew how to provide, I think. Something more than Maning could provide. So even though the school said he was failing, in my view it was the school that failed him."

I nod, remembering Jun's intelligence. Of course he was restless and bored.

"It turns out," Tita Ines continues, "that he is going to the library every day."

I smile. "You're saying that he was skipping school . . . to go to the library?"

Tita Chato says, "Ines, do you remember how he even went on the computer and showed us the checkout history on his account?"

Tita Ines nods. "The boy reads more books in those three weeks than I read in my entire life!"

They both laugh for a while at the memory, and I laugh with them. It's the easy happiness of remembering better times.

But the laughter is short-lived because we all know the story doesn't have a happy ending. I clear my throat. "So, what happened next?"

Tita Chato rubs her jaw. "He left."

"Why?"

"We do not know exactly," Tita Ines says. "We come home from work one day, after we discover he is not going to school, and he is not here. We think he is maybe at a friend's house even though he does not have so many friends. Then we see that almost all his possessions are missing, and we find a letter in his room. In the letter, he is thanking us for letting him stay for so long, but he is saying it is time for him to go. He is saying he is done . . . ah . . . *ano*?" She looks to Tita Chato for the word.

"Pretending," Tita Chato provides. "To be our son, I think." She closes her eyes like the words are physically painful.

Tita Ines scoots over, wraps an arm around her shoulder, and leans in so their heads are touching. It's an intimate moment, so I drop my eyes to my feet.

I think on all of this for a few beats and then say, "Maybe it was bigger than that. When we used to write each other, he'd sometimes talk about how he felt like everyone was pretending. Maybe he didn't mean it against you guys, specifically, but against how our world is, in general."

"Maybe," Tita Chato says.

"Any idea where he went?" I ask.

She shrugs.

"Ever hear from him?"

"We received letters every now and then. He told us he had found a place to live and some work. That he was safe."

"What about the return address?" I ask.

"Fake. And sent from different post offices in different cities. One would be from Makati, another from Bacoor, another from Naga, another from San Pablo. And so on."

I have no idea where any of those cities are. "Was there a pattern?"

"Only that they are all in the southern half of Luzon. But there are over fifty million people on this island, so knowing that did not help."

We fall quiet. An oscillating fan set up next to the door hums. The rain softens to a light pattering for a minute or two then picks back up, drumming heavily on the street and on the roof.

"You said *almost* all of his stuff?" I ask.

They nod. Tita Chato says, "There is a box inside with all he left behind. We kept it in case he returned. . . . If you want to look through it later, you can take what you want."

"Thank you," I say. And then, because it seems like my aunts are on my side—on Jun's side—I pull out my phone, bring up the blurry photo of the note, and then show it to them. "By the way, I found this in Tito Maning's office yesterday."

They lean forward and read it.

"On the other side was a list of names—suspected drug dealers, I think. Jun's name was on it."

"Ay." Tita Chato sighs, leaning back. "So it was true."

"But, Tita, I don't think he belonged on that list."

She lights a new cigarette. "Then why was he included?"

"A mistake, maybe? Or maybe Tito Maning was looking for Jun and knew adding him to the list would be a surefire way to locate him."

She shakes her head. "He would have hired someone privately."

There's another possibility. One we're all thinking. One we're unwilling to say aloud.

That Tito Maning thought Jun deserved to die.

Instead, I show them the DMs from Jun's friend. Their faces betray no emotion. I zoom in on the guy's profile pic. "Do you recognize him? Anyone Jun was close to while he lived with you?"

They both shake their heads.

"Maybe someone he met after he left," Tita Chato says. "But there is nothing to be done."

"What do you mean? If we can prove that Jun's name didn't belong on that list, that he was killed unjustly, maybe we can—"

"Sue the government?" she finishes.

I nod. "You were a lawyer."

She looks to Tita Ines and then back to me. "I know you mean well, Nephew, but the courts in the Philippines are not like the courts in America. Here, you cannot trust them. They are very corrupt. Even if we had the best lawyers in the country, the police or the government only need to put money in the hands of the judge and he will say what they want him to say."

"Maybe you're wrong."

"Oh, have you practiced law in the Philippines?"

"Shouldn't we at least try? We owe Jun that much."

"There is no point. There is no chance of winning such a case, let alone seeing it go to trial. In fact, attempting to do such a thing would put our own lives at risk. Because you do not live here, you fail to see that I am not exaggerating."

"This is true," Tita Ines says.

"Then we could protest," I say, without any idea of how to do such a thing.

"It would be a small protest," Tita Chato says. "People here like the president. They like his policies—especially this one. Even if Jun were innocent, most will not believe it. Or they will say that he must have had friends involved with drugs and it is his fault for having such friends. Or they will say a few mistakes are to be expected. That the overall benefit is worth it."

"A few?" I ask. "Thousands of deaths—whatever the body count is now—are a *few*?"

"In a country of over one hundred million, yes. It is a very small percentage. I am not saying I agree, but that is the way many Filipinos view it. It is the rhetoric that has been in use since the beginning."

"How many 'mistakes' have to happen before people realize it's not worth it?"

Tita Chato puts out her cigarette. "What happened to Jun is a tragedy, whether or not he was a drug pusher." She pauses, gathering her thoughts, then continues. "But he is dead. We cannot bring him back to life. You need to accept that. There is nothing we can do about it except mourn."

I clench my jaw.

She's not all that different from Tito Maning. Though her words were delivered with more compassion, they were the same: I am not truly Filipino, so I don't understand the Philippines. But isn't this deeper than that, doesn't this transcend nationality? Isn't there some sense of right and wrong about how human beings should be treated that applies no matter where you live, no matter what language you speak?

I'm alone in this. Somebody needs to clear Jun's name, even if nothing comes of it. We failed him in life. We should not fail him in death.

THIS POEM IS A TYPHOON

After dinner, I sit cross-legged on the thin mattress in Tita Chato and Tita Ines's guest room, Jun's abandoned possessions spread out around me:

A tortoiseshell guitar pick.

A tangled pair of earbuds.

Some clothes.

A small stack of pirated DVDs and CDs.

And three books: *America Is in the Heart* by Carlos Bulosan, *Selections from the Prison Notebooks* by Antonio Gramsci, and *The Collected Poems of Audre Lorde*.

"That is everything," Tita Chato says, standing next to the bed. "I am going to help Ines clean up. As I said, feel free to take what you want."

"Okay. Thank you. I'll probably take the books."

After my aunt leaves, I pick up and reexamine each item. Flip the guitar pick off my thumb like a coin. Unfold and refold the clothing. Untangle the headphones. Leaf through the books—none of which I've read, as I'm more of a dragons and spaceships kind of guy.

It's only a collection of random stuff Jun didn't deem worthy of taking when he ran away for a second time, but I can't shake the feeling that it's a coded language waiting to be deciphered, to be unlocked.

But the events of the day, the new information about Jun, and my jet lag are a cocktail that have me feeling worn-out and foggy.

I move the things back into the box and set it aside. Then I lie down.

Unlike Tito Maning's, Tita Chato's house doesn't have AC. There's just a small oscillating fan mounted in the corner near the ceiling blowing warm air on me every few seconds. Disembodied voices, barking dogs, passing traffic, and other night sounds float through the open window clear as if I were standing on the street. The rain continues, relentless.

I wake a few hours later, and it takes me a moment to remember I'm no longer at Tito Maning's. From the muffled sounds of the TV coming through the thin walls, it sounds like my aunts are watching one of those singing performance shows because there's music followed by applause followed by the low sounds of judgment and then either more applause or a chorus of boos.

I check the time on my phone to find it's after midnight. I try to go back to sleep, but I'm wide awake now. I sit up, wipe the sweat from my forehead, and reach across to my book bag on the floor. I grab the Tagalog phrasebook I brought with me, which I haven't opened since I was on the plane. I read the first chapter on introductions, the fan rustling the pages whenever it swings around. I whisper the Tagalog phrases to myself over and over until I feel like I'm reciting prayers during Mass.

But it doesn't feel right.

English is a language that lives in the middle of the mouth, but Tagalog is more of an open throat song that dances between the tip of the tongue and the teeth. My mouth feels too heavy, too thick, too slow to produce the light, rapid syllables Filipinos spit with such ease. I curse my parents for not teaching me the language when I was young, when the struggle would have seemed more like a fun game than an identity crisis. I put the phrase book away, reread Mia's last text, and begin typing one in reply, letting her know what I found out tonight from Tita Chato. But I hesitate before pressing send.

You don't text someone who has a boyfriend after midnight.

But this is completely innocent. She showed interest in what happened to Jun, and I'm merely updating her. What's wrong with that?

As my thumb hovers over the send button, my mind goes to AP chem last year, when I was lab partners with this black girl named Sierra. She was the captain of the volleyball team and a freaking genius who had pi memorized to three hundred and fourteen decimal places and a perfect math score on the SATs. Didn't hurt that she had beautiful dark skin and long, lean legs.

Suffice it to say she was way out of my league.

Also suffice it to say I was in love with her.

We had to message each other every now and then outside of class to work on lab reports and stuff, and when the first test was approaching, she texted to ask if I wanted to study with her at the coffee shop by our school. I quickly agreed, and we spent the night before the test at a small café table balancing chemical equations over lattes. We both got perfect scores, so after that, our study sessions at the coffee shop became a regular thing.

We were studying for the upcoming AP exam at the coffee shop toward the end of the year when I took a deep breath and looked up from my notes. She was drawing the Lewis structure of the nitrite ion. "Hey, Sierra . . . you . . . um . . . want to go to prom or something . . . with me?" I asked.

She froze, mid-drawing, and stayed that way for a couple seconds that felt like a century. If it hadn't been for the background sounds of the coffee shop's other patrons, I would have thought someone hit pause on the world.

Slowly, Sierra looked up. I could tell by the *Oh, honey* expression on her face that asking her had been a mistake.

"Um," she said, "I'm sorry—I'm kind of waiting for someone to ask me."

"Oh," I said, trying to wrap my mind around the implication that I, in fact, was no one.

She put her pencil down and reached across the table to take my hand. "No offense, Jay. You're a really nice guy and an awesome lab partner . . . but I don't think of you like that."

"Why not?" I asked.

She seemed surprised at my question. "I don't know . . . I just don't. You can't, like, force these things, you know?"

"True," I said because she was right. If she didn't like me, she didn't like me. Nothing I could say in this moment would change that.

"You know who you should ask?"

"No."

"Lara. You know Lara, right?"

"No."

"Sure you do. She's in our class—she's the one with the . . ." Sierra went on to describe the girl I didn't know in great detail, but I stopped listening.

When she finished, I said I'd think about asking this "Lara." Satisfied that she had offered me a more suitable match, Sierra cleared her throat, let go of my hand, and picked up her pencil again. She completed her drawing and turned her notebook to me. "Does this look right?"

Staring at Mia's last text, I realize that I'm as comfortable with her after only a couple days as I was with Sierra after several months. Sierra and I never even texted like this. But how does Mia feel? Would it end the same way it did with Sierra?

MIA HAS A BOYFRIEND, I tell my brain.

She's studying to be a journalist, so helping me find out what happened to Jun is probably nothing more than a project to her.

Whatever. That's okay. I need her help.

I send the text.

Then I put my phone aside and stare at a brown stain on the ceiling that kind of looks like Spock in profile. While I wait for a response, I pick up the book of poems from Jun's stuff and begin reading some of them at random. The language is beautiful, and I imagine Jun sitting at the end of the bed, reading the words aloud and then asking me what I think they mean. Not like how English teachers do, where they basically try to get you to guess what *they* think it means, but like how I know he would have, like he genuinely wanted to know my thoughts.

Grief—that sneaky bastard—returns, and I'm suddenly sad as hell again. I turn to the next poem for a distraction, and something flutters from between the pages. I pick it up from where it landed on the bed. A business card for a bookstore. There's a number, an address, and the owner's name. Strange there's no website or email address.

My phone buzzes. It's Mia.

WOW, she replies to my update. *That's crazy. . . .*

I send a pic of the business card. *And I just found this in one of his old books . . . . Maybe we can check out the store tomorrow?*

Sure. I'll stop by in the morning.

We text for another half hour about nothing in particular before saying good night. Then I read more of the poems. I've never been a big poetry fan, but these are blowing me away. Why don't we ever read this kind of stuff in school?

Then I reach "A Litany for Survival." And, my God. There's nothing I can do after finishing it besides close the book, stare at the ceiling, and soak in her words. This poem is a typhoon.

LET'S DO IT

I wake early the next morning long before the alarm I set, because my brain hates me. Peering out the window, I see the rain has stopped and the clouds have cleared, but the world is still damp. I wander out of my room and find Tita Chato and Tita Ines in the kitchen making breakfast.

"Magandang umaga, Jay," Tita Chato says.

"Magandang umaga po," I say, trying it out for myself and adding the marker of respect.

"How do you sleep?" asks Tita Ines, cracking some eggs into a frying pan.

"All right," I answer.

"Not too hot?"

"No," I lie. "It was fine." I turn to Tita Chato. "By the way, I'm sorry if I was disrespectful last night."

"It is okay," she says. "I understand. He meant a lot to you, as he did to us."

I don't say anything. She hugs me.

"Sit," she tells me. "Breakfast will be ready soon."

So I do. As I wait, I partially browse the Internet on my phone, and partially watch my aunts in the kitchen. They speak quietly to each other in what I think is Tagalog, taking turns laughing. Tita Chato's laughter is always sudden and loud, the kind that would draw looks out in the public, while Tita Ines's is quiet, most of it occurring in her eyes. As they move around the kitchen, they constantly touch each other. A hand on the center of the back as one moves around the other. A hip-check to punctuate a joke. A touch on the shoulder to warn of a hot pan. Fingers lingering as something is passed between them.

#RelationshipGoals, I think to myself.

Eventually they finish cooking and set the rice, fried eggs, and tocino onto the table along with some fresh mango and instant coffee. I put my phone away, they sit down, and then we all dig in.

As we eat, they apologize several times for not being able to take off work while I'm here, but they assure me we'll do something fun together as soon as they get home each day. I tell them that it's no problem since I have some homework assignments to complete anyway. After we finish the meal, they say good-bye and head out.

While I wait for Mia to text to let me know she's on her way, I spend some time wandering around the house. It's much smaller than Tito Maning's—only two bedrooms and one bathroom on a single level. And unlike Tito Maning's, the place is exactly as I remember it from the last time I visited. There are cracks in the plaster walls, and you can see the shadowy forms of dead insects collecting inside the light fixtures. The furniture is modest, the TV a reasonable size. There's no religious paraphernalia except for a single wooden cross above the main door. There are a couple of bookshelves filled with nonfiction, and a variety of art prints hang on the walls depicting abstract versions of such Philippine imagery as roosters, Bahay Kubo, and rice fields.

What draws my attention most, though, are the framed family photos. Tito Maning has basically no such pictures except for one of those awkward studio shots of his family—minus Jun—that hangs in the living room. But Tita Chato and Tita Ines's house is filled with images of all of us. There are lots of photographs of Tita Chato and Tita Ines doing things like walking on the beach, posing in front of buildings in foreign countries, holding hands. There are a couple of Lola and Lolo. There are shots of my parents, Chris, Em, and me from holidays and family vacations. There are a couple pictures of Tito Danilo in his priest's garb looking all holy, and even a few of Tita Baby, her husband, and my cousins Prince and Rhian, who we never see since they live in the UAE. And, of course, there are several photos of people I don't recognize—Tita Ines's relatives, I assume.

My eyes linger longest on the pictures of Jun. There are four of them throughout the house. One, which hangs in the living room, is an old shot of his entire family gathered around a straight-faced Tito Maning standing in front of Malacañang Palace, apparently Tito Maning's favorite place in the world. Jun's hair is buzzed low, and he looks maybe six or seven. He doesn't seem too thrilled to be forced to pose in the picture. The second, on a shelf next to the TV in the living room, is a shot of Jun and me on the basketball court just down the street, under the lights. We're all sweaty, each with an arm slung around the other's shoulders, and we've got these huge smiles on our faces, the kind of smiles I don't think anyone can make once they're past a certain age. I remember when Tita Chato took that one—we had just finished playing a game with some of the neighborhood kids. At one point, I was driving through the lane when a bigger kid fouled me hard and then denied it. Jun stepped right up in his face, even though the kid was probably four or five years older than us, he backed down and walked away.

The third photo hangs in the hallway and features a shot of an older Jun by himself, hair hanging over his eyes as he sits with his fingers on a keyboard—which I didn't even know he knew how to play. The last picture sits on the dresser in Tita Chato and Tita Ines's room. It shows the two of them attacking Jun with a hug. He's got this lopsided smile on his face and his eyes are downcast. You can see the first signs of what he would have looked like as a man. His shoulders are broad, and his jawline is well-defined. He's several inches taller than Tita Chato and Tita Ines, but he doesn't yet have the facial hair or the tattoos like in the photo his friend sent me on Instagram.

My thoughts are interrupted by the buzz of the doorbell. I set down the picture and glance at the time on my phone, surprised to find an hour has passed and that there was no message from Mia. I dip into the guest room quickly, spray some cologne on my neck in case it is her, and head outside.

When I open the door, Mia is standing in the sunlight on the other side of the front gate. As when I met her at the mall, she's wearing a plain black T-shirt and tight-fitting black jeans. Guess it's her thing.

"Oy, Jay," she says, smiling. "Good morning!"

"Magandang umaga po," I say, as I unlock the gate and invite her in.

"Ooh," she says, brushing back her hair. She rattles off some Tagalog as she walks in and takes a seat in one of the plastic chairs with an air of familiarity.

I rub the back of my neck and sit down across from her. "I have no idea what you said. I've only got, like, three phrases."

She laughs. "It is a good start, I think. But you don't need to use 'po' with me."

"But you're older, right?"

She holds out her right hand, downturned in such a way as to present the back of it to me. "Would you like to do mano, too?" she asks, referring to the Filipino custom of pressing the back of an elder's hand against your forehead for their blessing.

"Opo." I bow my head forward and move to take her hand, but she pulls back at the last second and slaps my arm.

"I'm only older by two years!" she says, mock-offended.

I laugh and fold my hands over my stomach as I lean back. "Sorry po."

She shakes her head, smiling. A few moments later, the smile drops from her face, replaced by a look of sympathy. "So your Tito Maning kicked out you out, eh?"

I nod.

"It is better here, I think. I love your titas—they are much kinder than your tito. And I admire so much your tita Chato's work."

I know she used to be a lawyer, but I don't actually know what she does now. I don't admit this. "Yeah, they're pretty awesome." There's an awkward moment of silence I feel compelled to fill, so I add, "I wish it was legal for them to marry here."

"It may take some time. We're the only country in the world where it is still illegal to divorce."

"Damn," I say, feeling stupid for how little I know about the Philippines yet again. I change the subject. "Anyway, I think my dad is going to kill me when I get home."

"Really?"

"He made me promise not to bring up Jun with my uncle."

"Why?"

"He knew it would upset him. Didn't want me to rock the boat, as we say in America."

She shakes her head. "I think it's good that you finally talked to him about your cousin. I think you were brave."

I drop my eyes to the edge of the table. That's not the word I'd use to describe how I felt during that conversation. It's not the word I'd use to describe how I feel when I think about the calls and texts from Dad, still unanswered. "Don't you think it's sometimes better not to say anything, not to dredge up those feelings for no reason?"

"No," she answers immediately. "If you have something to say, you should say it. If you are to figure things out, you can't hide from them. Silence will not save you."

"You should tell that to my entire family." I consider asking Mia about her boyfriend, but I go with a different question instead. "Did you tell Jessa about Jun, then?"

"Of course."

"Did she talk to Grace about it?"

"She did."

"And?" I ask.

186

"Like her father, Grace didn't want to talk about Jun. She's mad at Jessa now."

"Oh . . . but they're still cool, right?"

Mia sweeps her hair to the other side of her head and shrugs. "If they're going to work as a couple, they need to be able to talk openly about things like this. If they can't, then they should not be together. I taught Jessa this, and she understands it. It's why she broke up with the last boy she dated."

In the face of such confident maturity, I feel more like I'm ten years younger than Mia instead of only a couple. This advice strikes me as the kind that makes logical sense but is too impractical to follow. But I don't know anything about relationships, romantic or otherwise.

"So," I say, "ready to go to this bookstore?"

"No need. I looked up the owner's name, found his number, and called him this morning. Apparently, Jun was one of his best customers. Used to special order hard-to-find books all the time that would be very difficult for the guy to track down. But he was glad to do it for someone who loved the written word so much. . . . He said to tell you he was sorry to hear about his death."

I swallow hard. "I don't suppose he knows where Jun went after he left my aunts' house?"

"He didn't know about that. But he gave me the last address where he mailed a book—and it wasn't your tita Chato's house."

"Are you serious?"

She nods.

My heart soars. Finally, a lead.

Her expression darkens, though. "I don't know if there's some mistake, maybe? The address he gave me is in the slums. I called one of my professors who does a lot of reporting in that area, and we're going to meet up with him so he can help us find the place safely."

"We really need a guide?"

"Yes," she says, dead serious. "We do."

"I guess you know better than me."

"Yes," she says. "I do."

"Okay, then." I lean forward and offer a fist bump. "Journalism skills for the win."

She bumps it, cracking a smile.

"Can we go there now?" I ask.

"Yes. But there's something else."

"What?"

"Before I hung up, the bookstore owner asked, if Jun's dead, who's been updating the site?"

I freeze. "What site?"

"That's what I asked. But he became very nervous. Mumbled something about it being a mistake, said good-bye quickly, and then hung up."

"Wait—you're telling me Jun was running a website?"

"Seems like it."

"What do you think it was?" I ask, having a hard time believing this fact about someone who insisted we handwrite our letters.

"No idea."

"Do you think if you called him back he'd tell you?"

Mia shakes her head. "When I'm interviewing someone and they let something slip that they know they shouldn't have, they instantly put up a wall. I could hear it happen in this guy's voice. But we can try to figure that out later. For now, let's follow up on this address."

I stand. Take a deep breath. "Let's do it."

THE WIDE EYES OF THE LOST

When we hop out of the jeepney, Mia takes my hand. I raise my eyebrows at her forwardness, until I realize she's doing it to help me cross the ridiculously busy street to where we're supposed to meet her professor, Brian Santos, on the other side. Much to my surprise, we survive. And then she lets go of my hand.

It is here, behind the infinite line of kiosks and vendors selling an infinite variety of products, where the slums begin to fill the city several blocks deep, creeping almost all the way to the shining high-rise apartment buildings and skyscrapers in the distance. The air is filled with the sounds of motors and honking horns and the scent of cooking street food.

"I don't see him," Mia says, scanning the faces gathered around the intersection. "Guess he's on Filipino Time."

As we wait, I try to take in our dizzying surroundings. I've only seen the slums of Metro Manila in photographs and documentaries, but I realize in an instant that they've done nothing to convey what it's like to stand before them. The entire country is crowded, but there are so many people and cars and motorcycles and buildings that the word "crowded" fails to contain all of it.

It's a mass of shacks, attached to one another and stacked three or four levels high. At the ground level, they're bare cinder blocks and mortar, but those higher up seem to be pieced together from plywood, corrugated sheet metal, bamboo, tarps, and stolen advertisement banners. There is a sense that nothing was planned, that everything was cobbled together by hand as the need arose. Walls, roofs, and staircases are crooked, slanted, sloping. Thousands of power lines fill the air overhead, converging in tangled clumps at transformers that sit atop utility poles tilting under the impossible weight.

The number of safety hazards is mind-boggling. It seems like it would all collapse with a strong enough gust of wind, like it would all go up in flames with a single tipped candle.

"Ah, there he is," Mia says, pointing with her lips.

A middle-aged man approaches, wearing Nike tennis shoes, jeans, and a tucked-in polo shirt, from which a formidable belly bulges. His hair's more gray than black, and his skin's a medium brown. He seems to have two different cell phones in holsters attached to his belt.

"Mia!" he says, face lighting up. Up close, crow's-feet wrinkles suggest he laughs a lot while bags under his eyes reveal an undercurrent of exhaustion. "Kumusta ka na?"

They hug and exchange greetings in Tagalog that I actually understand.

Eventually, I catch Mia say my name, and then Brian Santos glances at me before turning back to her and asking something that includes my name and the word "Tagalog."

Figuring he's asking her if I speak the language, I step in and say, "Kaunti," which I've learned means "a little."

"Hindi po," Mia says, shaking her head.

And, yet again, a flush of shame washes over me.

Her professor turns his attention back to me and shakes my hand. "Brian Santos."

"Jason Reguero. You can call me Jay."

"I don't suppose you are related to Chief Inspector Reguero?"

"That's his tito," Mia explains. "His cousin's father."

Brian Santos raises his eyebrows. Instead of commenting on this fact, though, he simply says to me, "I'm sorry about your cousin."

I don't know how to respond, so I go with, "Me too."

"Thank you for agreeing to meet with us on such short notice, Sir Santos," Mia says.

"Lucky for you, the Danish photographer I was supposed to show around today canceled last night."

"Sir Santos often guides the foreigners who come to the Philippines to report on the drug war," Mia explains.

"And I get about as much credit as the Sherpas who carry white men to the top of Mount Everest."

Mia laughs. "Of course, he does his own work, too. He wrote a very important exposé on sex trafficking."

"The one that made you want to be a journalist?" I ask.

"Ah, you remembered," she says.

I smile. "Of course."

"Yes, that was the one."

Professor Santos nods with an expression of exaggerated pride. "I guess you can say I am her hero!"

"I wouldn't go that far," Mia says, laughing. "But I do aspire to be so fearless in pursuing the truth."

"But you must be careful," Professor Santos says, looking around as if to check for anyone who might be listening. "Those who are in power do not like the truth to be known if it does not make them look good. During the Marcos regime, hundreds of journalists and other critics of the administration disappeared into thin air. Right now, any investigation involving the drug war that seeks to tell a story other than how effective it is—is dangerous. One of my colleagues wrote such a piece. Then he wrote another. And then he was arrested on some tax-related charges I'm certain were fabricated. Think that is a coincidence?"

"I'm surprised the government lets those stories be published at all," I say.

"They can't do much about the foreign pieces except dismiss them as sensationalism. As for the domestic reporting, they can't do anything directly because we have freedom of the press," he says. "But don't think for a moment that they don't keep track of every single person who criticizes them, that they don't find ways to apply pressure on these individuals when it suits them."

He pauses to let his words sink in. Mia nods.

Then he turns to me. "So, Jay, are you a journalism student back in America?"

I shake my head. "High school senior. This is a matter of personal interest."

He considers this. "Most people are content to let things be. With all the digging Mia has told me you've been doing into what happened to your cousin, perhaps you are meant to be one of us. The first sign of a good reporter is an unhealthy obsession with the truth."

The compliment makes me feel proud even though he's overestimating me. To be honest, it's not like I would care about any of this if it didn't happen to Jun.

"Enough chatting," he says, taking out a small notepad. He flips through it until he lands on the page he was looking for. "Ready to go?"

We nod.

"Stay close. It should be safe since it's daytime, but you never know."

With that he's off, and we follow him past the stalls that border the street and into the actual neighborhood.

"I was surprised when Mia first told me the address," he says as Mia and I try to keep up. "I spend a lot of time here when I moonlight as a crime reporter, so that is not a good sign. Tell me, Jay, what do you plan to do with the information we discover today?"

I think of the conversation I had with Tita Chato about trying to start a protest or something, but I only shrug. "I just need to know."

"Do you know how many death threats I have received in the last two years?"

We step over a stray dog sleeping in the middle of the narrow street.

"I don't know."

"Hundreds," he says. "Every time I write an article that can be construed as critical of our Dear Leader, my in-box is inundated with vile messages. They call me a traitor. They say they will beat me if they come upon me in the street. They say they will rape my wife and slit my children's throats as I watch."

He pauses again, I assume so I can appreciate the gravity of the situation.

"Nearly all of them are hollow, empty threats, of course. Words from loyalist fools meant to scare me away from telling the world about what is happening here." He laughs. "These idiots don't even know enough to do some research and discover that I am not married and have no children. Even so, I am always aware that it will only take one such fool"—he holds up a finger—"one, to end my life. So, with each story I consider pursuing, I ask myself if I am willing to die to bring that truth to the world." He stops and turns around, and Mia and I almost bump into him. "Tell me, Jason Reguero, are you willing to die to find out what happened to your cousin?"

I clench my jaw as I consider my answer. Part of me wonders if this is all that serious. It's not like I'm writing some investigative piece that will be published for millions to read. Finding out the truth about Jun isn't going to change the world.

But then again, this feels important and part of me is sick of never doing anything of significance in my life. I go to school. I do homework. I play video games. I'll be going to college in the fall, where I'll pretty much do four more years of the same—and for what? If I died right now, I will have died having done nothing and having helped nobody.

"Yes," I finally, say, trying to imbue the word with the heaviness of the conviction I feel in my soul.

Brian Santos nods. Then he turns to Mia. "And you, Mia de la Vega," he asks, as if prompting for wedding vows, "are you willing to risk your life to help this boy find out the truth about his cousin?"

"Yes," she says, looking at me. Then she offers her fist.

I bump it, enjoying that maybe this is becoming our thing.

But then Professor Santos holds out his fist and leaves it up until both of us have knocked our knuckles against his. "Okay, okay," he says after we do. "Let's go."

We continue following Mia's professor through the slums, guided by his notes and his frequent queries for directions from people we pass since it turns out finding someone here is not as simple as a street name and number. The farther we go, the narrower the streets become until the space between the rickety structures are less alleyways and more low-ceilinged, mazelike passageways or tunnels, only a few feet wide and blocked from the sunlight for long stretches.

Clotheslines are strung across any open spaces. Bundles of power lines siphoning electricity from the transformers snake across the tops of walls, while hoses carrying water to shared spigots run along the damp, uneven ground. Stray dogs scratch and wander and sniff and urinate. Chickens and roosters peck the ground within trapezoidal wire cages. Cats lie across high, flat surfaces. Flies follow us everywhere. The air is laced with the scent of fried food, sweat, laundry detergent, rotting garbage, river water. Threaded through the air are the sounds of TVs tuned to different stations, water splashing, radios playing American pop music, someone strumming a guitar, children laughing.

And people are everywhere. Bathing, washing laundry, hanging clothes. Selling food. Throwing dice. Drinking soda from straws poking into plastic bags. Dribbling basketballs. Talking on small stoops. Arguing in shadows. On their way to or coming home from work.

Within the shacks and shanties, people are staring at their phones, reading, napping, eating in front of the TV—living their lives almost entirely on display. Inside one structure we pass there's a row of boys at computers playing the same game, while within another people are singing videoke. If there is an empty space somewhere, children fill it before long with their smiles and laughter and tears, only to chase one another somewhere else a few moments later. Some people look up to watch as we pass, but most seem oblivious to our intrusion.

I'm ashamed to admit that I expected more misery. Expected it to feel like one of those commercials where they play mournful music and some white actor's compassionate voice-over urges you to sponsor a child because it's the only way they will be saved from their hellish third-world country.

But, basically, those here are living their lives. Doing the best they can with what they have, I suppose. Doing the same things any of us do—only in smaller spaces with much less privacy. They're finding ways to survive.

Still, even amidst the surprising normalcy, I can't stop thinking about the health issues and safety hazards, the poverty and hunger. I can't help picturing my own family's house superimposed over all of this to know that there are probably forty to fifty people living in the same amount of space. I can't stop wondering if the children who run past me—and their eventual children—will ever know anything other than this.

"Are you okay?" Mia asks, looking at me with concern.

My heart roils like the ocean. I have no idea how to answer, how to sort through the conflicting emotions. I shrug.

She takes my hand.

"Almost there," Professor Santos calls over his shoulder.

We follow him around a corner, and the buildings give way to an open area the size of a basketball court. In fact, it takes me a moment to realize that we *are* standing on a basketball court—half of one, at least. The cement ground is smooth and level, painted painstakingly with regulation markings. The single hoop even has a net that looks new and a backboard that's well taken care of.

We cross the court, enter a new passageway on the other side, and then stop in front of a metal door. Brian Santos raps on it with his knuckles, drawing a few stares from the passing people. An old woman's face appears from behind the barred window next to the door, which appears to double as a sari-sari storefront where people can buy everything from shampoo to pain medication in single-use packets.

Brian Santos speaks with her for a few minutes, with occasional interjections from Mia. It seems like they're trying to convince her to let us in, but she doesn't seem so excited about that possibility. I stand there waiting for them to figure everything out, unable to comprehend, unable to contribute.

Eventually, the woman's face disappears from the window. Brian Santos nods at me. There's the heavy metallic sound of a lock sliding out of place, then the door opens, groaning on its hinges.

"Come," Brian Santos says, tucking his notebook away and slipping the woman who opened the door a few folded bills.

Mia and I follow him into a low-ceilinged corridor so narrow that we have no option but to proceed single file. Then we climb a staircase that's only a few degrees away from being a ladder. The steps themselves are too short to fit an entire foot, so I walk up with my body angled sideways and my hands gripping what they can to keep my balance.

We pass doors set into the walls without landings, stepping over the sandals that sit on the steps. Through the thin barriers separating the living spaces come the muffled sounds of TVs or the shifting of pots and pans. After we pass a couple of levels, the concrete steps become planks of wood I don't entirely trust to hold my weight let alone all of us at the same time. But we continue climbing until we reach a door at the topmost level.

"This is the place?" I ask.

Mia nods.

Brian Santos knocks loudly as he announces himself in Tagalog, like someone accustomed to announcing himself to closed doors. There's the sound of footsteps shuffling across the plywood floor. A woman's muffled voice calls from the other side, and then Brian Santos responds with a few sentences.

There's the sound of several locks sliding back, then the door opens, but only as wide as the remaining chain lock. A young woman's face peers out at us through the crack. Late teens or early twenties, maybe.

Her eyes dart between the three of us, then she says a few words to Mia, who replies at length. When Mia stops speaking, the woman offers a short reply. Mia glances at the professor with a look of realization. When she starts speaking to the woman again, her words have a choppier rhythm than the Tagalog I've gotten used to hearing.

The woman's attitude seems to shift, and she replies at length in the same staccato cadence. They continue to go back and forth fluidly. I'm starting to think they're arguing until Professor Santos whispers to me, "They're speaking Bisaya."

I nod, remembering that when we met Mia said she grew up in Mindanao. Maybe this woman is also from there.

The exchange continues for a few minutes. Professor Santos jumps in occasionally, but it's clear he's limited in this language. So mostly it's Mia and the woman conversing rapidly. I wait for a translation, impressed by Mia's fluency in at least three languages. Although I think it's pretty common here, I can't help but think of all my classmates back home who proudly put forth the minimum effort required to get through the two years of Spanish or French or German they need to graduate.

Finally, Mia motions for me to come forward. "Show her the picture. The last one of Jun."

I pull it up on my phone, squeeze past Mia on the narrow staircase, and turn the screen to the woman. The glow lights up her face, and grief arrives after a single beat.

This, I understand, is not some random person who took over the apartment after Jun moved out.

The door slams shut, the chain scrapes back, and then the door swings fully open.

Late-morning light at her back, the woman stands just beyond the threshold. Threadbare cotton T-shirt, long skirt, and bare feet. Hair, short and wavy. Skin darker than any of ours.

And at her legs, a small child staring at me with the wide eyes of the lost.

A UNIVERSE WHERE PEOPLE
DO NOT DIE FOR DOING
WHAT IS RIGHT

"This is Reyna," Mia says. "She says your cousin used to live here."

"With her?" I ask, mind reeling, attention fixed on the kid, a girl of maybe two or three. She's wearing an oversized, dingy tank top but no pants or diaper.

Mia nods. "For almost two years."

"Is that . . ." I start to ask but hesitate. I'm not ready to know.

Instead, I take in my surroundings with new eyes, trying to grasp how my brilliant, compassionate cousin who was bursting with energy could have ended up in the slums. I try to imagine him begging for money, playing cards, selling cheap merchandise, or silently watching from the shadows. I try to put his face onto these people I've regarded as faceless until this moment.

But I can't. I can't picture Jun in such poverty. And suddenly, as the reality of this place sinks in, all of this seems improbable. Maybe she's lying, trying to scam money out of us.

The woman named Reyna says something.

"She's not comfortable with both you and me going in," Brian Santos explains to me.

"Why not?"

"We are men. I understand—this happens more than you might think. But I'm basically useless in Bisaya, anyway. I will wait downstairs." Then he turns to Mia, holding up his notepad. "Make sure to take good notes."

Mia holds up her phone.

"Kids," he mutters, smiling, and then descends.

With that, Reyna steps aside and gestures for Mia and me to enter the home where she lived with Jun, to enter the space they shared.

We slip off our shoes and walk in.

If it were more structurally sound, I might call this place a loft. It's in the middle of the slums, but it rises above the other structures, overlooking a patchwork sea of rust, green, and metal on all sides, encircled by the smoggy Manila skyline. The living space seems two or three times the size of the homes we passed below, and with an open floor plan—though nothing here seems planned—air flows freely and natural light pours in. Overall, it is a jarring contrast to the cracked-casket atmosphere from which we climbed.

As impressive and surprising as it is, though, it still carries the same air of impermanence and instability as the other improvised structures in the neighborhood. The floor is uneven planks of scrap wood, the walls are sheets of plywood, and the roof is corrugated aluminum. The skeleton of wooden beams is dark with age and rot, and the "windows" that allow for the 360-degree view of the city are merely gaps in the walls.

Reyna gestures for us to sit in the plastic lawn chairs around a small table, so we do. The child sits down in front of the TV, which is playing some melodramatic Filipino teleserye, while Reyna rustles around in a small kitchen that's stocked with old, mismatching appliances that I'm guessing were scavenged. At the other end of the space, there are two sets of bunk beds, a hammock, and a cot. Next to them a lidless toilet (where does it drain, I wonder) and a plastic bucket of water with a tabo bobbing on the surface. A couple different clotheslines draped with damp laundry span the length of the apartment—if that's the right word—from one corner to the other.

After a few moments, Reyna sets a sleeve of crackers on the table. She then goes back to the cabinets and returns a second time with three old plastic cups of cloudy water and sits down with us. I'm ridiculously thirsty, but I notice Mia give a small shake of the head to indicate that it is not safe to drink. Though I'm not hungry, I follow Mia's lead and eat a few of the crackers to show my appreciation of the woman's hospitality. They're stale and make my mouth dry, but I smile. "Salamat, Ate," I say, using the elder sister designation.

Mia asks something, Reyna nods, then Mia takes out her phone. She pulls up an audio app, hits record, and then sets the phone on the middle of the table.

Then they begin talking. I try to follow along, hoping Bisaya overlaps enough with Tagalog that I might be able to catch a word here or there. But if they do share any vocabulary, the words slip past me in the air like blackbirds at night.

As I wait for translation, my eyes wander. Again, I try and fail to imagine Jun living here—for two whole years—before he was killed.

If it is true, then that only leaves one year unaccounted for. Still, I find the claim of this woman named Reyna hard to swallow. I consider asking Mia to see if there's any proof that Jun lived here, but I decide it best to let her steer the conversation.

After several minutes, Mia finally turns to me. "She's from a part of Cebu that speaks the same Bisaya as we do where I'm from in Mindanao—so she can tell me her story in her own language. That's important in journalism."

"But Jun didn't speak that," I say.

She shrugs. "He must have learned."

"Oh," I say, wondering if Reyna's Tagalog came from Jun.

Before I can ask, Mia continues telling me about Reyna. "She was the oldest of nine children. When she was eleven, some men came to her village. They were traffickers."

I don't say anything.

"But nobody knew that at the time. The men said that they were looking for young girls to work overseas as domestics. If any went with them, they would pay the family up front, and the girls could send remittances home once they had worked off their initial debt. Beyond that, they claimed the girls would have a better life abroad in Saudi Arabia or America or Singapore or wherever they would be placed."

"Debt?"

"For training, transportation, employment placement. Things like that."

"Oh."

"So her father sold her to these men—as a slave. Reyna used

kinder words to describe the arrangement as her father understood it, but I will name it for what it is. The men did not have any intention of helping her find work as a maid. They brought her to Manila and forced her to work as a . . ."

I look at Reyna, but she lowers her eyes. I turn back to Mia. "Oh."

She nods. "Right. But after five or six years—she doesn't remember exactly—your tita Chato's organization rescued her."

"What do you mean?"

Confusion crosses Mia's face. "You don't know what your tita Chato does, do you?"

I shake my head, ashamed.

"Your tita is the director of an organization that helps girls escape such situations as the one Reyna was in."

"Oh," I say. A sadness like sickness settles in the pit of my stomach at the realization that this woman's misfortunes are far from unique.

"After she was first rescued," Mia continues, "she spent several hours in the organization's office. They let her take a shower and gave her new clothes. Then your tita asked her all kinds of questions to try to find out more information about the men who took her from her home, and the men who . . . visited her, and so on. Then, when she was finished that first day, she went home with your tita to stay there until they could find a more permanent situation for her."

"And that's how she met Jun," I say.

Reyna adds a bit more and smiles. Mia laughs. "She said he was very cute."

I don't smile with them. Reyna was one of Tita Chato's clients—if that's the right word. She came to Tita Chato's house to heal, not to be taken advantage of by another guy. It doesn't seem right that Jun should have done anything with her. But he clearly did.

My eyes go back to the little girl watching TV.

Mia goes on. "She said that Jun was very considerate, very sensitive. He probably knew how to act properly because Reyna was not the first rescued girl that had stayed with Tita Chato as she had. Anyway, Jun was not around much. He attended school during the days, and eventually, Reyna started helping Tita Chato at the office. Preparing mailings, calling or emailing to thank donors, and other such tasks. At night, Tita Chato and Tita Ines taught her to do various household chores, but Jun kept his distance, going out of his way to make sure they were never alone in the same room together. He avoided eye contact and never spoke to her unless she addressed him first. Even then, he kept his voice soft and his words kind. She says that she appreciated that more than she can say."

Reyna speaks some more. Mia translates.

"After a few weeks, Tita Chato told her she had found a place for her to live. It was with a family that had just had a baby. In exchange for place to live and a small wage, she was to care for the child. It was a good arrangement. She thanked your tita for giving her the opportunity to live a new life, said good-bye, and went off to live with the family."

I feel a flush of pride in Tita Chato.

Then Mia's face darkens. "But the husband . . ." She goes quiet, shakes her head, and shifts her gaze to me. "You can probably guess what started to happen." She curses under her breath. It must be Tagalog because I catch, "mga lalaki," the phrase for "men," somewhere in there.

"Hey," I start to protest. "We're not all—"

"Stop," Mia cuts me off. "Don't make it about you. Just listen."

I burn with shame at the instinct to defend myself. But I hold my tongue because I know she's right.

"During this time," Mia says, "she only spoke with your tita periodically for check-ins. She thought of telling your tita what was happening, but didn't. She stayed silent."

"Why?" I ask.

"She was ashamed. Your tita's organization had already helped her so much, she did not want to trouble them again. And, of course, she was afraid of what the husband might do to her."

"She should have told Chato. Maybe even gone back to her family."

"To the ones who sold her into slavery? And how was she going to get the money to travel?"

"It would have been better than staying in that situation."

"You haven't *been* in her situation, Jay," Mia tells me with more anger than I expect. "You will never be, so you can't possibly understand. Don't be so quick to judge."

I keep my mouth shut this time.

Mia resumes her conversation with Reyna. Several exchanges and several minutes later, Mia continues the story.

"Eventually, Reyna decided she couldn't take it anymore—she couldn't wait for the next check-in. She swallowed her pride and called your tita Chato. Soon as the call was answered, she said her emotions were like water rushing over a burst dam. She started talking, confessing everything that the husband had done to her as if they were her own sins. But when she stopped speaking, she realized it was not Tita Chato at the other end of the line, but Jun. She felt overwhelmed with shame that she had told him what she had, but he only asked where she was. She told him the address of the house, and he was on the doorstep an hour later."

Again, I think about what my life was like when I was the age Jun was in this memory, the age Reyna must have been, and I feel so young.

"Jun asked her if she wanted him to take her back to Tita Chato's house or to the organization's offices. But Reyna said neither. She didn't want to burden your tita's family any more when she thought there were other girls that might need the space, and she didn't want another job with another family."

"So where did they go?"

Mia gestures around us. "Here."

I shake my head in disbelief. How in the world could someone choose to live in the slums instead of with Tita Chato? But I guess it's like Mia said—I can't understand.

Mia goes back and forth with Reyna a bit, and then continues the story. "She had Jun drop her off in these slums so she could make her own way, and she made Jun promise not to tell Tita Chato since she didn't want Tita Chato to spend any more of the organization's time and resources trying to help her. But Jun didn't think it was safe and came here whenever he could. He helped her find a spot to live, he brought her food and water, he helped her ask around for work."

As Mia speaks with Reyna some more, I shift my legs and think about how this must be that last month Jun was living with Tita Chato when he was ditching school. I guess the library was a cover. I can also guess where this story is headed—why he left Tita Chato's house.

Reyna starts crying. Mia reaches across the table and takes her hand. "They fell in love," Mia says. "Well, she fell in love with him first. She said Jun was so respectful, so kind and gentle. He helped make sure that she was safe and had enough to eat. He made sure the neighbors looked out for her. He was unlike any man she had ever known, and Reyna said maybe that's why she started to feel so affectionate toward him. One day, after about two weeks, she asked if he wanted to have sex with her."

"Oh," I say.

Reyna speaks. Mia translates. "But Jun said no. He said he was not helping her because he wanted to have sex with her but because it was the right thing to do. He told her that she was beautiful and kind, but that he could not be with her. That she needed to be alone for a while, to learn to care for herself. And things resumed as they had been."

"Not for long, though," I predict.

She nods. "About two more weeks passed. Then one day, after he had brought her groceries, he confessed that he loved Reyna. He asked if he could live there with her, and she agreed."

I lean back, shaking my head. It's wild to imagine all this happening to Jun while I was on the other side of the world debating strangers on the Internet about whether the new Avengers movie would live up to the hype. My heart breaks all over again for my cousin.

"Why didn't he tell Tita Chato at that point?" I ask. "Why leave and cut off all contact? I think she would have understood."

"Ate Reyna doesn't know why," Mia says. "I am thinking maybe he felt too guilty. He probably knew it was not appropriate to be involved with one of her clients in that way."

Reyna stands up suddenly and starts rummaging through a drawer. She pulls out a folded piece of paper and hands it to me, then she smooths down the front of her skirt and sits back down.

I unfold the paper and recognize Jun's handwriting immediately. It looks like a poem, with line breaks and stanzas. But it's in either Tagalog or Bisaya. "What does it say?" I ask Mia, passing it to her.

Her eyes skim the page. "It is a *kundiman*. A love song." She reads some more. "It's actually pretty good."

I almost ask her if I can have it, but it's hers in the same way the letters I lost were mine.

"Jun used to write her songs and play them for her on the guitar."

"Did she record any of them?" I ask.

Mia asks, then listens. Her face falls when Reyna finishes speaking. "Yes. Many. But she had to sell the phone the videos were saved on . . . Jun's guitar she also had to sell to avoid starving."

Starving. She probably means it in a different way from how everyone uses it back home.

Mia asks Reyna something, and Reyna talks for a few minutes. She smiles several times as she talks, but there's an undercurrent of sadness in her voice. Finally, she falls quiet.

Mia says, "He left school. They both found whatever work they could. He often took odd jobs like working on construction crews or painting buildings, and she washed laundry, cleaned houses, things like that. She said that they were not making a lot of money, but they were making enough to get by. They continued getting to know each other, and they fell more and more in love. Those were the happiest times of her life."

The question I traveled over eight thousand miles to ask tumbles from my mouth: "Was Jun a drug pusher?"

Mia asks.

I lean forward, holding my breath.

Reyna makes a face and then shakes her head emphatically. "*Wala*."

"No," Mia says.

I knew it. I fucking knew it.

The Jun who hugged me after that puppy died, who became a best friend more than a cousin, who wrote me letters for years, whose heart was bigger than anyone else's I've ever known—there was no way he would have sold drugs. He was too good. He was the best of us. He wouldn't have been able to live with himself knowing and feeling the pain and destruction those drugs would have caused.

But . . .

I lean forward. "Did he use?"

Mia asks.

"*Wala*."

Another wave of relief washes over me. I exhale, lean back, and look at the underside of the metal roof as I run my hands through my hair.

Mia continues translating. "It was not enough for Jun to live his own life. He was always trying to help people, and around here, there is no shortage of those who need help. In particular, he was drawn to the addicts. She said that when your cousin wasn't working, he spent less and less time with her, and more and more time trying to help people get clean or at least find something to eat." Then she looks to me with a question of her own. "Maybe his name ended up on the list by accident? If he was spending all this time visiting addicts, someone easily could have thought he was a pusher."

"Maybe," I say, gazing at the empty space across the table. I'm simultaneously bursting with pride at my cousin's integrity and hating him for his inability to suppress it like the rest of us do with such ease.

Even though Mia's theory makes sense, I can't shake the feeling in my gut that Tito Maning had something to do with all of this. Did his hatred for his son truly run that deep?

I glance at the little girl. "Reyna said he lived here with her for about two years?"

Mia nods.

"It's been three since he ran away from Tita Chato's. So what happened?"

Mia turns the question to Reyna who looks away. We sit in a heavy silence waiting for her to answer.

Instead, she starts crying. The little girl, concerned, comes over and hugs Reyna then asks something in a small voice. Reyna nods, kisses the girl on the top of the head, and then motions for her to return to the TV. She does, and Reyna watches her.

Reyna wipes her eyes and nose. Then she says something curtly without looking at us.

"Are you fucking kidding me?" Mia says.

"What?" I ask.

"He left her," Mia says, pissed.

They speak a bit more, then Mia adds, "She woke up the day after Christmas, and Jun was gone. He left a pile of cash and a note apologizing, saying he had to go, that it was what was best for her. But he didn't say why he was leaving, where he was going, or how she could reach him."

"He must have had a good reason," I say.

"Maybe there was another woman," Mia says with the bitterness of someone who's been replaced before.

"Jun wouldn't have done that."

She shoots me a withering look. "You haven't noticed a pattern?"

"What do you mean?"

"With Jun."

"What are you talking about, Mia?"

"He's a runner, Jay. It's obvious. Things get hard, and he leaves."

I shake my head.

"He shouldn't have left like that. He should have spoken to her, and they could have figured out whatever was going on together. It wasn't fair of him to make that decision himself. He did the same exact thing when he stopped writing you, when he left his family, when he left your tita Chato."

As much love as I have for my cousin, she's right. He was an escape artist.

Still, I don't want to acknowledge it. Instead I gesture with my head toward the little girl sitting on the floor entranced by the TV. "Is that his daughter?"

Mia looks at me sympathetically. "Are you sure you want me to ask?"

I nod.

She asks Reyna. Reyna answers. Mia translates.

"No. She's the child of one of the other women who live here now. There's a group of them who share the space and support one another."

I blink and keep my eyes closed for a few extra moments until a sense of relief and a sense of loss pass through me.

Reyna says something as she rises out of her chair, and even without the translation I understand that it's time for us to leave.

Mia and I exchange a look, and then Mia stops the recording on her phone and slips it into her pocket. We both stand, even though I still have so many questions about what happened in the year between when Jun left Reyna and when he was murdered by the police, about what he was like away from everyone else.

They start speaking again, Mia not bothering to translate any of it into English for me. While they're distracted, I take the opportunity to leave all the pesos I have with me on the table. I know it's not really going to help too much in the long run, but I feel the need to do something. Maybe I'm starting to hear the same voice Jun did.

Mia and Reyna embrace one last time. I want to hug her, too, for sharing a piece of Jun with me. But given her history, I just give her a small nod, and then we walk over to the door.

"One more thing," I say before we leave. "Mia, can you ask her if she knows anything about Jun running a website like the bookstore owner mentioned?"

She asks, but Reyna shakes her head.

"Damn." I turn to Reyna. I wish I could speak her language so I could offer words of substance, of healing, of light. Instead, All I can say is, "Salamat, Ate." But I say it like I truly mean it because I do.

Then I turn and walk away, imagining some parallel universe where Jun is still alive and married to Reyna and they have a daughter who feels like a niece to me. In that universe, people do not die for doing what is right.

EVERYONE LOSES THEIR SHIT

I don't speak much at dinner, and Tita Chato believes it's because I'm sad she and Tita Ines left me alone all day. I tell them that I'm fine, and I mostly am. I learned Jun wasn't a drug pusher or even an addict like Tito Maning claimed. In fact, he helped those struggling with addiction. But he's still gone.

If I'm honest, though, Jun's absence isn't the only reason I'm feeling off. Not knowing why he left Reyna nags at me like when you're almost finished with a jigsaw puzzle but discover you're missing a couple of pieces. You overturn the box, search under the furniture, and look everywhere else you can think of, but they don't turn up. Of course, you can still see 99 percent of the puzzle's image, but the inability to click those last pieces into place irks the soul.

Anyway, I stop short of telling my aunts about my day because it's the path of least resistance. They think I stayed at the house all day doing homework, so I'd have to admit that I lied. Also, Mia told me after we left Reyna's home that Reyna asked us not to tell my aunt that she was the reason Jun ran away from home. So even though I desperately want Tita Chato and Tita Ines to know the truth, I haven't figured out how to do so in the best way.

Tita Chato decides she'll call in sick tomorrow and Tita Ines agrees to do the same. I tell them not to, but they hold firm to their decision. I feel guilty considering the importance of Tita Chato's work, but I can't find the courage or whatever it is that I need to speak up.

After dinner, Tita Chato declares, "I know what will cheer you up." She marches me out to the front patio and instructs me to sit down. She disappears inside the house and returns a few moments later with the TV, which she sets up on the table across from me. She dips back into the house, and I'm confused as to what's happening until she comes back out with the karaoke machine.

I'm not really feeling this, but I help bring out a few of the chairs from the dining room and set them up around the screen in a semi-circle. When I ask about the extra seats, I'm told it's in case neighbors join us. It's not long after we turn on the machine and the corny menu music starts playing that those neighbors indeed arrive like moths to the flame.

The first is a middle-aged woman who introduces herself to me as Tita Bibi. She's holding a baby to her chest, while a skinny, silent girl who looks to be four or five clings to her leg. Tita Bibi claims to remember me from my last visit and marvels at how much I've grown. Another one of the neighbors is a man in his twenties named Gregory. He's stocky, with light-brown skin and neatly styled hair shiny with gel. He has the kind of smile that's infectious, and I like him immediately. The third person who joins us is a super old man everyone calls Lolo, but it's unclear to me if he's related to anyone. Everyone presses the back of his hand to their foreheads to request the mano blessing when he arrives, so I follow suit, and then he apologizes to me in broken English for not being able to speak English. I tell him it's okay, that he knows more English than I know Tagalog. Lolo nods, Gregory translates my words, and then Lolo laughs wide enough to reveal he's missing several teeth.

As everyone settles in, Tita Ines brings out a couple bags of chicharon—the Filipino version of pork rinds—and then passes a bottle of San Miguel to each of the adults, including me. I've gone to a few parties with Seth, but I'm usually the kid who spends most of the time petting the host's dog or browsing their video game collection, not the kid doing keg stands or playing beer pong. In other words, I don't drink much. But I play it cool, cracking it open just like everyone else and keeping a straight face after I take a sip even though all beer tastes like ass to me.

People start flipping through the laminated pages of the song-book. I'm not planning to sing, so I sit back thinking about how strange it feels to drink with family. My own parents would never allow it. Whenever we travel abroad to places where the drinking age is more of a suggestion, they insist that I'm American and need to follow American drinking laws. Meanwhile, Tito Maning would probably deny me based on my insufficient manliness.

I know it's a superficial thing, but it's nice to be treated like an adult. I lean back and take another sip as Gregory takes the mic first and has Tita Chato key in his song choice. He stands up and demands we clear an absurd amount of space for him, so we do, laughing all the while. He clears his throat as the first chords of his song start play-ing in that weird digitized instrumental karaoke music kind of way.

I don't recognize the tune, but everyone else seems excited. The song title appears, informing me it's "Harana" by a band called Parokya Ni Edgar, and images of Philippine beaches start showing in the background. Tagalog lyrics appear on the screen a moment later, the words turning from white to yellow marking the timing. Gregory has an impressive voice with decent range, and he's got us all nodding and smiling as he hams it up, swaying his hips with the rhythm and clutching a fist in the air and leaning his head back with closed eyes as he belts out the more passionate parts. Everyone else except me sings along, but not so loudly as to steal the spotlight.

As the song reaches its final chords, everyone claps. And then a huge number 92 appears on the screen—his score—and Gregory shakes his head. In English he says, "Ay, ninety-two? That should have been a perfect one hundred!" Everyone laughs again and he passes the mic to Tita Ines. A few more neighbors have gathered around now, some standing behind those of us who are seated and a few leaning against the gate on the street side.

Tita Ines sings Celine Dion's song from *Titanic* and ends up scoring a 97. Gregory claims the videoke machine is rigged, and she slaps him in the back of the head. Then she passes the mic to Tita Bibi, finds the songbook, and shoves it into my hands.

"Pick one," she says.

I shake my head, pass the book along to Lolo, and finish off my beer. Tita Ines offers me another, and I take it because I'm having a good time and the first one's making me feel warm inside.

We all start cracking up as Gregory wrangles the mic back into his possession to try to redeem himself. When his score of 88 appears at the end, he throws his hands up in frustration as everyone else busts out in sarcastic applause. I'm laughing so hard that my sides hurt.

"Ay, you are laughing at me, are you?" Gregory says, looking at me with a mischievous smile on his lips. "But it is your turn, I think." He holds out the mic.

"Nah," I say, wiping tears from my eyes. "I'm cool."

"Come on, Jay!" Tita Chato says, clapping.

"Yeah, Jay, sing for us!" Tita Ines says.

Others start egging me on and soon everyone's chanting, "JAY-SON! JAY-SON!"—even those who didn't know my name moments before.

Gregory tries to force me to take the mic, but I hide my hands behind my back. "I don't know any of these songs!"

"I will pick one for you," Tita Chato says. "An easy one. You just read the words!"

Everyone starts chanting my name again.

I down the rest of my beer, set the bottle on the ground, and hold out my hand. "Fine."

Gregory passes me the mic and then pulls me to my feet. The world sways a little, almost making me fall back into my chair. But Gregory steadies me, and everyone laughs. The music starts playing, and I recognize it immediately: "Call Me Maybe" by Carly Rae Jepsen, that song that wouldn't go away back when I was in elementary school.

I'm nervous at first, self-conscious of my shaky, off-key voice being amplified through the speakers. But people start clapping along with the beat and singing along loudly with me to boost my confidence, and soon I'm feeling it. I'm even dancing a little as I shout the chorus more than sing it. At the end of the song, I fall back into my chair, out of breath and sweaty as people pat me on the back. Then my score shows up: 65.

Everyone groans with disappointment and assures me the machine is broken. But then we're all laughing and smiling again. Someone hands me another beer. I wipe the sweat from my forehead with the hem of my shirt and take a drink, suddenly understanding that beer tastes better the more you drink.

As more and more people take their turns, I stop paying attention to the scores, stop paying attention to the fact that everyone here sings a million times better than I do. I bob my head with the beat and sing along from the background even when the lyrics are all in Tagalog and eat the chicharon and drink my San Miguel and refuse the balut that has appeared from somewhere and lose myself in the moment.

Then Tita Bibi and Gregory sing a duet of "Bakit Ngayon Ka Lang." I'm not sure what they're saying since it's all in Tagalog, but it sure as hell sounds like a love song. It's really crowded now and everyone's got their arms around one another, swaying with the tune, and for some reason, I start feeling really fucking sad about Mia having a boyfriend and the fact that Jun isn't here singing with all of us. I'm feeling so sad, I'm on the verge of crying as the song ends. When everyone removes their arms from around one another, I hug myself and keep my eyes on my flip-flops.

A song I recognize starts up next: "My Way" by Frank Sinatra. Whoever's singing sounds exactly like Sinatra. I look up to see who's got the mic and am blown away when I realize it's Lolo. The old man's leaning back in his plastic chair, holding the mic by his wizened fingertips, belting out all of Sinatra's lines perfectly. When he finishes, the machine scores him the first and only 100 of the night, and everyone loses their shit.

TO FLOOD

We're all a little slow the next morning. After a late breakfast, we end up driving for about an hour to a spot called Katungkulan Beach Resort to take full advantage of my aunts' sick day. We have to pass through a military base to access it, and there's an entrance fee, which I insist on paying, much to Tita Ines's disapproval. After we park in a grassy area alongside a couple jeepneys and a few cars, I look up at the sky. The sun is still out, but there are more clouds than when we left. Its not too hot, but there's a warm breeze carrying the briny scent of the ocean.

We grab our stuff, walk past a few small buildings and a thin copse of trees, and then emerge on the beach. It's set in a small cove, with towering cliffs on either end and jungle behind us. The water is a deep blue green, and there are a few mountainous islands silhouetted on the horizon. The sand is more gray than white, but when I take off my sandals, it's soft between my toes.

"This is a good beach," Tita Ines says. "No Australians."

I'm not sure if her comment is racist, but the last part appears true. There aren't too many people here yet, and the ones that are seem to be mostly Filipino families. The adults lounge in the shade of little thatched cottages, while the kids play in the waves wearing basketball shorts and T-shirts instead of swimsuits, the wet cotton stretched out and pasted against their bodies.

Despite my desire to set up in the sun so I can work on my tan as proof that I did indeed visit a tropical nation, Tita Chato and Tita Ines overrule me and do a day rental of one of the cottages on the beach, which is basically a small hut made from bamboo with a nipa roof. Nearby, a couple men chop away at coconuts with a machete.

"Anyone want to go in with me?" I ask, gesturing toward the sea.

They laugh as they set out our stuff on the built-in table. Tita Chato readjusts her hat and sunglasses and then lies on one of the benches, using an extra towel as a pillow. "We will leave the water all for you, Nephew."

"Oh, thanks."

Tita Ines stretches out on the bench perpendicular to Tita Chato, their heads touching. They settle in like they're going to sleep, so I walk by myself toward the water's edge.

The waves roll in and out, in and out. Some small, colorful flags strung from poles flap in the wind. A couple of kids run past me, kicking up sand. A stray dog, its mangy, copper fur matted with the ocean's water, chases after them.

I stop just shy of the water's reach and look from the sky to the horizon to my feet. The water is quiet as it gathers, and then it comes roaring back in a low wave that breaks twenty or thirty feet out. Then it pushes ashore, sliding over my feet with surprising warmth and rising to cover my ankles. A moment later it slips away, leaving my toes sinking into the sand.

And it sounds stupid to say this, but I feel like I'm home.

Maybe everyone feels like this when they leave a place like Michigan and kick back on a sunny beach a few degrees from the equator. Maybe in the same way I find myself suddenly considering unenrolling at U of M, they dream of quitting their 9-to-5 jobs, moving here, and opening a beachfront restaurant or something. The overwhelming peace of waves in the sunlight makes everything else seem inconsequential.

But I can't help but feel like it's something more for me than a tourist's fantasy.

Most of the time when I tell someone I was born in the Philippines, they look very interested for a moment. "When did you move to America?" they'll ask.

"When I was one," I'll answer.

Their interest will fade, like I was just messing with them. Then they'll say something like, "Oh, it doesn't really count, then. You don't remember anything."

"I guess not," I'll say because I never know what else to say.

But standing here with my feet in the water, listening to the sound of Tagalog and maybe other languages mixed with laughter and the crashing of the waves, smelling the chicken inasal or pork inihaw grilling behind me as swallows flit past overhead to their nests high in the surrounding cliffs, I feel like that first year mattered in a way I've never felt it did before.

Surely the air your lungs first breathe matters. The language your ears first hear. The foods your nose first smells and your tongue first tastes. The soil you first crawl upon.

My conscious brain might not remember, but something in me does.

I step farther into the water until small waves break against my chest, pushing me back toward the shore. But I keep pushing forward as if headed for those distant islands. Sand and small shells crunch underfoot. I shiver. I dunk my head, stay under as long as my lungs will allow, and then break the surface. The water runs down my hair and my face, the salt tingling on my lips.

I go out a bit farther until my feet can no longer touch the bottom. Treading to keep myself afloat, I look back at the beach and wave at my titas chilling in the shade. They wave back, and one of them shouts something I can't hear. I wave again. Turn to face the open sea. It starts to rain lightly even though the sun's still out.

I should tell them what I've found out about Jun. They'd be happy to hear he wasn't the drug pusher Tito Maning claims. On the other hand, I'm not sure how they'd feel about what went on between him and Reyna. Maybe they'd be glad that he had found love. Maybe they'd be upset and ashamed that he crossed boundaries he shouldn't have, especially for someone he eventually abandoned.

Staring at the sea, it seems impossible that at this moment this country contains countless girls in the same situation as Reyna was in, countless men whose unchecked appetites serve as the teeth of that trap.

It strikes me that I cannot claim this country's serene coves and sun-soaked beaches without also claiming its poverty, its problems, its history. To say that any aspect of it is part of me is to say that all of it is part of me.

I'm not sure what all that means at a practical level, but I do know it at least means fuck Tito Maning. Fuck those people who say being born somewhere doesn't count if you didn't grow up there or because half your ancestors are from somewhere else. Fuck anyone who tries to tell you who you are and where you belong.

The rain picks up. An expansive gray cloud covers the sun now. It doesn't seem to be going anywhere any time soon, and darker clouds gather on its tail. Everyone in the water heads for the shore, while those on the beach start packing up. Tita Chato motions for me to come in.

I close my eyes and float on my back. My body lifts and dips with the waves as the rain patters lightly on my face, my chest, my stomach.

"Come on, Jay," Tita Chato calls. "*Alis na tayo!* Let's go!"

As if the universe agrees, thunder rumbles and the rain starts falling harder. A fresh gust of wind rustles the trees. I swim to shore, and then Tita Ines hands me a towel that the wind almost carries away. I pat myself dry, even as I'm newly soaked.

"I like it here," I say. The gray sky. The water falling on water. The emptying beach. There's something holy about this moment, this place. "Can we stay a little longer?" I ask.

"Maybe it is passing," Tita Ines says.

"Look at that sky," Tita Chato says, trying to brush back the loose strands of black hair dancing about her face. "It will only get worse."

We finish packing up and jog to the car. We hop in, wet sand still clinging to our feet, and close the doors right as the clouds let loose. Heavy rain beats upon the vehicle, the water cascading down the windshield and blurring the world. This is a different kind of holy, I think.

"Whew," Tita Chato says, removing her sunglasses. "I think it is too heavy to drive right now. We wait until it lessens."

Tita Ines says, "The beach is wanting us to stay."

I laugh.

"*Ulan,*" she says. "Do you know this word?"

I shake my head, hair soaking.

"Rain," says Tita Ines.

"*Ulan,*" I repeat.

"Good," Tita Chato says. "*Umuulan*: it is raining."

I repeat.

"Now: *Baha.*"

"*Baha,*" I say. "Doesn't that mean 'house'?"

"You're thinking of *bahay.*"

"So what does *baha* mean?"

"To flood."

We listen together.

"I like this," I say. "I like being here with you guys. Thank you for bringing me." And it's kind of silly, but I imagine Jun sitting next to me, the four of us comprising our own little family.

"You are a good kid, Jay," Tita Ines says over her shoulder from the front passenger seat as she towels off her hair. "You remind me so much of him."

I don't say anything because I don't believe it. His courage was like this storm. Mine is like a single raindrop. His life was defined by his constant drive to do what he thought was right. Mine is defined by everything I don't do.

"It is a shame you have made such a long journey to stay for such

229

a short time. You will have to come back. You are always welcome to stay with us," Tita Chato says. "Maybe next time we will not have to work so much."

The car falls quiet again. Eventually, I say, "I'll ask my parents to start donating to your organization, Tita Chato."

"Your parents are already among our most generous donors," she says.

"Really? *My* parents?"

She nods.

"You sure?"

"Your tatay is a quiet man, but he is not without a heart."

He could have fooled me.

"For years he has also paid the school fees for many of our cousins' children."

"Oh."

Eventually, the rain relents and then stops altogether a few moments later as if God turned off the tap. The clouds shift. The sun reemerges. We decide to stay a bit longer since the storm passed sooner than expected.

"Baha," I say to myself as we climb out to reclaim the beach. "To flood."

ITS CENTER UNSOLVED

Late that night, I lie awake atop the sheets sweating in the dark, still smelling of salt. The increasingly familiar night sounds of the barangay float through the open window. I brush a bug off my face at one point, then I keep having that phantom feeling of insects crawling over my sunburned skin.

I try to quiet my mind so that I can fall asleep, but my brain runs through everything I've learned about my cousin so far on this trip—and everything I still don't know.

Why did Jun leave Reyna, and then where did he go? While I was across the world filling out college applications, what was his life like in the last year? How did he end up on that list? What happened in his final moments?

Who took my fucking letters?

I tell myself it doesn't matter if I never find out any of this, that I've learned the core of what I wanted to learn: Jun was who I knew he was. He helped. He was selfless. He ran, but he did not destroy. Everything else is detail.

Still, it bugs me.

Reyna said she never heard from Jun after he left her, so I'm not sure how I might find out anything else. I got lucky with that business card in the book, but nothing points where to go next.

And unfortunately, my time here's running out. In a couple days, we'll go to the province to stay with Lolo and Lola for the last leg of my trip. Not much of a chance I'll find out anything there, considering how, from what I remember, they don't even have Internet access or indoor plumbing.

I take out my phone and open Instagram. Not only is my inbox empty, but Jun's friend's account has been deleted. At this point, I didn't think it was likely he'd reply to any of my messages, but it still stings to know there's no hope whatsoever anymore.

So I pull up GISING NA PH!, the account with all the pictures of people holding photos of their loved ones killed in the drug war. I scroll and scroll, the feed seemingly infinite. In truth, I'm hoping there will be a post for Jun, but I know I won't find one. Who'd hold his memory?

Eventually, I put my phone away and try again to fall asleep.

As I continue to toss and turn, sirens sound in the distance. Something—hopefully only a butiki—scuttles across the ceiling. Two people argue in the street. And every time I close my eyes, I see that puzzle, its center unsolved.

ANOTHER DAY
IN THE MINEFIELD

The next morning, I wake to an empty house and a crushing sense of loneliness. There's a note on the table from Tita Chato apologizing for her and Tita Ines having to return to work today and saying that I could help myself to whatever I want in the kitchen.

I skip over a few new texts from Mom and Dad and then text Mia, but she doesn't reply. I DM Seth, but he doesn't answer. So I power on my computer and hop online. Except for the season finale of some popular reality show I don't watch, I haven't missed much.

My email in-box is mostly a bunch of spam. The only real message is from Mom, which some measure of guilt compels me to read. Apparently, Tita Chato told Dad that I came to her house a day early because I'd gotten into an argument with Tito Maning. They still don't know what it was about, though, since Tita Chato had no idea at the time, and they're not happy about how I've gone incommunicado. She lays the guilt trip on thick, talking all about how they agreed to trust me letting me go by myself and how I've broken their trust and there will be consequences when I get home and whatever.

Email feels safer, more removed, so I write her back. I tell her not to worry, that I'm fine and all that. To explain what happened with my uncle, I toss in a vague lie about sharing some memory of Jun and him getting pissed about it, counting on my parents' familiarity with his volatility to believe it. As for not responding to their texts or calls, I claim that I lost my charger and my phone died. I close by apologizing and saying I didn't intend to break their trust because I appreciate them treating me like an adult and so on.

I read it over. Tita Chato might end up telling Dad what I told her last night, but this will serve as damage control for now. Future-Jay can deal with what may come.

Send.

Next, I pull up the list of school assignments I need to complete. I get as far as opening a Word doc and typing my heading for an English essay before deciding I can work on all this stuff when I get to Bicol since there won't be much else to do there. I save the file to make myself feel like I accomplished something.

I head to the living room and turn on the TV. I flip through the channels before landing on a teleserye. Though there's a bit of English every now and again, it's mostly in Tagalog, so I don't know what's going on. From what I gather, this guy with a man-bun and scar on his face and this other guy, who only vaguely looks Filipino, do not seem to like each other. There's a confrontation where the camera keeps cutting back and forth between their set jaws and glaring eyes. Then there's a flashback, to some woman playing with two boys. Their mother, maybe? I don't know. The screen returns to the stare-down.

Before either of them says anything, it cuts to commercials.

I check my phone again. Still no reply from Mia.

Then I get an idea. I grab my laptop, open Facebook and search, "Mia," cursing myself for not remembering her last name even though I know Brian Santos said it at one point.

Of course, there are hundreds of hits. I was hoping she might appear in the "Friends with Your Friends" category because of Grace, but then I remember that Grace doesn't have an account.

I navigate away from Facebook and find a new article from the UK about the drug war in the Philippines. Now that I've been digging deep into Jun's personal life, the piece rings vague and impersonal, detached from reality since there's so much the bird's-eye-view statistics fail to capture.

I close my laptop and check my phone to see if maybe Mia texted me yet and I didn't notice, but nope.

However, there's an Instagram notification. I open the app and find a DM from Seth.

Yo, is all it says. And it's stupid, but it makes me feel a little less alone.

I reply, **Hey, man, how's break?**

Boring af, he says. **Almost wish we were still in school.**

Lol what about the D&D campaign?

Can't play without our healer, he says. And then a few moments later, **So thanks for that.**

I type out an apology and then I delete it. I go with, **lol.**

He asks, **How's the motherland?**

I'm surprised that I find myself wanting to tell him. I think for a few moments, debating how much I should say. Maybe because

235

it's easier for me to write things out than say them aloud, or maybe because there are no real stakes in telling him, or maybe because I feel so damn lonely and need someone to understand what I'm going through—but I start typing out a lengthy reply confessing everything about Jun.

But I'm on, like, paragraph three when another message from Seth comes through: **People are like super poor there right?**

I sigh. Highlight everything I'd written. Delete.

Instead: **Every country has poor people.**

I hope that will settle it, but then he replies, **Yeah, but not to the same extent. I watched this YouTube video about the slums over there. SUPER effing depressing.**

Hey, man, sorry but I've got to go, I type.

Um ok? he says.

Later.

I'm about to exit Instagram but stop. I start scanning the posts that are location tagged with my aunts' barangay, on the insanely slight chance I might come across something from Mia.

But do I really want to get that intense?

Turns out I do.

And it actually doesn't take long before I stumble upon Jessa's profile. Her timeline's filled with selfies and Stories about her fashion and makeup and the books she's reading. Grace is even in a few of the posts, though the profile name that's tagged is nothing like her actual name. She has a secret phone, so it doesn't surprise me too much that she has secret social media. I try to follow her, but her privacy settings are set so that I'll have to wait until she approves it.

I go back and start scrolling through Jessa's impressive number of followers, hoping Mia will have an account with a straightforward screen name or a profile pic that's obviously her. So, I scroll and scroll and scroll, the names flying upward and offscreen. A few minutes and hundreds of profiles later, I finally come across a profile pic with Mia's image, hair swept to the side so that it's covering one of her eyes completely and showing off her undercut.

Unfortunately, like Grace, her profile's set to private. My thumb hovers over the Follow button for a few seconds. I tap it. Resigned to wait in the purgatory of requests.

But a fraction of a second later, a notification appears—except it's not Mia but Grace who's approved my request, and she now follows me.

Damn. That was fast.

I waste no time scrolling through her posts. Mostly shots of food, scenery, and selfies with friends and with Jessa. Angel appears in a few of her shots, and it seems she even has her own account, too, also set to private, and also with a profile name that's nothing like her real name. I request to follow her as I smirk at the fact that Tito Maning doesn't have as much control over any of his kids as he thinks he has.

But then my heart almost stops.

Because in one of Grace's posts dated about four months ago, there is Jun.

He's got one arm thrown around her, while the other holds the phone to take the selfie. They're both smiling wide and flashing peace signs at the camera, hanging out in what seems like the food court at the mall. Jun looks happy enough, but his face is gaunt and there are shadows under his eyes. His facial hair and tattoos tell me this isn't one of those #ThrowbackThursday posts.

Jun cut me out of his life. His parents. Tita Chato and Tita Ines. Even Reyna eventually.

But not his sisters—at least not Grace.

Why didn't she tell me?

Maybe for the same reason I never asked.

I keep scrolling through Grace's posts and find a few more of Jun—all untagged and uncaptioned. Each shot is a few months apart. Angel even appears alongside them in a couple. They're all taken in a mall food court.

Except for one.

In one, he's sitting on a curb, leaning back on his hands.

Holy shit—

It's the same photo that his friend DM'd me a couple weeks ago.

My mind reels for a moment as the truth dawns on me.

There is no friend.

Grace sent those DMs. She must have created a fake account to reach out to me, to tell me that her brother had done nothing wrong.

She approved my follow request knowing I'd see these photos, knowing I'd figure it out. I take a deep breath and shoot her a message. **It was you.**

A minute passes. Then her response arrives: **Yes.**

Why?

I wanted to see if you cared.

Why would you think I didn't?

You stopped writing, she says.

My thumb hovers over the onscreen keyboard, caught off guard.
He told you about that?

Yes.

I didn't know where he was, I offer, like I had even tried to find him.
Why didn't he reach out to me?

**You stopped answering his letters before he left home. He figured
that you were like your tatay.**

What's that supposed to mean?

**That you had your life there. You did not really care about what hap-
pened to any of us here.**

I feel like the wind's been knocked out of me. I can't speak for
Dad, but it was true about me. I didn't really, not back then. I was a
stupid kid.

I'm here now, I text.

It's too late already.

That hurts, Grace. And it's not fair, but I add, **It's not like you even
told Jessa that he existed.**

A few moments pass. **You do not know what it is like to live with this,**
she messages.

I do.

**You do not. I have to deal with the pain all the time. This is your vaca-
tion.**

Her words sting. **I cared about him, too.**

She doesn't reply.

I ask, **Why use that fake account? Why not tell me it was you?**

I didn't know if I could trust you yet.

But you trust me now? You trust that I care?

I do, Kuya.

He left Reyna because he was in trouble, wasn't he? I ask, thinking about the list from Tito Maning's locked drawer.

Yes.

He was criticizing the government online. Running a website or something, I text, piecing everything together finally. **They found out it was him. He knew he was in danger, so he left because he didn't want something to happen to Reyna.**

She doesn't respond.

Am I right?

Yes, Kuya.

My eyes well with tears. I clench my jaw. I'm alone—why am I still trying so hard not to cry?

What was the site? I ask.

She replies with a link that opens an Instagram account I immediately recognize.

I scroll through the posts with new eyes, gazing at picture after picture of Filipinos holding photographs of their loved ones killed as part of the drug war, all of them joined by their shared sorrow. My heart breaks in a new way as I imagine Jun behind the camera, risking his life to document and broadcast the devastation to the world.

Jun was running GISING NA PH!.

How did the police find out??? I ask.

I do not know. He was always very careful.

Then I remember what the bookstore owner asked Mia.

You've been updating it, I message.

She doesn't reply.

You have to stop, Grace, I say, fear coursing through me. If someone finds out . . .

No, she says. Kuya Jun always said it was important that we remember everyone's humanity. The world needs to know that all the people dying here are not nothing.

I'm serious. It's not safe . . . look at what happened to your brother.

I am doing this to honor him.

I rub my temples trying to figure out how to persuade her to give this up, how to convey the gravity of the potential consequences to a sixteen-year-old.

I'm typing out a reply when she messages me, I have to go.

Wait, I text.

See you tomorrow, Kuya Jay.

Right. Tomorrow—the trip to Bicol. I had completely forgotten Tito Maning's family was going with us. But every minute that account stays up, Grace is risking getting added to some list just like Jun did on fake charges.

Promise you'll delete the account!

But there's no response.

Grace?

Nothing. She's gone.

I drop my phone and lean back against the wall. I don't know what to do. I don't want to lose another cousin.

I go back to the GISING NA PH! a few minutes later and start scrolling through the posts again.

A middle-aged woman with a birthmark on her cheek is holding a picture of a man climbing a palm tree while laughing.

A kid who looks like a teenager is carrying a baby with one arm while holding a photo of someone who looks like his little sister in the other.

A woman in her twenties or thirties is standing at the front of a classroom filled with children holding an image of what looks like one of their classmates.

A man holds a photo of himself kissing another man on the beach.

A large family posing together beneath a cross together holds a photo standing in for the father.

All of these people, dead—yet alive again in these images thanks to my cousin. In all of this, there is both beauty and sadness, light and darkness, pain and something that might be healing.

Maybe Grace is right. Maybe it is worth it.

The right to due process is so ingrained in me as an American that I've taken it for granted. Up until now, I've never fully understood that such a right is nothing but ink on paper, paper that can be shredded and tossed in the garbage, paper that can be ignored if people don't demand its application. And it doesn't even take some great evil to do that. The promise of safety is enough.

Confused and overwhelmed, I close Instagram and shoot Mia another text. **Can you talk?**

There's no reply.

It's important.

Still nothing.

After staring at my phone for a few more minutes, I put it aside, let out a long sigh, and rub my face with my hands. I know so much more than I did only a few minutes ago. I am so much more lost than I was a few minutes ago.

After Tita Chato and Tita Ines come home from work, they insist on taking me out to dinner. We end up at an American-style restaurant, and it strikes me as strange to come all this way to eat burgers and fries.

Throughout the entire meal, I consider telling them what Mia and I found out yesterday about Jun, what I found out today from Grace. But I'm still so afraid and confused about what I should and shouldn't say.

So I eat my burger. Avoid the topics that matter.

Another day in the minefield.

GO BACK TO SLEEP

"Ay, how are you so tired?" Tita Chato asks, reaching back from the front seat of the car to pinch my knee. "It is morning."

Pain shoots up my leg. Tita Ines giggles from behind the wheel. I make a half-assed attempt to swat her hand away, and then I nestle deeper into the pillow I've propped up against the window and try to go back to sleep. Except now I'm wide awake. I sit up, rub my eyes, and look around.

The impossibly dense housing of the city and its surrounding suburbs has given way to lush, green countryside. Squared plots of rice paddies lined with palm trees and nipa huts slide past. Mountainous jungles loom on the horizon. I'm just as struck as the last time I was here by the contrast between the smoggy, overpopulated cities with their garbage-choked waterways and the rural provinces where farmers wearing wide-brimmed salakot still plow fields with carabao. It feels like two different worlds.

According to the clock on the dashboard, we've only been on the road for a couple hours. We still have another seven or eight to go, depending on traffic. Tito Maning's family is leading the way in the black SUV ahead of us, Tomas driving.

"Good morning, sleepyhead," Tita Chato says.

"Magandang umaga po," I say, checking my phone. No signal.

"Did you not sleep well last night?"

"Not so much," I say. I don't say that I spent the night waiting for Mia or Grace to respond. I killed time by copying and pasting those captions from GISING NA PH!'s posts into Google Translate. Most came out as garbled nonsense, but some of it made sense.

"Did you know Jun was an insomniac?" Tita Chato asks.

"Really?"

"Oo. Most nights he slept only a few hours, if at all. Sometimes, I would wake up at two or three in the morning to the sound of him playing the guitar. Of course, he would be strumming very quietly. Singing very softly. But our house is small, our walls thin. I never had the heart to tell him to stop."

"It drives me crazy," Tita Ines says. "He plays the same song over and over and over again. What is the name of the band he really likes?"

"Eraserheads." Tita Chato chuckles at the memory.

"That's it," Tita Ines says, shaking her head.

"I didn't mind so much," says Tita Chato. "The repetition was because he always wanted to perfect the songs. He was talented and had a beautiful voice."

"More beautiful than Lolo's?" I ask, and everyone laughs, recalling the old man who rocked that Sinatra song the other night.

"No," Tita Chato says, "but it was close."

"What was his voice like?"

She stares out the window and rubs her chin. After a few moments she says, "The ocean right before a typhoon."

It sounds poetic as hell, but I have no idea what this means. "Do you have any videos of him playing or singing?"

"Unfortunately, no."

"That's a tragedy," I say.

She reaches back and pats my leg. "I wish he were still with us. You two would have been very close, I think. Like brothers."

A wave of guilt washes over me as I yet again think about never writing him back, about how even now I'm failing to find any tangible way to bring his memory justice. And beyond that, Tita Chato shared this tiny piece of Jun with me freely, while I'm hiding enormous portions of his life she knows nothing about. I think about what Mom said about how the truth can cause unnecessary pain, but I also consider what Mia said about the need to be open with one another in order to grow. They both seem right somehow.

Maybe soon I'll tell them everything. I will tell everyone the truth and clear his name. Except when I get to the part about Reyna, maybe I won't mention that she was one of Tita Chato's clients since she asked to be kept out of it.

I fluff my pillow and try to fall back asleep because these narrow, winding Philippine mountain roads scare the hell out of me. Vehicles race up and down, ignoring all speed limit signs, passing each other left and right despite oncoming traffic and blind curves.

The last time we drove this way, I remember peering over the edge of a particularly steep drop-off and spotting an overturned coach bus in the ravine below that didn't look like it had been there for very long. While this by itself was disturbing enough, it happened to be the third crashed vehicle we had passed on that journey—the first, a jeepney, and the second, a car. When I pointed out the bus to my dad as I envisioned our own doom, he shrugged and said, "What do you want me to do? That happens here."

"Why?" I asked.

"It just does."

"Oh."

"Go back to sleep."

BRAVERY AS IF
IT WERE MY OWN

The sun is setting by the time we approach Lolo and Lola's barangay.

"There it is," Tita Chato says, pointing out the front window as we crest a hill, even though I'm already looking.

Their village sits beneath the blazing red and orange sky, eclipsed by the shadows cast by the enormous Catholic church that stands in the center. Beyond the edge of town are fields and jungles, and beyond those, the silhouette of Mount Mayon volcano perches on the horizon like a sleeping goddess saving her wrath.

As we wind through their neighborhood, we pass buildings that bear the architectural scars of colonialism in the form of terra-cotta roof tiles, terraces, and other turn-of-the-century Spanish features. But the paint is faded, the plaster walls are crumbling, and the vegetation is overgrown. The streets are paved, but not maintained. The word "quaint" pops into my mind, replaced a beat later by "forgotten."

Even though I was just a baby when I lived here with Lolo and Lola for the first year of my life while my parents tried to figure out what our family was going to do next, the place looms over my memories in a way that Tito Maning's or Tita Chato's houses do not. There's room to breathe here. Fences here are not topped with barbed wire, and the ditches are not filled with litter. The old homes are interesting in a way the rushed, boxy concrete structures of the cities are not, and they're more spread out with green filling the spaces between. The same empty lots I remember from my last visit remain undeveloped. Carabao graze in the tall grass, children play wherever they want without fear of getting hit by a speeding car, and chickens and street dogs trot around peacefully.

When we pull into Lolo and Lola's driveway, they're waiting for us on the front porch. Lolo is wearing basketball shorts, and a dingy white undershirt that looks two sizes too large, while Lola is in a flower print dress with a lace collar. They look like smaller, faded versions of the grandparents I remember.

"Where's Tito Danilo?" I ask my aunts, noticing his absence.

"Legazpi," Tita Chato says.

"Is he coming later?"

"Something came up. 'Church business,'" she says with a skeptical tone.

"Oh," I say, disappointed. I was looking forward to seeing my kinder uncle, and to his presence serving as a buffer for the weirdness between Tita Chato and Tito Maning.

When I step out of the car, I stretch and yawn. The air is warm, but not hot. Humid, but not unbearably so. I fill my lungs and taste the countryside, a welcome contrast from the city's fumes. As Tomas starts unloading the luggage, the rest of us climb the four or five stone steps to meet our family on the raised porch. We take turns receiving Lolo's and Lola's blessings. I go last, and after

I touch the back of Lola's hand to my forehead, she embraces me.

"Welcome home, Apo," she says, going up on tiptoes to kiss me on the cheek.

Then she holds me for a long time, wrapping me in her scent of sweat, laundry soap, soil, and old person. There is a familiarity to the combination of smells that strikes me in a way I can't explain, in the same way as when I first stepped off the plane.

When she finally lets me go, Lolo looks me up and down and says, "Oh—you are a man now!" He smiles wide, revealing several missing teeth.

And I want to say more to both of them, but their English isn't so good anymore and my Tagalog doesn't go beyond greetings and basic words.

Tomas starts taking our bags inside, but we stay out on the porch. Lolo talking to Tito Maning's family on one side and Lola talking to Tita Chato and Tita Ines on the other side. I'm stranded in the middle, unable to understand any of the words floating in the air. I wander away and sit down on the edge of the porch facing the house and stare at ants crawling in a line across the cement.

After a while, Grace breaks away from her family, sits down next to me, and follows my gaze to the marching insects. "You will not be able to talk to Ate Mia until we go back to the city," she says quietly enough that the others can't hear.

"No?"

"No cell towers, Kuya Jay. And no Internet. It's like going back in time. Only old people and babies live in this village now."

"Why?" I ask.

She shrugs. "No jobs. No colleges. After people finish high school, they move closer to the cities."

I breathe in deeply. "But it's kind of nice to be away from all of that noise."

We watch a butiki skitter up and over the low wall a few inches away from where we're sitting. A cock crows somewhere in the distance. I imagine Jun sitting with us.

"They're speaking something other than Tagalog, right?" I ask because I can't catch any familiar words, just like when I was trying to follow Mia and Reyna's conversation.

She nods. "Oasnun. It's the local dialect of the Bikol language."

"Do you speak it?"

"A little since we visit often. But I didn't grow up here."

I check my phone out of habit to distract myself, but as Grace assured me, I have no bars. As nice as the quiet is, I do wish I could at least text with Mia. I'm irritated she never replied to my latest messages because there's a lot we need to talk about.

"Grace, about—"

She shakes her head. "Not now."

Everyone starts heading inside. Tito Maning says something to Grace in Tagalog before disappearing through the front door, and she translates for me, "Tatay said it is time for Pasalubong."

"Guess he's still giving me the silent treatment," I say.

"He'll get over it."

"Oh, yeah?"

She doesn't answer.

I follow everyone inside. I leave my sandals in the pile that takes up most of the entryway, and when I look up, I'm unsurprised that the inside of the house is as unchanged as the outside. The same white walls and tile floors. The same couches, coffee table, fans, and boxy TV. The same framed, sun-bleached photos on the walls. The same dusty Santo Niño figure presiding over it all from atop a bookshelf in the corner.

As with the first night of my trip, everyone circles up in the living room. Tito Maning carries my second balikbayan box over from wherever it was and sets it down in front of himself. But as he's reaching for his keys to cut the tape, I pull the box away from him.

"I got it."

I don't look up to see his reaction as I finish opening it myself.

I don't really know what I'm doing, so I guess at who gets what. Cigarettes? Lolo. Toothpaste? Also Lolo. Body wash? Lola. A bag of fun-size Kit-Kats? Lola. A magnet in the shape of Michigan? I set it aside for Tito Danilo. And so on and so forth. They examine what I pass them, turning each item slowly in their hands. Sometimes they nod in what I hope is appreciation and approval, sometimes they laugh for reasons I don't understand, and sometimes they set the item aside also for reasons unclear to me. I get into a nice flow, when I reach the last item in the box: a University of Michigan T-shirt that I didn't know Dad put in there. I end up handing it to Lolo, who immediately slips it on.

As we're finishing up, other people start randomly walking into the house. They greet my family, and then they're introduced to me as the cousins or nephews or nieces of my aunts and uncles or whatever. I nod and smile, pretending to remember them, pretending I understand the complex web that connects us. Then a little girl who looks like she's six stands in front of me expectantly. Except the box is empty.

But then Tita Chato gathers the items they had set aside and dumps them back into the box, and now I get why they did that. I scan the renewed contents for something for the girl and decide on an action figure. She thanks me, smiling, and then others take their turn. Each one thanks me, and each time I don't know what to say since I'm playing Santa with gifts I didn't pack. This parade of my distant relatives quickly becomes a blur, and soon I can see the bottom of the box again, which makes me worry there's not enough for everyone.

A small panic blooms in my chest after I give out the last of the items, but when I look up, there are no new visitors. I breathe a sigh of relief and lean back on the couch. The house is filled with people chattering away, but I stay where I am, taking a moment to collect myself.

"Good job," Tita Chato says, slapping my knee.

"Thanks?" I say, still guilty that I played no part in the process until now.

"You did good, Nephew," she says.

I feel a flush of warmth. Pride, maybe. My own inaugural participation, however slight, in the balikbayan ritual.

After some time, the distant relatives thin out until it's back to my aunts, uncles, grandparents, cousins, and me. I try to catch Grace's eye, hoping we can slip away to talk, but she avoids me. Eventually, at Lola's signal, we transition to the backyard for dinner.

Though evening has fallen, the back is lit by a bright light attached to the rear of the house. This part of the property is also the same as what I remember. The back door opens to the outdoor kitchen with a hard-packed dirt ground, where they cook nearly all their meals. There's a long table where the food waits for us in bowls and platters covered with plastic wrap. It's too dark to see much beyond the table, but I know there is the cacao tree and a doghouse where that mutt gave birth to its doomed litter of puppies, then a row of rooster cages probably covered with tarps since it's nighttime, the outhouse, a thicket of trees, and a pit where they burn their garbage. I remember Jun fell in once when Chris dared him to try to jump over it.

Everyone takes turns washing hands in the outdoor sink and then sits down in the plastic chairs arranged around the table. When everyone's settled in, we join hands and Tito Maning leads us in reciting the prayer of thanksgiving. After the amen, everyone uncovers the dishes and digs in—except for me because I don't recognize any of the food beyond the steamed rice and fried fish. Ashamed, I keep leaning over and asking Angel what everything is in a low whisper. She points out Bicol Express ("Careful, it's spicy"), *dinuguan* ("Pig intestines boiled in blood and soy sauce—Lola says it was your favorite as a baby"), and *kandingga* ("Minced pig heart and lungs sautéed in vinegar—they don't like to waste anything here").

I help myself to a lot of rice and just enough of everything else so that I don't seem like a snobbish American, but I end up enjoying most of the dishes, especially the Bicol Express.

As the meal begins to wind down, conversation restarts. I stay silent, my thoughts turning, of course, to Jun, that star around which I orbit like a distant planet.

I remember how the last time I was here, the entire Reguero clan went to the fishpond. Lolo unrolled an enormous hempen net and each male member of the family was given an edge of it to hold, while the females watched. We then stepped through the tall grass and into the greenish brown pond. I remember the soft feel of my feet sinking into the muck, and the earth sour scent of stagnant water. Mosquitoes and other tiny insects buzzed around me, drawn by my sweat. For most of the men, the water came up to their waist, but for Jun and me, it reached high on our chests.

At Tito Maning's command, we started walking through the water from one end of the shallow pond to the other, each of us gripping our end of the net tightly. Though I remember smiling and laughing at first, the net became heavier and heavier with each step. I began to fall behind. In my efforts to catch up, I swallowed a mouthful of water. I dropped my edge of the net as I began to gag, eyes watering. Jun let go of his side, too, to help me ashore.

"It is okay, Kuya," he said, one hand on my arm and the other on my back, "you will be safe."

By the time we pulled ourselves out of the water, my gag had turned into a wet cough that felt like sandpaper cutting up my throat. My mom and aunts rushed over to make sure I was okay, as the men continued dragging the net the rest of the way through the pond. Jun sat next to me, staring at his legs—which were covered in leeches. They clung to his calves, his shins, his thighs like so many fat, wet, black worms. In my mind, I see a couple dozen of the bloodsucking creatures, though in reality the number may have been half that.

In any case, I felt myself start to panic on Jun's behalf. But he just gazed at them, unfazed, angling his head to examine each one. Tita Ami called for Tito Maning, but he said Jun would be fine.

After a moment, Jun pinched one leech between his forefingers and pulled. Like rubber, it stretched to an impossible length—expanding from maybe one or two inches to a foot or more—before it popped off his skin. There was nothing at first, then a spot of blood beaded where it had been attached and ran down the length of his calf like a drop of condensation on a glass of water. Then, he tossed the leech back into the pond and said, "Back home you go, my friend."

By the time the men dragged the net fat with shimmering fish out of the pond, Jun had removed almost all of the leeches. Lolo, Tito Maning, Tito Danilo, my father, and Tita Baby's husband walked over to us then. None of them had a single leech on their bodies.

"Ay, Jun," Tito Danilo said, face colored with concern, "are you okay?"

"He's fine," Tito Maning said and kept walking.

My father stood by but said nothing.

Jun shrugged and turned to Tito Danilo. "It is life."

I emerge from the memory to someone calling my name. I blink, look up from the fish bones, and realize that it's Tita Chato.

"Jay—are you feeling okay?" she asks. "You look like you are going to be sick. Maybe you need some medicine?"

I'm not sick, of course. Just sad. But I don't say this.

"Maybe we should have picked up McDonald's for him," Tito Maning says and lets out a sarcastic laugh.

"I'm fine," I say to Tito Maning. Then, to Lola, "The food's delicious."

She smiles.

I finish what's on my plate, wipe my mouth, and then start for the outhouse.

"There's a bathroom inside now," Grace says.

"Oh," I say, relieved. "Thanks." And then I leave the table, which has grown loud with conversation and laughter, and head into the quiet of the house.

With three bedrooms, the place is bigger than Tita Chato's but smaller than Tito Maning's and my family's. Though I have vague memories of its layout, I don't remember exactly where each room is, and I don't know where the new bathroom was built.

In the first room I check, my aunts' high school pictures hang on the walls, and Tita Chato's and Tita Ines's bags and mine sit in a pile next to the bed. The second door leads to a linen closet that exhales the scent of mothballs and must. The next one I peek into is Lolo and Lola's room. And behind the fourth door I find Tito Maning's family's luggage in what used to be his, Tito Danilo, and my dad's room. I start to back out and close the door when a corner of yellow paper catches my eye—a yellow I recognize. It's peeking out of Grace's backpack, which lies sideways on the floor in front of the rest of the luggage and must have come unzipped when Tomas dropped it off.

I step fully into the room, crouch next to the bag, and pull out the paper, which turns out to be a folded page.

I unfold it and angle it so that I can read it by light that's spilling into the room from the hallway behind me.

My breath catches. I recognize the handwriting immediately.

It is one of Jun's letters. One of *my* letters.

I read it.

11 June 2014

Dear Kuya Jay,

I think I am going to become a vegetarian. I decided this today as I watched Tatay kill a goat. First, he strung it up by its feet. It wriggled and cried like a human child. But then Tatay slit its throat with a knife, and it became still and silent after a final shiver ran through its body. Blood poured from its neck and into a large metal bowl that Tatay had placed underneath its head.

It was not the first goat I saw slaughtered. So I do not know why this time it affected me so. But it did. I felt really sad watching it. I thought, what if that goat had a wife and children? What if the rest of his goat family was back in their pen waiting for his return? This is not a very Filipino thing to think, I know, to imagine the goat like a person. To us, animals are animals. Humans are humans. But there I was thinking it, anyways. Maybe it is your fault—maybe your American attitudes are infecting me! Ha!

Back to my story . . .

That night, when the goat appeared before me as chunks of cooked meat in a stew, I pushed the bowl away. "Tatay," I said, "I do not eat meat anymore." Everyone at the table froze.

I am sure you are already predicting that Tatay said, "Okay, Anak. I love you no matter what," and that dinner proceeded without incident.

Just kidding.

I am sure you know that is not what happened.

Everyone was silent. Tatay glared at me for a long time. His jaw clenched. Even before he said a word, I could feel the hatred and disappointment in the way he looked at me.

Finally, he said, "You eat whatever we feed you."

"No," I said. "I don't eat meat anymore."

He took a deep breath. "Do you know how many people are starving in this country? And you sit here refusing to eat perfectly good food?"

"Oh," I said, then, getting an idea, "can I take my bowl to one of them?"

I really meant it, but Tatay's face grew red. His eyes moved from me to the bowl I had pushed away and then back to me. "Eat it."

I took a deep breath, folded my arms over my chest, and met his gaze.

"Kuya, do as he says," Grace whispered.

Angel began to cry.

Nanay said, "Maning, I am sure Jun only means that he is not very hungry today. Yes, Anak?"

"No," I say. "I am a vegetarian."

(Though the rest of this conversation I have translated for you from Tagalog, I actually do say that last part in English because there is no Tagalog word for someone who doesn't eat meat.)

Tatay then said, "No son of mine is bakla"—I think you probably remember that this is a word for those men who love other men. *"As long as you are living under my roof, you will eat the food we cook."*

I did not point that out the fact that it is Ate Nina who cooks, not him or even Nanay, because I was trying not to be disrespectful. Instead, I told him, "Maybe I do not want to live under your roof anymore."

At that, Tatay sprung out of his chair, grabbed me by the collar of my shirt, and dragged me outside. He tossed me onto the porch and slammed the door shut, and then I heard the lock click into place. From within, Angel's crying turned into wailing. Nanay started to yell at Tatay, but Tatay yelled back louder.

As for me, I walked away. I went to the house of a quiet boy in my class who lives in our village and asked him if I could stay the night. I do not know him very well, but his family gave me permission, and that is where I am writing you this letter from now.

Even though it makes Tatay so angry, I am going to stay a vegetarian. It does not seem right to me anymore to kill and eat other living things. And besides, if someone like Tatay feels it is so important to eat meat, then it makes me feel all the more certain it is a good idea not to. And if we do not live according to what we feel is right in our hearts, then what is the point of any of this?

Sorry this letter was all about me. I hope you are doing well, and I hope you will write me soon about your life.

Sincerely,

Jun

When I finish reading, I bite my fist partially to stop myself from crying and partially to stop myself from running into the backyard and knocking Tito Maning out cold.

After a few moments, I move my hand away from my mouth and take a deep breath. I set the letter down on the floor next to me, unzip the backpack the rest of the way, and find the rest of the letters that had been stolen from me on the first day of my trip bundled together in a thick stack bound by a rubber band.

"Kuya Jay?" Grace's voice calls from the hallway. She appears in the doorway a moment later. "I—" She falls silent as her eyes land on her open backpack and the exposed letters.

She starts to speak then stops.

"You?" I ask, even though the answer's obvious.

Grace checks over her shoulder, steps all the way inside the room, and closes the door. She sits down on the floor next to me. "I'm sorry," she says, and starts to cry. It is not the shaking sobs, runny-nose kind of crying. It is soft and quiet. The world after a storm.

My anger melts. In its place a shared sorrow arrives. The cousin I've been mourning is the brother she lived with for sixteen years. I put the letters aside, slide next to Grace, and wrap my arms around her.

"I loved him so much," she says, our heads touching.

"Me, too," I say.

"I . . ." Grace starts to say after a few moments, but her voice falters. She tries again. "I remember when we were little, a boy at school lifted up my skirt so that everyone in class could see my underwear. I was

261

still crying at the end of the day when Jun and I met to walk home together, and he asked me what happened. I told him. He turned around, found the little boy, and brought him back. Then he made the boy listen as I explained how it made me feel embarrassed and humiliated and angry when he did that. The boy cried and then apologized. He never did it again, not to any other girl."

She laughs at the memory, and I laugh with her. "Kuya Jun had a way of making people pay attention, of making them realize that others existed outside of themselves and getting them to care. But I don't . . . and I failed him. I stayed quiet whenever Tatay yelled. I left the room whenever they argued. I never asked Nanay to let him live with us again. I never even protested when they told us there would be no novenas, no vigil, no lamay, no funeral."

"Why not?" I ask, even though I know the answer because it's the same one I'd give.

"I was afraid."

I'm not sure what to say. Maybe I should tell her it's not her fault, maybe that it's all okay because he's with God now? I try to channel Jun because I think he always spoke the truth as he felt it, but I don't have that ability. I offer no reassurance, no wisdom. I only hug her tighter and start to cry with her. Maybe that's what we both need right now.

"Tatay commanded us to never speak about him again," Grace goes on. "It seemed so easy for Nanay to abide by this rule, but it was so hard for Angel and me. We kept asking about him that first month after he left, and when we did, Tatay would yell and get so angry, then Nanay would get angry that we upset Tatay, angry that she had to think of her lost son again. I would feel so guilty. Eventually Angel and I learned it was easier for everyone if we stopped talking about Jun."

She looks down.

"I can't forgive myself for that. Even though I stayed in contact with him, I was a coward to pretend at home as if he were already dead . . . and when he actually died, it didn't feel real. It still doesn't. It still feels like I'm pretending."

Quiet settles between us.

She pulls away from me but holds on to my hand, eyes on the stack of letters. "When I went to wake you for dinner that first night, one was on the nightstand next to the bed. I think you were reading it before you went to sleep—so I went through your bag to see if you had any others. You did . . . and so I took them."

I stand there, speechless, feeling like a fool for having completely overlooked this possibility, and for having almost completely forgotten about the letters with everything else that's been going on.

"I'm sorry," she continues. "I can't imagine where you thought they went."

I squeeze her hand. "It's okay."

"Tatay threw away everything of Kuya's, so all I have are his online messages. It's not the same as holding on to something physical, something real. It was like he was alive again in a way. Do you understand?"

I nod. "You should keep some of them."

Her eyes widen. "Really?"

"Really. Later, I'll pull out the ones I want to keep. The rest can be yours. But you have to promise me something."

"What?"

"Share them with Angel."

"Of course. Thank you," she says. "That means a lot."

I nod. Even as it hurts to think about letting some of his words go, it feels right.

"I stopped writing him because I got a girlfriend," I say, admitting it for the first time. And it sounds as trite as I knew it would.

"Oh?"

I nod. "Her name was Briana. She was my first girlfriend, and I kind of fell off the face of the earth for a few months. It wasn't only with Jun. I even stopped hanging out with my friend Seth because I basically spent every free moment I had hanging out with her or watching her run."

Grace gives me a confused look.

"She was on the cross-country team," I explain. "Long-distance running."

"Ah."

"Which, by the way, is pretty much the worst sport to spectate. You basically go to the starting line, everyone takes off, then you're, like, 'Okay, see you later.' The crowd trots over the halfway point, claps when the runners pass, then shuffles back over to watch all these skinny kids cross the finish line looking like they're about to faint."

"Sounds intense."

"Indeed."

"Are you still together?" Grace asks.

I laugh. "No. We broke up after about four months."

"Why?"

"I don't think we were ever really right for each other. I mean, we had the same tastes in video games and TV shows and stuff. But I think we disagreed on a lot of the deeper stuff, the stuff that really matters."

She considers this. "I think Jessa and I are the opposite."

"That's probably better."

"So why did you and Briana stay together for that long?"

I shrug. "Because I was in high school. I wanted a girlfriend."

Grace laughs, then leans back into me. I put my arms around her again. It's nice—to be here for her in Jun's place. To love and to be loved. In the short span of a few days, she's become a new sister instead of a cousin I've seen only a handful of times in my life. But, hell, even Em and I never hold each other like this. Nobody in my family does. I don't know why. This, too, feels right.

We stay like that for a few minutes. I wonder at our hidden depths. We all have this same intense ability to love running through us. It wasn't only Jun. But for some reason, so many of us don't use it like he did. We keep it hidden. We bury it until it becomes an underground river. Until we barely remember it's there. Until it's too far down to tap.

But maybe it's time to dig it up. To let the sun hit the water. To let it flood.

Baha.

After a few moments, Grace says, "I know you want me to delete that account, Kuya Jay, but I can't. I feel like I am finally doing something for him in a way I never did while he was alive."

"I get that," I say because I finally do. "But do you really understand the risks?"

"I do."

"You're only fifteen."

"I know what's right," she says with the conviction of her brother.

"That's what worries me."

I think again about how Jun deserves a post of his own. I consider snapping a shot of me or her holding up the picture of Jun on my phone, the one she anonymously texted me. It would be an important gesture. But if Grace is going to continue updating the account, either one of us appearing on it would be stupid.

Grace wipes her eyes and combs her fingers through her hair a few times, gathering herself. "We should probably get back," she says and lets out a small, sarcastic laugh. "Back to the fakeness."

We help each other stand. I shake my head. "I'm done pretending."

And though my words are borrowed from Jun, I feel the bravery as if it were my own.

THE DARKNESS
UNINTERRUPTED

Nobody notices us return. Lola, Tita Ines, and the maid are at the outdoor sink washing the pots and pans. Tita Ami is putting the leftovers into old plastic containers that have been reused so many times their original labels have faded. And Angel is at one end of the cleared table still reading, while at the other end, Lolo and Tita Chato are leaning back in their chairs, chatting and taking sips of San Miguel while Tito Maning stands by himself in the far corner of the yard. He's facing away from the house as he alternates between drinking a beer with one hand and smoking a cigarette with the other, which surprises me since his idol is so critical of the habit.

"Are you sure about this?" Grace asks.

I nod, even though I'm not. She follows me past everyone else in the family and across the yard. We stop a few feet away from Tito Maning. He turns slowly. Then his gaze shifts from Grace to me. He doesn't look away and neither do I, even though I know that's what he wants. He sucks deeply on the cigarette and then exhales the smoke out of the side of his mouth. He drops the butt and steps on it. The entire time, none of us breaks eye contact. None of us speaks.

"Do you want something, Nephew?" Tito Maning finally says, spitting "Nephew" out like it's meant to remind me of my place.

"What really happened to Jun, Uncle?"

He continues staring at me for what feels like a full minute, face set like stone. Right when I think he's about to stay quiet until the end of time, he takes a drink of his beer, swallows, then says in a low voice, "We have already had this discussion."

I clear my throat. I'm not backing down this time. "You didn't tell the truth."

He looks up and watches the sky for a few moments, as if tracking a bird or passing plane. Another drink. Then he meets my eyes again. "You are calling me a liar?"

My instinct is to mumble an apology and say never mind. But I don't. I hold his gaze. "Yes. I found the note in your desk."

Tito Maning lets out a huff of air through his nose like a snort, then he shakes his head while smirking and takes another swig of beer. "Americans," he says. "So disrespectful. This is why I keep my family here. In this country, children know how to behave."

He lifts the beer to his mouth to take another drink, but then Grace steps forward and slaps it out of his hand, sending the bottle flying.

The rest of the family whips their heads in our direction.

Tito Maning's hand stays stuck in midair like he's still about to take a drink. Like a snake slithering from branch to branch, his gaze slides from me to Grace to the bottle lying on the ground a few feet away, unbroken and spilling into the soil. I expect him to strike at any moment, to rear his hand back and hit her or grip her up by the collar like he did to Jun all those years ago. My muscles tense in preparation, ready to throw myself between them even though he's my uncle, even though he's a regional police chief. I was never there for Jun, but I'm here for Grace.

Everyone else has gathered around us now.

"He had his subordinates keeping tabs on Jun," I tell them. "He always knew where Jun was, right up until the end."

"Is it true?" Grace demands.

Tito Maning balls his hands into fists and then crosses his arms over his chest. "Of course I knew everything. I knew he lived with Chato. I knew when he left her to live with that prostitute. I knew when he started that website. I knew when he ran away because he suspected—correctly—that the authorities took notice." He looks to Grace. "I even knew that you continued to meet with him. It is my job to know things."

"So you knew he wasn't involved in drugs," Grace says, shaking and eyes wet with tears.

"He was," Tito Maning says.

"You're lying," I say.

"I promise you I am not."

"You had him killed—not because of the drugs, but because he was showing the world what you and Duterte's other thugs were doing."

Insects drone. A dog barks. Stars burn.

Tito Maning starts to chuckle while shaking his head in disbelief.

"Ay," Lola says, pulling Tito Maning by the elbow. "You are all tired from a long day of travel. You need to rest, I think."

He shrugs her hand away.

Nobody else moves.

"So," Tito Maning says, looking only at me now as if I'm the instigator of his daughter's rebellion. "You have invented some story about my son, have you? Some conspiracy theory, that I ordered his death to stop him from fighting the good fight?"

I don't say anything.

He laughs again. "You Americans and your stories. Always looking for a hero. And if you don't have one, you create one." His face darkens. He steps up to me so that we're almost chest-to-chest, so close that I smell the smoke and alcohol on his breath. I sense everyone else tense up, unsure if they should—if they even could—intervene.

But I hold my ground.

"Maybe you," he says, "are wrong. Maybe *I* am the hero. I am the one fighting to rid my country of a poison that has ruined more lives than you can even begin to comprehend."

His words hang in the air between us.

"You're a madman's butcher," I say. "And you murdered your own son."

In a flash, his hand clamps around my throat. I feel my feet come off the ground as he shoves me backward until I slam against something hard, pain jolting through my spine. I try to pry his fingers off my throat, but his grip is too strong. I can't breathe. The world blurs. My feet kick in the air. There's the chaos of shouting and movement all around us, but Tito Maning's face—pinched with rage—is the only thing I see in my shrinking field of vision . . . my brain feels like it's floating away, my lungs like they're on fire, my heart like it's going to burst.

I'm on the edge of completely passing out when the pressure suddenly releases. There's a cry from somewhere, and I collapse to the ground, gasping for air on my hands and knees. As Tita Chato and Tita Ines rush to my side, I look up and see the reason for my release: At the end of Lola's arm, Tito Maning is bent and writhing in pain as she pinches and twists his earlobe between her thumb and forefinger.

"Are you okay, Apo?" she asks me, calm as her oldest grimaces and curses in Tagalog or Bikol, still at her mercy.

I feel my neck, cough a few times, then nod.

She releases Tito Maning and he stumbles away and straightens up, rubbing his now bright red ear. Tita Ami reaches out for him, but he swats her hand aside.

"I did not kill Jun, and I did not order anyone to kill Jun!" he says bitterly to no one, to everyone. "Do not believe me? Ask Danilo."

His words land like a shock wave. Time stops. Nobody speaks for a few beats, as we all wonder what Tito Danilo has to do with any of this.

"Even if you didn't kill him, you didn't stop it," Grace says, breaking the spell but blowing past the part about Danilo.

Tito Maning spits on the ground. "He was an enemy of the state."

I stand up as if ready for round two. "He was your son."

He shoots me a murderous look—but then glances at Lola and storms away. Tita Ami calls for the girls to follow, but only Angel obeys. The screen door slams into its frame like a gunshot as they disappear.

Everything's so fucked up. I try to calm down, to make a little deal

271

with myself like I used to when I was a kid: if I look up and see the clouds have moved at least enough to show a single star in the sky, it will be a sign that maybe this will all turn out okay.

But I close my eyes. I don't want to look up. I'm too afraid that overhead I'll find the darkness uninterrupted.

NEW LIFE

The next morning, I wake up before anyone else and slip out of the house. The streets are silent and empty and the cocks haven't even started crowing. It's foggy and dark, so I use my phone's flashlight to light the way.

"Wait for me," someone calls from behind.

I turn around and see a figure approaching in the darkness. She steps into the small spotlight cast by my phone, shielding her eyes against at the brightness.

"Grace?" I ask, my voice small in the predawn hush. "What are you doing out here?"

"I heard someone leave the house, so I looked out the window and saw you. Where are you going, Kuya?"

I continue walking. "Legazpi."

"Ah," she says. "It's the other way."

I turn around.

"Are you planning to walk there?" she asks, stepping in line with me as I pass her. "It might take a while."

"I'm going to find a taxi."

"At this time?"

"Yes."

We walk side by side in silence for a while. We pass several stray dogs curled up in the middle of the street, who look up to see what's going on and then drop their heads to return to sleep. Then Grace asks the obvious question.

"You're going to speak to Tito Danilo, yes?"

I nod.

"Then I'm going with you," she says.

I shake my head. "I think this is something I need to do alone."

"He was my brother."

We keep walking.

Grace adds, "I am guessing you do not even know which church to go to."

I don't answer. Grace takes the lead. We make a few turns and then come upon a street with a row of parked taxis and tricycles. All are empty and still, and I start to lose hope. But then Grace calls me over to a taxi with a driver asleep behind the wheel. She knocks on the window until he wakes up.

I take out all three of the thousand peso bills I have in my wallet and hold them up. In a flash his eyes are open and he's unlocking the back doors.

We climb in, and then Grace tells him the name of the church in Legazpi where Tito Danilo serves. He nods, and then we're on our way.

Most likely, we'll end up in trouble for leaving without telling anyone. But if we did, they wouldn't have let us go. After Tito Maning walked away last night, I tried asking the rest of my family what they thought he meant by the Tito Danilo comment. But nobody wanted to talk about it. They kept telling me it doesn't matter, to let it go, to let things blow over.

So here we are.

It's warm inside the car, so I roll down the window and let the wind rush through my hair as we careen down the province roads. The air feels damp and cool and carries the scent of wet grass and moist earth. All I can see is the patch of road illuminated by the head-lights, though I know rice paddies and dense jungle are rolling by in the darkness on either side. We only pass a handful of vehicles along the way, and roughly an hour and a half later, we reach the city as dawn lightens the sky.

As the driver navigates through the city, more and more people appear on the streets. Some look like they're on their way to work, others, on their way home. Doors are being unlocked, shopfront gates rolled up, sidewalks swept. A light rain starts to fall and the wind picks up, rustling the palms overhead.

My phone buzzes in my pocket, probably alerting me to new messages since it finally has a signal again. But I don't want to pull it out right now in fear I'll drop it, so I make a mental note to check it later.

Eventually, we come to a stop in front of an enormous stone cathedral illuminated with recessed lighting that looks like it's been plopped down in the middle of the block from another century, some hybrid of Spanish and Roman architectures. Maybe four or five stories high, it's all columns and balustrades and arcades, statues of saints and stained-glass windows. In the rear to the left there's a bell tower with a dome topped by a white cross, while in the rear to the right is a peaked spire, stone stained dark with soot.

"This is it," Grace says.

I hand over the three thousand pesos, which I think is about sixty dollars. After exchanging a few words with Grace in Tagalog or Bikol he drives away.

"You overpaid," she says. "Maybe that was more than he makes in one month."

That fact blows my mind. The U of M hoodie Seth bought me probably cost about the same amount.

We make our way to what seems like the main entrance, expecting to find the door locked. Except when I yank on the heavy iron handle, it pulls wide open, revealing a spacious sanctuary filled with light and smelling of frankincense.

Much to my surprise, the inside of the church looks brand-new and is smaller than I expect. The marble floor is freshly waxed, the walls unblemished, the pews polished. Square columns line either side of the sanctuary like a rib cage, a circular depiction of each Station of the Cross and a stained-glass window between each one. There's a tray ceiling overhead with a painting of the Last Supper along the front edge, while on the altar is what looks like five connected glass display cabinets topped with an ornate vase. The center section, which is the largest, contains a statue of Christ being taken down from the cross. The two on the left and the two on the right hold statues of other saints, the only one of which I can confidently identify is the Virgin Mary. Finally, above the altar is a circular opening in the ceiling with blue lighting that makes it look like the portal to Heaven itself.

"Beautiful," I say.

"And funded by the poor," she says, sounding a bit like her brother.

The heavy door swings shut behind us, sealing out the sounds of the street and wrapping us in the hush of the sanctuary.

"Hello?" I call. My voice bounces around the space and then fades.

There's no response. We walk farther inside, the sound of our steps echoing in the quiet. After calling out a second time to no reply, we make our way down the wide center aisle. Strange that the church would be open with nobody home.

"Wait here," Grace says. "I'll check the rectory."

I nod, slide into the back pew, and then read the texts I received while we were on our way here. They're all from Mia, mostly asking if we arrived safely and what else I found out about Jun. I slip my phone back into my pocket without answering them. I know it's immature, but I can't help it since I'm still annoyed she never replied to any of my messages from the other day.

A few moments later, Tito Danilo appears from a hallway off to the opposite side of the altar from where Grace went. He's larger than I remember, and now sporting an impressive beard for a Filipino. He doesn't notice me at first because he's reading a book and wearing a large pair of noise-canceling headphones over his ears. But then he spots me out of the corner of his eye and stops short. He slips his headphones down so they hang around his neck and offers a confused smile.

"Jason?"

"Hey, Tito."

He closes the book, walks over with a puzzled expression, and hugs me. "It is good to see you . . . but what are you doing here?"

This, of course, requires a long-ass answer. So instead, I cut to the heart of the matter. "I need to talk to you. About Jun."

His smile falters, and I swear his face pales. "I don't—"

"There you are," Grace says, returning to the sanctuary. She makes her way over to where we are, hugs Tito Danilo, and then sits down next to me.

Tito Danilo slides into the next pew, turned around so he's facing us. He tries making small talk, but I'm not here for niceties.

"Tito Maning insists the police killed Jun because he was selling drugs," I say. "But that's a lie. He was only spreading the word about all the people that were being killed."

Tito Danilo is speechless. We go ahead and tell him everything, from the moment Grace sent me those DMs to how we snuck out this morning, leaving out only the specifics about the Reyna situation to honor her request. Our voices echo throughout the empty chapel, and judging by his reactions, it seems like most—but not all—of what we reveal is new to him. It takes a long time, and when we finish, Tito looks up at the cross. Then he closes his eyes and lets his gaze fall to the floor. A new sadness seems to settle upon his shoulders.

He lets out a long sigh. He doesn't explain how much he already knew about what we've shared with him about Jun. Instead he says, "What's done is done. It was a tragedy, but there's nothing more to say."

"There's the truth," I say.

"Tito, we need you to come back with us and tell everyone that Tatay is a liar," Grace adds.

He's silent for a long, long time. So long that I start to think it didn't work, that this information, this story, will not serve as the catalyst I hoped it would, will not inject him with the courage to stand up to his big brother.

But then he picks up his head, opens his eyes, and starts to speak.

"It is a shame what is happening in this country. And it is a shame that the Church has been so quiet. That all of us have been so quiet. That the world has been so quiet."

We wait for him to say more.

He goes on. "Manoy Maning called me a few months before Jun's death. He told me that his men had informed him Jun was in Legazpi."

"You serious?" I ask.

He nods.

"What did he want you to do?" Grace asks.

"To find him . . . to save him."

I sit up, disbelieving that my uncle still cared about Jun at that point. "Maning called to ask you to save Jun from the police—the police that Maning was in charge of, that he could've ordered to fall back at any time?"

"No," Tito Danilo says. "He had already bribed someone once to remove Jun's name from the list. But he found his way back onto it. He wanted me to save Jun from himself . . . from the drugs."

Grace and I exchange a look and then I say, "But Jun didn't use them, and he wasn't a pusher. That was their excuse for murdering him."

Tito Danilo is quiet for a long time again. Then he continues his story instead of responding to what I said. "I searched the streets for weeks, but I couldn't find him. I carried his picture with me everywhere I went and asked everyone I came across. But nobody had seen him. Or, at least, nobody was willing to tell me they had. Three months passed before I gave up hope, even as I continued carrying his picture."

I say, "He probably wasn't even in Legazpi, Tito. That must have been another lie."

Tito Danilo's face takes on an even more sorrowful expression. He goes on. "And then one day, Jun came into the church. 'Is it you?' I asked, because he looked so different. 'It is,' he said, then we embraced. I was so happy, even though it was painful to see him like that."

Grace clutches my hand. "See him like what, Tito?"

"He had become small. Skinny as a stick. And he couldn't stop rocking back and forth. His voice was shaky and . . . broken. He was broken."

Grace doesn't say anything to this.

"What did he say?" I ask.

"That he wanted to go for a walk," Tito Danilo says. "To speak."

"About what?"

Tito Danilo is quiet for a long time. A very long time. Rain begins to patter against the stained-glass windows. A breeze stirs the air, blowing out a few of the candles on the altar burning no more for lost souls.

Then, he says, "I tried to convince him to go back home. To come stay with me, at least. But then he grew angry. He wanted me to listen, he said. That nobody ever listened. That all they ever did was try to tell everyone else what to do."

"Tito," Grace says, "what did Kuya Jun tell you?"

He sighs and bows his head. "He did all that you think he did not do."

My heart skips a beat.

"No," Grace says, shaking her head as tears well in her eyes. She squeezes my hand harder.

Danilo sighs. "It is true. He told me as much himself."

I shake my head. "He was on the list because of GISING NA PH! Not because of drugs . . . That's why he left the woman he loved—so she wouldn't be in danger."

"That may have gotten him onto the watch list, but he told me that he ran away from her because he had started using. He did not want to drag her into that life."

I don't say anything. I was so close to feeling like I had Jun's story nailed down. But no. That's not how stories work, is it? They are shifting things that re-form with each new telling, transform with each new teller. Less a solid, and more a liquid taking the shape of its container.

Tito Danilo continues. "And later, he started selling."

"But why?" Grace asks, desperate.

"Shabu is a hunger suppressant. You see, it is cheaper than food, so many of the poor start for this reason, and then they become addicted. As for why he started selling? Your guess is as good as mine. Maybe to make money to keep feeding his addiction."

I close my eyes, as if doing so will rewind the story, erasing everything Tito Danilo has just told us. As if it will stop the warping truth. I can't reconcile this version of Jun with the one I had come to know, to love, to admire. Even as I sit still, I feel like I'm falling.

I try to pull my hand away from Grace, but she tightens her grip.

Tito Danilo steeples his fingers and touches the tips to his lips as if in prayer. "Nephew. Niece. I am sorry to be the one to tell you this. But it is all true. I know you cannot believe Manoy Maning because of his position, but you must believe me when I say I have nothing to gain by telling you all of this."

Grace stays silent.

I shake my head.

"I again offered for him to stay with me," Tito Danilo continues. "He refused. He promised that he would return, that we would talk more. But then a few days later, he was dead."

My heart thrums. My hands tremble. My uncle's words are like waves, only I don't know if they're pulling me to shore or carrying me out to sea.

"No," I say, closing my eyes. I think of GISING NA PH!.

Tito Danilo must be wrong.

Jun wouldn't live that life in a million years.

I lift my eyes to Tito Danilo, and he looks at me as if for the first time since I've arrived. His expression is filled with sorrow as deep as the ocean. And in that instant, I know he's telling the truth.

My heart breaks for what feels like the hundredth time in two weeks. I look away.

I search for an excuse on Jun's behalf, desperate to justify, to exonerate. "Maybe he was using the money to help people," I suggest. "Maybe he . . ." I trail off.

Nobody says anything.

"Who killed him?" Grace asks, breaking the long silence.

"Does it matter?" he asks.

"Yes," Grace answers.

"Why?" Tito Danilo asks gently. "What will you do?"

Neither of us answer.

"It doesn't matter who killed him," Tito Danilo says. "Jun is already dead. You can't save him anymore. And his murderer is one more poor soul trying to make a few pesos to feed his family. If he did not pull the trigger, someone else would have eventually." He hesitates and then adds, "But if you must know, I was told it was a vigilante."

"A vigilante?" I ask.

"Someone who kills drug pushers of their own accord."

"Was this 'vigilante' arrested?"

"He was paid," Tito Danilo says. "For making the city 'safer.' In most people's eyes, Jun's death meant one less drug pusher on the streets."

"And everyone here is okay with the fact there are people running around and killing whoever they want? Without a warrant, without due process?" And I know my tone's disrespectful, but I can't help myself.

"If they are pushing drugs, then yes," Tito Danilo says. "This isn't America."

"Don't people care about all of these lives being taken?"

"Did you?" he asks. "Before Jun?"

I look down, burning with shame. Then I deflect. "Why doesn't the Church do anything? Whatever happened to 'Thou shalt not kill'?" I let out a sarcastic laugh. "It's been a while since my Catechism classes, but I don't remember an 'unless' tacked onto the end of that commandment."

He considers this for a moment. "The Church tends to souls. Not the affairs of the state."

Great.

Tito Danilo thinks it's not the church's job. Tita Chato believes there's nothing to be done. Tito Maning actively assists in these murders. And Dad doesn't care.

All of the adults are failing us.

Tito Danilo lets out a heavy sigh and then stands. "I'm going to go call the family and let them know you're here. Then we will take breakfast together, and I'll drive you back."

He leaves Grace and me alone in the sanctuary. We sit in the silence together, crying quietly. There's the familiar pain, but there's a fresh hurt, too. In losing the story we had told ourselves about Jun, we've lost him all over again, in a new way.

"I'm not hungry," I say eventually.

"Me neither," Grace says.

A few beats of silence pass.

"I can't believe it," I say. "I can't believe that he used . . . that he sold . . ."

"It isn't right," Grace says.

"Which part?"

"Any of it."

I nod and let my graze drift upward. A bird flits across the rafters to a nest high in the corner. It reminds me of when I heard the baby birds chirping outside the window the day that the puppy died in my hands. What was it Mom told me in that moment? Something about death making way for new life. But what new life has come from Jun's death? I don't know.

I imagine souls trapped overhead, bouncing against the steepled ceiling like invisible balloons whose strings have slipped from careless hands.

HEADFIRST ACROSS THE MUDDY GRASS

The last time I came to the Philippines, Jun and I spent one entire day in the open field by the church a few blocks away from Lolo and Lola's house. We started out trying to play soccer with Chris and Em, using palm trees at either end to mark goalposts. I say "trying" because it rained the night before, leaving the field a muddy mess. We played barefoot so we wouldn't ruin our shoes, but we kept sliding all over the place. I also say "trying" because while Chris and Em both played in competitive leagues back home, Jun and I had no idea what we were doing. Still, he insisted that we be on the same team.

My brother and sister clobbered us, of course. And it wasn't long before they lost interest and returned to the house. Jun and I kept playing, though, transitioning to a pathetic one-on-one game. I don't remember keeping score. I only remember laughing until I was out of breath, smiling until my cheeks hurt, and staying outside under the sun until I held my forearm next to Jun's and we were almost the same shade of brown.

Eventually, a bunch of kids started to gather around to watch. Not just a handful, but maybe a couple dozen ranging in age from five or six to fifteen or sixteen. Jun invited them all to play because that's how he was. That's how I want to remember him. We began a new game with these massive, uncoordinated teams. Since nobody understood positions, it was basically just twenty-something kids chasing the ball at the same time.

But everyone had fun. Nobody cared who won, and the older kids made sure to let the little ones kick around the ball for a while every now and then. Teams became meaningless.

Eventually, the clouds covered the sun, and it started to rain again. Most of the kids wandered home at that point, and I picked up the ball to leave. But Jun popped it out of my grip and began kicking it around the field in the opposite direction. I chased him down through the rain and when I was about to steal it, he slid headfirst across the muddy grass to knock the ball out of the way. My foot swung through the air, and I slipped onto my back. When we stood up, we were covered in so much muck we both looked like Swamp Thing. We stayed out another hour or so, running around and sliding in the mud before heading back to Lolo and Lola's house. But when we returned, they wouldn't let us into the house since we were so dirty. Instead, Lola brought out soap and shampoo and then Jun and I showered outside in the rain, laughing.

TO RESURRECT

In the car with Tito Danilo and Grace on the way back to Lolo and Lola's, I think about how there's a new grief in remembering Jun now, knowing what eventually happened, knowing that he was more than my idea of him in ways I do not like, knowing that there's probably so much more I'll never know.

I was determined to find the truth. And I did—at least a piece of it.

But was it worth it? What do I even do now?

This didn't play out how I thought it would.

I expected the truth to illuminate, to resurrect.

Not to ruin.

HOW TO LIVE WITHOUT HIM

When we arrive at the house, our family is gathered out front. Most everyone seems relieved that we've returned safely, and there are a lot of hugs when we step out of the car. But Tito Maning stands on the porch with his arms crossed and a smug look on his face, probably because he knows he's been vindicated by what Tito Danilo told us. As we enter the house, Grace and I walk right past him without a word.

I'm retreating to my room and Grace to hers when I stop. I turn to her in the hallway before she disappears.

"Are you okay, Grace?" I ask.

She stops, hand on the doorknob. Then she turns, leans back against the doorframe, and bites her lower lip like she doesn't know what to say. Outside, the rest of our family is still talking on the porch.

"I keep thinking about the last time I saw him . . . I keep trying to remember if there were any signs I missed . . . if there was anything I might have done for him."

I think of the weed Tito Maning found in Jun's room all those years ago. I was quick to dismiss it, but was there something unnamed going on with Jun even then? Maybe all of this didn't begin later in the slums—maybe it was always there, lurking under the surface with a tentacle already wrapped around his ankle.

"It's not your fault," I say. "People are good at hiding things from one another. Especially in our family."

She sighs. "I know. But I still wonder." Then she asks, "How are you, Kuya Jay?"

I hesitate. "Honestly? I have no idea."

"What are you feeling?"

"Confused."

"Why?"

"I don't know what to think anymore, Grace," I say, then I fall quiet for a few beats. "Do you regret sending me those DMs? Do you wish that I never came?"

She tilts her head. "Why would you say that, Kuya?"

I shrug. "If I didn't come, if I didn't push to find out what happened, we wouldn't have learned about that part of Jun's life. We could have held on to our own versions of him. But now it feels like his memory is . . . I don't know . . . tainted?"

"Tainted how?"

"Like we got him wrong."

"Just because we didn't know everything about him doesn't change what we did know about him, Kuya. What Tito Danilo told us—it made me question what I could have done to help, but it did not change how I feel about my brother."

"Even though he was guilty?"

"He was human," she says without hesitation. "He was struggling. Just because he was a user, a pusher, it doesn't mean that his life was worthless. It doesn't mean that there wasn't good in him."

I don't say anything, but I feel ashamed. How much of my life have I spent believing deep down exactly what she's challenging?

She goes on. "Jun and I sometimes talked about what our government was doing with the drug war. He always said that the administration was not trying to solve the problem, but only trying to make it seem like they were solving the problem. They used the poor to do this because the poor could not or did not know how to fight back. He told me that if the administration truly wanted to fix the drug problem, they knew what needed to be done."

"And what did Jun think that was?"

"He said that those suffering from addiction needed to be helped, not to be arrested, because their addiction was as much genetics as it was a choice. And that those pushing needed to be employed, not to be killed, because most of them were only trying to survive. He also said that none of these drugs could even make their way into our country to begin with if not for corrupt people in power—so they needed to be replaced, not reelected."

She's summarizing Jun's words, but they feel like hers. It is as if part of his spirit now belongs to Grace.

"I listened to him whenever he talked about these things," Grace goes on, "but I think it is only now that I understand what he meant. Because if enough people understand this, the victims will no longer be faceless criminals."

"There has to be something I can do," I say weakly, feeling like a failure in the face of her new resolve.

"No offense, cousin, but even though you are from here, you are also not. I know you want to help, but you have only recently learned about any of this. You are not going to be the one to save us."

I look down. It hurts my pride to hear this, but I know Grace is right.

"I am going to continue updating GISING NA PH! because I refuse to let Kuya's life have been for nothing, because I understand how important it is for the world to remember the humanity of those the government murders so easily. There is probably more that needs to be done if any of this is to truly stop, but I don't know what that is yet."

I look up, as if to confirm which cousin is standing across from me. As much as she sounds like Jun, as much as I see him in her eyes, it is Grace leaning against the doorframe, a blade of afternoon light falling across her shoulder.

"I miss him," I say. "So damn much."

Grace considers this. Her face falters, the revolutionary resolve slipping away. At least for now. "Me too," she says, voice cracking. Then she drops her face into her hands and starts crying.

I hold her. Then I start crying, and she uncovers her face and uses her hands to hold me, too. And it hurts so much to think of Jun—to think about all we could have done for him but didn't, to think about all that he could have done for the world but now never will. Somehow, I know that this is an emptiness I will carry forever. Like a stone rounded by the waves, the ache might soften over time, but it will never go away. Not completely.

And in Grace I finally realize that there's something important in sharing this sorrow, in not carrying it alone. I crossed an ocean to learn about what happened to Jun, but it's what I'm learning in this moment that gives me faith that we'll be all right, that we'll figure out how to live without him in ways where we will never be fully without him.

A moment later, we hear our family walking back into the house.

Grace and I hold each other for a moment longer, then break apart, wiping our tears and smiling gently at each other.

"It's too late for a funeral," Grace says, "and I don't think Tatay would even begin to allow a *lamay* . . . but do you think it would be a good idea if I asked everyone if we could hold a small memorial for him?"

"I do," I say without hesitation.

ALL THE DARKNESS
IN THE WORLD

At dusk, we gather in Lolo and Lola's backyard. Tito Maning was still too ashamed of how Jun died to join us or to allow us to follow the tradition of inviting the community. However, he didn't try to stop our family from following Grace's idea.

The insects are starting their evening hum, and birds or bats flit past overhead. The roosters at the side of the house move about restlessly in their cages, settling in for the night. It looks like it could start pouring at any moment.

We arrange ourselves in a semicircle around a framed picture of Jun set at the base of the tree. It looks like he was maybe thirteen or fourteen at the time. He's smiling wide with his arm propped up on the shoulder of someone just out of frame, someone I know isn't me but I pretend is. A lit candle sits in front of the picture, its orange flame swaying and flickering.

Tito Danilo carries a Bible and a rosary. The rest of us each hold an unlit lavender tapered candle. I also carry a folded letter.

Nobody says anything for a long time. Grace keeps shooting

glances at the back door as if she's expecting her father to change his mind. But it remains closed.

Eventually, Tito Danilo steps forward. "Usually, I would not be speaking English for this kind of service. But tonight I want all of our voices to rise together to God." He nods at me, then makes the sign of the cross and switches to a priestly tone. "In the name of the Father, the Son, and the Holy Spirit."

The rest of us do the same and reply, "Amen."

"The Lord be with you."

"And also with you."

"Lord, have mercy," he says.

"Lord, have mercy," we echo.

"Christ, have mercy."

"Christ, have mercy."

"Lord, have mercy," he says again.

"Lord, have mercy," we say again.

Tito Danilo then leads us in reciting an Our Father, a Hail Mary, and another prayer I don't know about eternal peace. We repeat each prayer so many times I lose count, then he clears his throat and looks down at the Bible. He opens his mouth to start reading, when a gust of warm wind flips the thin pages. He turns back to the correct page which is marked with a ribbon. "A reading from the book of Wisdom," he begins.

We bow our heads and close our eyes.

"'But the souls of the just are in the hand of God, and no torment shall touch them. They seemed, in the view of the foolish, to be dead;

and their passing away was thought an affliction and their going forth from us, utter destruction. But they are in peace. For if before men, indeed, they be punished, yet is their hope full of immortality; chastised a little, they shall be greatly blessed, because God tried them and found them worthy of Himself. As gold in the furnace, he proved them, and as sacrificial offerings, he took them to Himself. Those who trust in Him shall understand truth, and the faithful shall abide with Him in love . . . The Word of the Lord.'"

"Thanks be to God," we all reply.

As Tito Danilo closes the Bible and sets it down in front of Jun's picture, I contemplate the words still floating in the air. Even though I would like to, I'm not sure I believe them. Life, death—I still don't understand any of it. There was a time when I thought getting older meant you'd understand more about the world, but it turns out the exact opposite is true. I don't know anything about anything, let alone why Jun had to live the life he lived, why he had to die the way he died. The idea that it's all a test ensuring an afterlife reward has this fairy-tale feel that's hard for me to swallow. And if it is, did Jun even pass? If not, who possibly could?

My eyes settle on Jun's picture as Tito Danilo starts to speak again. "Somebody once said, 'All the darkness in the world cannot extinguish the light of a single candle.' Consider the truth, the implications, of those words for a moment."

I shift my gaze to the candle in front of Jun's picture. It continues to sway and flicker, but it keeps burning.

"Jun died a tragic death before his time. But that does not extinguish the good that he did on this earth. It lives on in the lives that he touched, and like a single candle's flame, it can grow and make what is dark light." He pauses to let that sink in. "I invite each of you now to light your own candle from his, signifying that his goodness, his love, has multiplied through the ways he touched each of us, will continue to multiply through those we will go on to touch. If you feel moved, please say a few words. If not, that is okay. You can keep them in your heart. They will still reach Jun."

Even though we all want to, nobody moves for several moments. The last light of the sky begins to fade. The drone of the insects grows louder.

Tita Chato goes first and touches the wick of her candle to Jun's until it lights. She speaks quietly for several minutes. Of course, I don't know what she's saying since it's all in Tagalog or Bikol. It is a strange thing to mourn in another language, but I figure everyone will probably speak their own language tonight. And though I want to ask for translation, I won't, because their words are not for me.

Eventually, Tita Chato is crying so hard that she can't go on. Tita Ines comes to her side and wraps her arms around Tita Chato, who manages to say a few more words.

Grace and Angel go next. They deliver good-byes in Tagalog and end with a "We love you, Kuya" that leads to a fresh bout of tears all around. Tears that hurt but heal.

Then Tito Danilo steps forward. "Even as a small child," he begins in English, "Jun challenged me in my faith more than anyone else. 'Bakit?' he was always asking. 'Why?'" Everyone laughs quietly. He goes on. "He was never satisfied when I told him, 'Because the Bible says,' so I had to keep thinking up responses to his questions. I had to admit when I did not know. But his challenges were never out of malice. He was not trying to disprove my faith, but to understand it. I do not know if he ever did, but in trying to explain it to him, I arrived at new realizations and new questions of my own. Even now, my faith grows stronger because of Jun. Though he is no longer with us, his voice will remain." Then he switches to Tagalog or Bikol and speaks for a bit longer before stepping back.

Then, Lolo and Lola step forward, holding hands. They light their candles at the same time. Lolo doesn't say anything, but Lola speaks for a while in what I think is Bikol because I recognize even fewer words than usual. When she finishes, there are again more tears.

I go next. I drop to one knee and light my candle using Jun's flame, and then stay like that for a while trying to sift through my memories for the perfect one that will convey what Jun meant to me—what he still means to me.

I carry a feeling like I've been trying to figure out how to map the islands of his life, trying to make sense of them, trying to figure out what right I have to do so. And maybe there are still some inaccuracies and gaps, but it's so much clearer than it was before.

I unfold the letter I've been holding. Scan the words illuminated by the candlelight. I wipe my eyes and clear my throat. Then I read it aloud.

3 May 2019

Dear Jun,

Eight years ago, you comforted me when I was crying because a puppy died. You wrapped your arms around me, touched your forehead to mine, and told me that it made you sad, too. What you did in that moment was real. You weren't saying what you thought you were supposed to say, doing what you thought you were supposed to do—like I think a lot of us do most of our lives. No. You saw my pain for what it was, recognized it as if it were your own, and gave me the love I needed to heal.

I will never forget that.

I don't want to believe there was another side to you. But I don't have any choice, do I? I will try not to judge because I have no idea what you were struggling with in your heart, what complicated your soul. None of us are just one thing, I guess. None of us. We all have the terrible and amazing power to hurt and help, to harm and heal. We all do both throughout our lives. That's the way it is. I suppose we just go on and do the best we can and try to do more good than bad using our time on Earth. I'd like to think your scales tip toward good.

Anyway, sorry for rambling. And sorry this reply comes so late. Too late. It took me a long time to figure out what to say.

You were my cousin, my brother, my best friend.

Wherever you are, know that I miss you, and I love you.

Wherever you are, know that I will try my best to make the people in my life feel how you made me feel that day eight years ago.

Wherever you are, I hope I will someday be, too. And when we meet, I will tell you about everything without paper and pen.

Love,
Jay

I refold the letter, pinching my fingers along the edges of the paper to straighten the creases. Then I place it on the ground before my cousin's picture.

When I turn around to rejoin the others, I stop short—Tito Maning is standing in the shadows just outside the back door. At first, I wonder if he's about to come over and put an end to the memorial. But his arms are crossed and he's posted up against the house like he's been there for a while. Then I remember how Tito Danilo said that Tito Maning called to ask for his help to save Jun. Truly, none of us is one thing.

I offer him a small nod. I'm not certain—it's difficult to see him clearly in the semidarkness—but I'm pretty sure he returns it.

When I rejoin my family, Tita Chato and Tito Danilo move to either side of me and each rest a hand on one of my shoulders.

Now there is only one person who has not lit her candle yet: Tita Ami.

We all wait, wondering if she will do so. She defied her husband by agreeing that this was a good idea, but how far will her defiance extend? After a couple moments, she doesn't move, and I start to judge her. However, maybe it's that her grief is too much to bear.

But then she steps forward and drops to both knees in front of the picture, letting her candle fall to the dirt.

"I love you, Anak," she says, and then begins speaking in Tagalog. She talks for a long time, longer than anyone else. She has to pause over and over again when her words give way to cries and wails that rend my heart. Her sadness triggers the rest of us to give voice and breath to our grief once more.

As if summoned by her sorrow, Tito Maning leaves his place by the back door and makes his way to her. Everyone's surprised, but it's clear by his face he means no harm. He kneels at his wife's side before the picture of his dead son. He wraps one arm around Tita Ami, and with the other, picks up the candle she dropped, lights it, and hands it to her. Grace and Angel join them. He does not say anything, but she leans into him and speaks for a few more minutes.

When she falls silent, we stand around together for a long, long time. I wonder at how, though the world may be darkening all around us, we've formed our own small sphere of brightness with the candles we lit from Jun's. Our sadness swells one more time before finally subsiding.

Eventually, Tito Danilo leads us all in another cycle of Our Fathers, Hail Marys, and the other one about resting in eternal peace. After our final amen, he sticks his candle in the dirt next to Jun's and we all do the same.

As we start to walk into the house, I look up at the sky. It's black and moonless but bursting with stars.

A SEED

There's a lightness to Saturday—my last full day in Bicol—that I haven't felt since before my dad told me the news about Jun. The sun is out and the sky is clear. We eat a huge breakfast of coffee, puto, fried eggs, tocilog, and all kinds of fresh fruit, like mango, bananas, and melon. Neighbors come by and we feed them. I talk to my parents on the landline. Nobody told them about what happened between Tito Maning and me, so when I recount my time in Bicol, I'm free to leave out nearly everything except for last night's memorial.

All day long, everyone is a little quieter, a little gentler, a little quicker to smile. Tito Maning avoids making eye contact with all of us, especially me, and speaks little. I know that Jun's memorial probably isn't going to make him turn his back on enforcing his president's policies overnight, but maybe it planted a seed.

Maybe.

After lunch, Tito Danilo takes Grace, Angel, Tita Chato, and me to a place where we rent ATVs and ride them to the base of Mount Mayon. On the way there, Tito Danilo tells me the story of Magayon, a young maiden who was saved from drowning by a man named Pangaronon. The two fell in love and planned to marry, but another man wanted to marry Magayon and fought Pangaronon. During the fight, Magayon and Pangaronon were killed. Magayon's father buried them together and the mountain that grew over them became Mount Mayon.

We're sitting in the silence of the story's ending when my phone vibrates with messages now that there's a signal. Most are from my parents, but there are a few more from Mia, wondering why I'm not responding. I'm not sweating it too much since she didn't respond to the messages I sent before I left for Bicol. But I no longer see the point in holding on to that, so I go ahead and shoot her a text letting her know that I haven't had signal. She asks if we can see each other before I leave, so we make plans to meet tomorrow night when I'm back at Tita Chato's before my red-eye flight.

Post-ATVing, my shoes end up muddy and my skin sunburned badly enough I know it will peel, but I don't mind. It is good to be laughing in the sunlight with family.

EVERY DETAIL OF
THIS FINITE MOMENT

After an obscenely early morning Mass on Sunday in Legazpi—which Tito Danilo dedicated to Jun—we say good-bye to Lolo, Lola, and Tito Danilo. I tell them how much I love them and how much my time with them has meant to me. When they say that they will see me next time, it fills me with sadness knowing that might be years from now, if at all. Yet I smile and hug them each in turn and try to will my brain to remember every detail of this finite moment because, in this world, there are no guarantees.

OUR SEPARATE WAYS

It's a long drive back to Tita Chato and Tita Ines's village in Cavite, so my aunts immediately head to bed to get some rest for a few hours before they have to drive me to the airport. However, I pack up all my stuff then sneak out to the community pool.

I lean back on my hands at the ledge, letting my legs dangle into the water, which is lit to a turquoise blue. The pool is chillier than I expected, but warmth lingers in the cement beneath my hands and butt from a full day of direct sun. The neighborhood is quiet except for the rhythmic drone of insects, the distant sound of cars, and someone singing karaoke far away.

"Hey! You're not supposed to be here!" calls a deep voice from behind me, making me jump. But then there's laughter, which I immediately recognize as Mia's.

"Hey," I say, as I twist around to look at her while pretending like she didn't just scare me.

It's only been a few days, but it feels like a decade has passed since I've seen her. Once again, she's wearing a plain black T-shirt, but her black jeans are replaced by baggy pajama pants with an intricate floral design. She walks over, steps out of her sandals, and rolls up her pant legs to right below the knee. But when she sits next to me, she crosses her legs instead of putting them in the water. Then she bumps me with her shoulder and casts a smile that makes my heart speed up a bit. "Miss me?"

"Meh," I say.

She smiles. "I'm glad you're back."

Her tone is light, like things are normal between us. Like she didn't ignore my messages for an entire day because she was hanging out with her boyfriend or whatever.

"For now," I say. "But I leave in a couple hours."

A car careens past the adjacent street, leaving K-pop fading in its wake. The quiet resettles. I kick my feet a little, splashing the water softly.

"So how was the trip?" she asks.

A lump forms in my throat as I gather my thoughts. I lean forward, resting my elbows on my knees and clasping my hands together as if in prayer. Gazing at the water, I tell her all about everything that happened in Bicol.

When I finish speaking, Mia is quiet for a long time. She scoots closer so the sides of our legs are touching, and then takes my hand, lacing our fingers together.

I look at our hands, confused.

Then she rests her head on my shoulder.

"Remember Brian Santos? My professor?" she asks after some time.

"Sure."

"After he took us to Reyna's, he messaged me."

"Oh?"

"He said your story was important." She pauses. "And that . . . if

I could write a good enough piece about it . . . there might be wider interest."

"You mean to get it published?"

She nods. "Even though you're not Filipino—"

"I am," I interrupt. "But I'm also American."

"Sorry," she says. "You're right. What I meant to say was that you have a unique perspective. It might show what's happening here in a new light."

I think of Grace's saying how I'm not going to save this country. "You really think anyone would care?"

"Some won't. But some will."

"So what did you tell your professor?"

"That I would only write it if you approved."

I don't say anything.

"We won't use real names . . . and Reyna already said it would be okay . . ."

"You've kept in touch with her?"

She nods.

I consider the additional pain the attention might bring to her, to me, to my family.

"I understand if you do not want me to," Mia says after some time. "I am okay with telling him no if you're not completely comfortable with it."

"The thing is, I'm not sure I'm in a position to give permission. After all, it's not my story—it's Jun's."

She sits up and shakes her head. "What happened to him, sure. But what's happened to you is yours."

I think of the GISING NA PH! account, and what Tito Danilo said about Jun living on through the ways we multiply his love. Maybe if it is told in the right way, our story can do something like that. But would people stop reading, stop caring, when they get to the part about him actually being involved with drugs? Would they stop seeing him as a full human being at that moment?

"Could you and I try cowriting it?" I ask. "And maybe Grace?"

She squeezes my hand and leans her head back on my shoulder. "Of course."

"Okay," I say. "Let's try it. But I'm not saying for sure that I definitely want to try publishing it."

"Of course." Mia squeezes my hand again. We stay like that for a long time. It's nice. Very nice.

But it doesn't feel right.

"Mia," I say, "why are you holding my hand like this?"

"When friends need to hold hands, they do," she says.

"Right," I say. "Friends. So there's nothing more going on here? Because it feels like there is to me."

She doesn't answer.

"I know you have a boyfriend," I say. "Grace told me after we first hung out. I think maybe you were with him the other day and that's why you weren't replying to my messages."

She doesn't deny it.

"You live on the other side of the planet," she says by way of explanation.

I have nothing to say. Do I expect her to break up with her boyfriend so she can Skype-date with someone she's only known for a few days?

Even so, I don't let go of her hand. She doesn't let go of mine. Instead, she nestles closer to me, and I wrap my other arm around her.

I want to ask about her boyfriend, but I also don't want to. It's easier to keep holding her right now if he's nothing but an abstraction in my mind.

Instead, I ask her about her life. Then she asks about mine. We talk for a long time, covering everything from major moments to random, mundane memories.

Part of me feels guilty. Jun will never experience anything like this anymore. He will never again hold Reyna, press his lips to hers, speak with her through the night. He will never do anything ever again.

But then I imagine telling him about Mia in a letter, and I imagine him smiling and laughing as he reads it. I imagine the reply he would write, the encouragement he would offer. The darkness I felt coming over me retreats. For now, at least.

It feels like only a few minutes have passed, but when Mia finally looks at her phone, we realize it's time for me to go.

We stand. Hug. Hold each other long enough that it's obvious we're both trying to prevent this from ending. And then we say goodbye and go our separate ways.

PATRON SAINTS OF NOTHING

The engines roar louder as we accelerate down the runway. There's a slight jolt, the plane leaves the ground, and then my stomach drops as we rise into the air. The lighted buildings and cars of Manila shrink away until they look like toys, and then ants, and then nothing at all. After a couple minutes, the sound of the engines lower to a steady hum and the wheels retract with mechanized whirring.

I gaze at the dark shapes of the Philippine islands dotting the sea below until they disappear below the clouds. I slip on my headphones to listen to a playlist of Filipino music Mia made for me, and then read what I have decided is my favorite letter from Jun.

1 Nov 2014

Dear Kuya Jay,
Today is All Saints Day in the Philippines. Do you celebrate this day in the United States?

Almost all Filipinos have this day off. Many of us go to the cemetery. We bring blankets, candles, food, drink, guitars, and so on, and spend the day at the tombs of our loved ones. We eat, we play music, we talk and laugh and tell stories about the dead. I know this probably seems strange. All of the graveyards I see in American TV shows and movies are always dark and scary and empty except when there is a funeral. But here it is a celebration. A time to honor our dead and remember their lives. I think this is a healthy thing to do.

The day is also meant to celebrate the saints, of course. For example, maybe you have already heard of St. Blaise, the patron saint of wild animals, veterinarians, and throat ailments. Did you know he lived in a cave with all these wild animals? I think that's really cool. Anyway, there are also many other lesser-known saints. There is St. Apollonia, the patron saint of dentists; St. Lydwina, the patron saint of ice skaters; St. Drogo, the patron saint of ugly people, and— another one of my favorites—St. Clotilde, the patron saint of disappointing children.

You get the idea. There are a lot of saints in our religion, more saints than there are days in a year. A saint for almost anything you can imagine. People pray to them to try to receive their oddly specific blessings. But, to be honest, I don't think the world works that way.

I often wonder why we have so many. I asked Tito Danilo, but he said he doesn't know, that maybe it's because there are so many good people. But it seems to me that maybe it is because there are so many problems in the world, many of which are out of our control. People want to feel like they can do something, so they pray to these saints. I can understand that. And even if there are not actual magical spirits listening and waiting to fulfill our wishes, maybe just the act of thinking about these things changes us in some way.

Anyway, assuming this is all real and you were canonized someday, what would you want to be able to help people with? I know it is hard to think of something for which there is not already a patron saint! Personally, I would like to be St. Jun, the patron saint of holding in your farts during Mass. I think I would be very popular. Ha-ha! Just kidding!

In all seriousness, I don't know what saint I would be. St. Nothing, I guess.

Anyway, I miss you, Kuya, and I hope you will come to visit soon here in the Philippines. You are always welcome.

Sincerely,
St. Nothing

I smile to myself as I put the letter away. I rest my head against the window and close my eyes. I drift off to sleep thinking of my cousin and me, of humanity and its problems, of oceans and islands. I imagine both of us, patron saints of nothing.

THERE ARE SO MANY WHITE PEOPLE HERE, I think as I stand on the curb of the passenger pickup area outside of Detroit International Airport, scanning the circling cars for my dad's.

It's a gray morning, cold even for May in Michigan. I'm shivering in my hoodie, khaki shorts, and Islander sandals.

Thankfully, it's not long before I spot Dad approaching. I flag him down and he pulls to a stop a few feet ahead of me where there's enough space, waving at me through the window. I heft my luggage into the back, traveling so much lighter without the balikbayan boxes, and then climb into the passenger seat. "Yesterday" by the Beatles is playing on the radio, reminding me of that videoke night at Tita Chato's.

"Hey," he says, and reaches across the center console and shakes my hand like I'm one of his coworkers instead of his son.

"Um. Hi."

He clicks on the turn signal, and then pulls back into the flow of traffic. I try to imagine him as the generous donor to Tita Chato's organization. As someone carrying his own unvoiced pain and guilt about leaving his homeland.

"Looks like you got some sun," he says.

I look down at the backs of my hands. "I guess. Mom working?"

"Yup. I took the morning off to come get you."

A few moments pass before either of us speaks again. It's only been a week and a half, but I feel like I've experienced an entire lifetime since I last saw him. There's almost too much to say.

It's weird to be back.

"How was the plane ride?" Dad eventually asks. If he's still angry about me breaking my promise to Tito Maning, he's hiding it well.

I shrug. "It was good."

He's quiet. I'm quiet. We pull onto the interstate.

I watch the world slide past and try to imagine tomorrow morning. Going to my classes. Sitting there, surrounded by people who don't even know who Duterte is. Talking about video games with Seth. Then, in a few weeks, prom and graduation. In a few months, starting college in Ann Arbor.

It feels like someone else's life.

"Dad?" I ask about twenty or thirty minutes into our drive, when we're halfway home.

"Yes?"

"I've been thinking."

"Congratulations."

I laugh, genuinely surprised at his joke. He laughs, too.

"Sorry," he says. "What have you been thinking, Jay?"

"The fall," I say, shifting my gaze from the side window to the road in front of us. There are a few other cars on the road, but not many since rush hour is still an hour or so away.

He waits for me to go on.

"Maybe . . ." I hesitate. I start to feel nervous, like what I'm about to suggest is a mistake. But then I think of all that I faced down in the last few days and come out with it. "I'm going to defer my enrollment at U of M."

He glances at me like I'm crazy, taking his eyes off the road for longer than seems safe. "Oh?"

I nod.

He faces forward, eyebrows still furrowed. "Why?"

I look out the window at the passing world. All my life, I assumed I'd graduate high school, go to college, and then get a job. But I realized I don't have to follow that path. I mean, what's the point if I don't understand why I'm doing it beyond the fact it's what I'm supposed to do? We have one life so we should live it in a way that makes sense to us.

"I've been thinking that maybe I could do something else instead. Something I understand, something I want to do."

"You don't want to go to college?"

"No," I say. "Not yet."

Dad raises an eyebrow. "So what would you do instead?"

I take a deep breath. "A gap year."

"A gap year?"

"Yeah," I say.

"As in you want to backpack around Europe or something?"

"I want to go back to the Philippines," I say.

He doesn't react.

"I'd like to see more of the country," I continue. "Learn more of its history. More Tagalog, maybe some Bikol."

He switches lanes. And I know he's about to launch into all the reasons why this is going to ruin my future. I can sense it like electricity crackling in the air before a lightning strike.

But then he says this: "Interesting."

Something between us shifts.

I go on. "I was thinking I could stay with Tita Chato and Tita Ines. They said I have a standing invitation at their place, and Tita Chato said she could always use help at her organization. And afterward, who knows, maybe I will go to college. But maybe at that point I'd know why I'm going. I'd know what I actually want to study."

He's quiet for a long time. But I don't press it. I let him turn it over in his mind.

Finally, he says, "You know, I moved us here to give you and your brother and sister a better life. Not so you could go back . . ."

"I know," I say. "I appreciate that. I really do. But I want to do this. I think it would be good for me."

"Chris and Emily didn't need to, and they're fine."

"Yeah, but that's them, Dad. I'm different, I guess."

He sighs. "So what's her name?"

"Whose?"

"The girl you met."

Feeling like a cliché, I answer, "Mia . . . but she has a boyfriend. And that's honestly not the reason I want to do this."

He looks skeptical.

"Fine," I concede. "It's not the *only* reason."

He sighs. "I'll speak to your mother. Then the three of us can sit down and talk about it."

"Salamat po."

Dad shakes his head and laughs. "What happened to you over there? You sound like you've aged a few years since you left."

"Feels like it," I say.

And then I tell him everything.

The words, the stories spill out of me. At first, Dad seems shocked at the sheer volume of it all because I don't think I've ever spoken so much to him at one time in my entire life. But eventually, he starts asking me questions. Real questions.

And when I give real answers, he listens without judgment.

It's weird to be this open with him, to not hold anything back. It's like we're characters in a cartoon who have continued to run over and past the edge of the cliff, defying the laws of physics. This is just not the kind of relationship we have, and I fear I'll eventually say something wrong, and we'll plummet.

But I keep talking because I'm determined to resist falling into the same pattern as always. This is my life, and I want my family to understand it in a way none of us truly understood Jun's. If we are to be more than what we have been, there's so much that we need to say. Salvation through honesty, I guess.

We're still talking as we reach the house, and we're still talking as we unload my luggage and bring it inside. But in the foyer, we falter. Dad gives me a look I can't read. I feel the tug of routine urging me to close the conversation so we can retreat to our separate spaces now that we're home. Maybe he's feeling it, too.

"You probably want to take a rest now," he says.

I drop my backpack by the door. "Actually, I'm all right."

He's quiet for beat, then asks, "Coffee?"

"Yeah," I say. "Okay."

He nods. Pats me on the shoulder. It's awkward, but whatever.

"Meet me out front," he says. "I'll brew a pot. Then I'm going to call the hospital to tell them I need the rest of the day off."

I smile. "Cool."

Then he heads into the kitchen, and I go outside and sit on the steps of the porch.

Our neighbor across the street emerges a few moments later with her black lab and her smaller dog that looks like a fox. She waves, then they set off on their morning walk. A car zips past. Our sprinklers turn on. Above it all, a sliver of blue sky and sunlight splits the clouds and then slowly expands.

As I watch the world wake, I try to sense the shape of it now.

Jun is gone. I will always carry the grief of that loss and the regret that I let him slip out of my life too easily. Nothing will ever change that.

But there are good things I can hold on to and there are other things I have the power to change. My family, myself, this world—all of us are flawed. But flawed doesn't mean hopeless. It doesn't mean forsaken. It doesn't mean lost. We are not doomed to suffer things as they are, silent and alone. We do not have to leave questions and letters and lives unanswered. We have more power and potential than we know if we would only speak, if we would only listen.

A few minutes later, Dad walks outside with two steaming mugs. He hands over one, then joins me on the steps.

I breathe in the scent of the coffee, the watered grass, the damp sidewalk. Even though we're not in church, this moment feels holy.

"So, tell me more," Dad says.

And the conversation continues, blessed by the morning.

AUTHOR'S NOTE

Although Jun's story is fictional, the war on drugs in the Philippines is not. As of this writing, the Philippine National Police reports that approximately 4,300 Filipinos have died as result of the campaign since Roderigo Duterte was elected president in 2016. However, the Human Rights Watch estimates that more than 12,000 people have been killed, and other data suggest that the number might be over 20,000. It is likely that we will never know the exact number.

RECOMMENDED READING

The Drug Archive at http://Drugarchive.ph from the Ateneo School of Government at Ateneo de Manila University, De La Salle Philippines, the University of the Philippines-Diliman, and the Stabile Center for Investigative Journalism at Columbia University's Graduate School of Journalism

"The Impunity Series" from *Rappler*
- " 'It's war': Murder in Manila conclusion" by Patricia Evangelista

"Residents from 26 barangays file protection vs police" by Arianne Christian Tapao for *VERA Files*

"The human rights consequences of the war on drugs in the Philippines" by Vanda Felbab-Brown for The Brookings Institution

"They are slaughtering us like animals" by Daniel Berehula for *The New York Times*

"Philippines secret death squads" by Kate Lamb for *The Guardian*

"President Duterte's war on drugs is a pretense" by Leila de Lima for *The New York Times*

"City of the Dead" from *CNN*

GET INVOLVED

Malaya Movement at https://malayamovement.com

Anakbayan-USA at http://anakbayanusa.org

National Alliance for Filipino Concerns at https://nafconusa.org

Kabataan Alliance at https://kabataanalliance.org

ACKNOWLEDGMENTS

Maraming salamat to all that helped bring this story to life:

To my agent, Beth Phelan—thank you for believing in this story early on, helping me find its shape, and then taking care of the business-y stuff. And thank you to the entire team at Gallt & Zacker for your help along the way.

Thank you to the Kokila and Penguin Random House crew for turning this into a real book. To my editor, Namrata Tripathi—I will always be grateful for your excitement about Jay's journey and for your insightful feedback that helped illuminate and refine. Thank you to Theresa Evangelista and Dana Li for an amazing design, and to Jor Ros for the stunning artwork. Thank you also to Sydnee Monday, Jasmin Rubero, Natalie Vielkind, Kaitlin Kneafsey, Rosanne Lauer, Cherisse Landau, Caitlin Taylor; to the sales and marketing teams; and to everyone else behind the scenes who help this story find its readers.

Thank you to Twitter for helping me fill my fictional karaoke lists and balikbayan boxes. Thank you to V & R for fighting the notorious Manila traffic so we could discuss Pedro.

To Ellen Tordesillas—thank you for the perspective of a journalist in the Philippines. And thank you to all those reporting on the drug war, and to those fighting for justice. Your important work is appreciated. Please, ingat palagi.

To the Gutierrez, Tresvalles, and Reboya families—thank you for all the rides and the meals and love whenever I visit.

To the Djerassi Resident Artists Program, Nova Ren Suma, and the Cornered Weasels (Alison Cherry, Kim Graff, Tamara Mahmood Hayes, Sara Ingle, Imani Josey, Nora Revenaugh, Leigh Shadko, Rachel Lynn Solomon, Cass White)—thank you for the inspiration and space while I worked on the first draft instead of working on the piece I brought to workshop.

Thank you to my Bay Area YA fam (especially Parker Peevyhouse, Kelly Loy Gilbert, Sabaa Tahir, Gordon Jack, Mimi Yu, Misa Sugiura, Sonya Mukherjee, and Evelyn Skye), KidLit Authors of Color, the Fearless Fifteeners, everyone at Kepler's, Hicklebee's, and Books, Inc., my #Beoples, and Mike Chen/In-N-Out Burger. It's nice not to do this alone.

Thank you to my Lions, Warriors, and Rams—past and present. To all the educators, librarians, booksellers, and book bloggers/booktubers/bookstagrammers helping to spread the joy of reading. You all inspire and motivate me every single day.

To Roberto Ribay, Jaclyn Reyes, Inah Peralta, and Sawyer Lovett—thank you for the reads near the end that helped me improve the story's authenticity and nuance. As always, any mistakes are my own.

Thank you to all the Ribays, Clores, Kimbrells, Seyfrieds, and Carders. No matter how many of these I write, I will never be able to articulate how much your support and encouragement mean to me.

And, of course, to Kathryn—thank you for everything, all the time. Even though I make things up professionally, I cannot imagine a better partner.

ABOUT THE AUTHOR

Randy Ribay was born in the Philippines and raised in the Midwest. He is the author of *After the Shot Drops* and *An Infinite Number of Parallel Universes*. He earned his BA in English Literature from the University of Colorado at Boulder and his Master's Degree in Language and Literacy from Harvard Graduate School of Education. He currently teaches English and lives in the San Francisco Bay Area.